FROM
NOWHERE TO
NOWHERE

COPYRIGHT © 2021 Bekim Sejranović
TRANSLATION Copyright © 2021 Will Firth
DESING & LAYOUT Nikša Eršek
PUBLISHED BY Sandorf Passage
South Portland, Maine, United States
IMPRINT OF Sandorf
Severinska 30, Zagreb, Croatia
sandorf.hr | contact@sandorf.hr
PRINTED BY Tiskara Zrinski, Čakovec
Originally published by Profil as *Nigdje, niotkuda.*

Sandorf Passage books are available to the
trade through Independent Publishers Group:
ipgbook.com | (800) 888-4741.

Library of Congress Control Number:
2020940942

National and University Library Zagreb
Control Number: 001067093

ISBN 978-9-53351-294-5

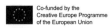

Co-funded by the
Creative Europe Programme
of the European Union

The European Commission support for the
production of this publication does not constitute
an endorsement of the contents which reflects the
views only of the authors, and the Commission
cannot be held responsible for any use which may
be made of the information contained therein.

This Book is published with financial support by
the Republic of Croatia's Ministry of Culture.

FROM NOWHERE TO NOWHERE

translated by **WILL FIRTH**

BEKIM SEJRANOVIĆ

SAN-
DORF
PAS-
SAGE

SOUTH PORTLAND | MAINE

This edition is dedicated to BEKIM SEJRANOVIĆ, *"the greatest post-Yugoslav nomad," who died shortly before publication at the age of forty-eight.*

Note on the pronunciation of names

We have maintained the original spelling of proper nouns. The vowels are pronounced as in Italian. The consonants are pronounced as follows:

c = ts, as in *bi*ts
č = ch
ć = similar to č, like the t in *future*
dž = g, as in *general*
đ = similar to dž
j = y, as in y*ellow*
r = trilled as in Scottish; sometimes used as a vowel, e.g. "Brčko," roughly "Birch-ko"
š = sh
ž = like the s in *pleasure*

I

The funeral

I WAS THE ONLY one standing. Towering above all the others. I stood and didn't know where to put my hands. Should I let them dangle feebly or hold them stiffly? Should I interlock my fingers and let that ball hang below my belly? All the others squatted, their arms half raised, their cupped hands toward their faces. The hodja was at the front, in the middle of the semicircle. He recited ritual prayers, and the men, staring into the grave over their bent fingers, sometimes repeated a few words after him.

I could make out the "amen."

It was too late now for me to join the others. To squat like all of them and lift my cupped hands to my face. To repeat a few words together with the men. I don't know why I didn't do that. I hesitated for a moment and looked for Grandfather to see what he was doing. Since I didn't notice the hodja straightaway, I was surprised when he began speaking the words of a prayer in his nasal voice. At that instant I also saw Grandfather squatting with difficulty and holding out his right hand in prayer. Alija's son supported him because the left side of Grandfather's body was paralyzed from his last stroke. The folds on that side of his face took on the expression of a sullen laborer. He squeezed his eyes shut but they shone a little through his sparse eyelashes. I could see by his lips that he wasn't saying the prayer aloud.

"Amen," hummed over the hummocky graveyard.

Dull, heavy clouds had settled on the surrounding hills. The clay earth seemed to pull the men in. The air they breathed smelled of the freshly dug pit.

The bier stood beside the grave on three-foot boards. Slightly listing, because it was hard to find a flat piece of land at that cemetery. Gravestones jutted out of the ground like tusks of extinct beasts.

This wasn't my first time at a funeral, though you couldn't say I'd been to many. Only two others, but never as an adult, which the men crouching around the fresh heap of yellow-brown earth now considered me.

I first went to a funeral when I was five. A boy from our street drowned in the Sava River. We called him Giraffe because he was thin and two heads taller than the rest of us. That was the first time that I saw a dead body in the flesh. It was laid out in a room. Whoever wanted to could go and say goodbye for the final time. I followed the others and all at once I saw Giraffe there in front of me, lying with eyes shut. He was yellow and his hair was bristly. The boy next to me stroked him on the head. I quietly farted.

The next time, my father's stepmother drowned herself in the Sava. She'd put up with severe pains in the belly and one day she couldn't stand it anymore. She put on her slippers and her dressing gown, walked down to the river, got into a rowboat, and jumped into the water.

I went to her funeral, like now too, with Grandfather, Mom's father, but I didn't want to see her body before the burial. We walked along Brotherhood and Unity Street. Grandfather and I were at the front of the procession. He put his shoulder under the bier and carried it for part of the way until somebody relieved him. And then all the men squatted down and held their cupped hands in front of their faces, whispered quietly, and repeated a few words after the hodja. When I asked Grandfather later why everybody squatted, slowly closed their eyes, stretched out their cupped hands, and sometimes passed them over their face like when a person washes himself, he told me that was what believers did. That was the way of paying one's last respects to the one who'd gone to the other world. I was small at the time and didn't really know what the difference was; I knew Grandfather wasn't a believer but a communist. But he squatted too. He answered calmly that he didn't normally do that, but now he did, out of respect for the dead. I didn't get the whole respect thing. What did respect have to do with squatting, communists, and the hodja? Grandfather said he didn't want to be the only one who stood. Everybody, or almost everybody was squatting in prayer, so it wouldn't be good for him to be the only one standing. That explanation made sense to me.

This time it was just me standing. My gaze shifted between the soft, trampled earth and the stony faces of the other men. There was no sorrow or theatrical mourning on those faces, just a wistfulness. Deeper than the grave where we'd bury Uncle Alija and heavier than the soil we'd cover him with. I sensed that one last "Amen" would hum from the throats of the men around me and that they'd slowly, almost reluctantly get up. Somebody, probably the gravedigger and his assistants, would lower the coffin into the ground on ropes. One of them would then get down into the grave. The two that remained above would hand him the boards to cover the green sheet with them like a roof.

Only then would everybody be able to take a clump of the sticky soil and throw it into the grave.

II

A MURMUR OF male voices filled my ears. The men had come to see Alija's body off into the black hole and his soul into the unknown. I closed my eyes and recalled a world that was no more.

1. *The Mercedes*

It was fall back then, and Suzana's dad, Uncle Slavko, had finally come home from Germany. He worked there, in Frankfurt, while Suzana, her mom, and elder sister Mira lived in a small three-story house at the beginning of our alley. Ours was at the end of the alley—the one with the red gate. It was the house of my mom's parents, where I lived with Grandfather and Grandmother. I called Grandmother "Mother." Mom and Dad got divorced, "officially," Grandmothe explained to her friends, simple women from the neighborhood. Dad went his own way, and Mom to a big city on the Adriatic coast to finish her education. Grandfather was a traveling salesman—and always on the road. Grandmother and I were at home.

I often played by myself because there was nobody for me to play with. All the children on the street went to day care, but I didn't need to because Grandmother looked after me. Once she asked the daycare lady if I could play with the children a bit while they were outside. She said yes, but I got into a fight with another boy and bloodied his head. After that, I wasn't allowed to play with them anymore. I didn't want to either. Sometimes I'd find a stray puppy and would play with it until Grandmother chased it away. She'd say that they fouled up the courtyard or were mangy.

When Grandmother had some business to attend to in town by herself, she'd leave me with Suzana's mom. Their apartment had a room full of things from Germany. It was always locked, and not even Suzana was allowed in. Only when it was her birthday—then we all could go in. It was like Ali Baba's treasure cave. There were all kinds of toys, little dresses, and decorations. Uncle Slavko would always come for her birthday, and then he'd dim the lights in the room and show us Disney movies on the projector. We ate German candies, which were always better than ours. Everything from Germany was better, we thought. Aunty Radmila, who lived by herself in the small white house across the street from Suzana's, once said that we'd eat shit if it had "Made in Germany" written on it.

I asked Suzana why we couldn't watch movies every day, and she said her mom wouldn't let her. We could damage something. Her mom locked away everything they got from her dad. It was a shame because of all the toys, but I felt especially sorry for Suzana.

When I was circumcised and lay in bed tearful and hurt, she came and sat beside me and held my hand. I sobbed and didn't want to tell her what'd happened because I was ashamed, and I didn't really know myself.

Suzana was slender, and a head taller than me. She had sparse black hair and looked like a sad heron. Nobody had such a big mouth as her, Grandmother said.

Every time Uncle Slavko came home, he'd bring a lot of presents for his daughters. Sometimes he'd have something for me too. We kids from the alley gaped with amazement when we saw a battery-operated toy dog for the first time. It moved just like a real dog, wagged its tail, and even had a squeaky bark. Suzana would turn it on and make it bark, wag its tail, walk, and stop again. It always obeyed. I was sure Grandmother would let me have a dog like that. It was neither mangy nor ill. But later the dog broke down. It didn't react to Suzana's commands anymore, and Suzana's mom locked it away in the room.

Once, Uncle Slavko brought Suzana a German bicycle. It looked like a rocket to us. It had three gears. We all wanted to have a go, but Suzana's mom wouldn't let us. In Suzana's basement there was also a red Mercedes with pedals. A two-seater. I was little when Suzana's dad brought that car for her and her sister, so I didn't remember it. You got in, pedaled, and turned the steering wheel, which looked almost like a real one. Later the pedals got damaged a bit, and Suzana's mom forbade us from playing with the Mercedes. Uncle Slavko had also forgotten about it, but he saw it when he went down to the basement and decided to give it to me. His daughters were big now anyway, they had bikes, and the car was spoiled. Suzana's mom didn't like the idea.

The pedals couldn't be repaired, but the steering wheel worked, and that was the important thing. Our courtyard was large and had a gentle slope. You went up to the top near the gate, gave the Mercedes a bit of a push, hopped in, and zoom! At the far end of the courtyard you'd lined up some boxes that you now bowled over, or you turned sharply and the momentum made you and the plastic car roll over. Like in a movie, except there was nobody to film it.

BEKIM SEJRANOVIĆ

2. Coal

I don't know when I saw Uncle Alija for the first time, but I remember well that he came every fall to carry in the coal for us. Grandfather would order five tons of coal, and we'd burn it all winter in a stove called a Kreka-Weso. The truck would squeeze into the narrow alley and dump its load at the gate. Then Uncle Alija would turn up out of nowhere to carry the coal down to the basement.

He didn't like me to help carrying the coal, and I soon found it boring too. So I came up with the idea of transporting the coal in the Mercedes.

"It'd be a shame, kid, to dirty your pretty Benz with coal," he told me.

But I knew that he only said that so I wouldn't bother him. I put a full bucket of coal on the passenger seat, gave it a bit of a push, and hopped in. The hardest thing was taking the sharp turn toward the basement halfway down the slope. In one attempt, the Mercedes overturned together with the bucket of coal, and I hurt my knee and elbow. Grandmother scooted out of the house and started shouting because I'd dirtied the courtyard with coal.

"It wasn't me who made the mess, it was Alija," I told her.

She glanced at me furiously and stormed back into the house. She didn't give me a smack on the bottom or look at my bloodied knee.

Alija kept carrying the coal and went past me as if I wasn't there.

Later we searched for wire. You always found a lot of different-colored wires in the coal, and afterward you could make slingshots with them. First you shaped a fork from the thickest wire, then you took out the fine elastic band from a pair of Grandmother's underpants. You made pellets for the slingshot by taking small, thin pieces of wire and bending them into a "U" shape. You couldn't break a window or bloody anybody's head with them. You needed a proper slingshot for that—a wooden one with a piece of bicycle tire you could fit a stone in. Wire slingshots were best for shooting at girls in tight pants. You could blind somebody with them, but a pigeon wouldn't be hurt if you hit it.

"D'you know why there's wire in the coal, kids?" Alija asked as he was loading it into the wheelbarrow.

We said nothing.

"From the blasting."

"Blasting?"

Alija stopped for a minute, took off his gloves, and rolled himself a cigarette. He sat down on a stone, pulled up his left leg, stretched out his right, and rubbed it a bit. He explained to us how they used the wire to do blasting in the mines.

"You should see the stones, earth, and everythin' go sky 'igh."

"How do you know, have you seen it?"

Alija threw away his cigarette butt and kept working, until there was only fine coal left, which he shoveled.

"Did they blast your leg there too? Is that why you have a limp?"

"'Ey, just gimme a break, okay?" he said to me in the end.

3. As if she was dead

After I made a slingshot and pellets, I shot at everything I could. Then I decided to shoot at Suzana. She laughed and teased me at first. She ran around me in circles and shouted that I couldn't hit her. I started to chase her, but she was much faster. When I hit her, she began screaming for help and begging me not to shoot at her anymore. I'd just started to have fun. I ran after her and aimed at her skinny legs. When I hit her again, she shrieked and crouched down, holding her calf. She covered the spot where I'd hit her and quietly cried. I stood over her in silence. I held the slingshot with another pellet ready to fire. Then Alija appeared. He walked past without even looking at us.

Uncle Slavko returned from Germany in the late eighties, but when the war in Bosnia began in 1992 he went back again, this time as a refugee. He took his wife, elder daughter Mira, and her deaf-mute son with him.

The big house they'd built with his earnings in the German factories was hit by several shells. One of them killed Suzana.

She didn't look like she was sleeping, she looked like she was dead, Uncle Slavko said after the funeral.

III

UNCLE ALIJA WASN'T actually my real uncle. He was Grandfather Kasim's brother, which actually makes him my mom's uncle. But if we want to get to the bottom of it, dot the i's and cross the t's, he wasn't her real uncle either.

1. *The billy goat*

Suljo, the father of Grandfather Kasim, was one of the most eminent men in the village, they say. He was as wealthy as the village was poor. He had a few goats and some forest, which he tried all his life to clear so as to gain an acre of arable land. He and his brother Agan owned that small hillside clearing in the middle of Salkovina forest.

In the village, they said of somebody who was haughty that he was "puffed up like Šehaga's billy goat." Šehaga was a term of respect for Suljo in his time, and the story about the billy goat goes like this:

Suljo had a herd of goats and one burly billy goat. He was the bellwether and carried a hard, clanking bell around his neck, on his hairy chest. When they came back from the pastures in the late afternoon, the billy goat led the herd. He'd stick out his chest, puff it up a bit, throw back his head, and quaver with his lower jaw. The bell would bump against his stretched chest with a dull, tinny clatter. People would peep out of their court-yards, come out in front of their gates, and children would stick their heads through the rickety fences—there was the proces-sion, with all the goats following Šehaga's billy goat.

And so the haughty billy goat would pass through the vil-lage, not suspecting that he'd remain in its collective memory for the next hundred years.

2. Kasim

Suljo married young and soon, several months after the wedding, his wife became pregnant. Suljo then began to clear the forest with his brother in an attempt to enlarge the area they could cultivate. Cleared land is known for yielding a good crop in the first few years, while the soil is still fertile, but after a time it be-gins to go yellow. During the summer droughts it turns to clods, afterward to dust, and in the end only a fine dirt is left. And in the fall and the spring, when the rains set in, everything turns to mud, an ooze that the rains strip away within several years. Then the first stones appear. First tiny ones, later ever larger. Then the cleared land has to be cleared again. This time of stones.

The pregnancy went perfectly and his wife Mejra, or just "Suljo's wife," because women in the village were known by the names of their husbands, bore him a large and healthy son, but she herself seemed to never fully recover from that birth.

She died of tuberculosis less than eighteen months later.

Suljo mourned and asked Allah, and the people he met, why it had to be her. God didn't answer, and the older, experienced women in the village would just sigh and whisper that Allah wanted it that way, and since it was the wish of Allah in His mercy, that was how it had to be. The men were mostly silent, and when they spoke they'd say the same. Wise Hadži Murat, too, said it was the will of God, who gave and took away. Sometimes the child died, sometimes the mother, and sometimes they were lucky and Allah spared both and breathed new life into them: the spirit to live and be happy, to work and to suffer, to torment and be tormented, and, in the end, to die at the appointed hour.

Suljo and his boy Kasim were by themselves.

3. Ahmet

Less than a year later, Suljo married again at the urging of his brother Agan, who said a house couldn't be without a female ear.

Try as they would, Suljo and his second wife simply couldn't have children.

There were astonished glances in the village and mutterings through the teeth. Some directed their barbs at Suljo, saying he shunned what God had made man for, others concluded that it was Allah punishing *her* for marrying a man whose former wife hadn't even had a chance to grow cold under the gravestone.

Be that as it may, eleven years later Suljo's second wife bore him a son, and they named him Ahmet.

That was the end of the malicious rumors, and people said happiness had finally settled into the house of Suljo, also known as Šehaga.

4. Alija

Before Kasim turned thirteen, Suljo suddenly fell ill—they said it was meningitis—and before anybody could become seriously worried, he died.

People cursed and swore. Some cursed the poor and barren earth that hardly provided sustenance and took away life all too easily, while others waved fatalistically and with a cosmic calm, citing Allah the Almighty's power to give and to take away, to separate and to connect, depending on a person's fate, and when their time was up.

Several months after Suljo's death, people in the village began to notice that his widow's belly was growing. Some said it was Allah granting Suljo one more life, but others thought it was Him punishing both the man and his unborn child.

There were also some who said it'd be better for the child not to be born.

Nine-and-a-half months after his death, Suljo's widow bore a male child and silence reigned in the village. She gave her son the name Alija.

5. Calamity

For some time already, Kasim had been big enough to do farm work. He tended the goats, sowed, reaped, and picked fruit. Sometimes he'd play with his half-brothers, who were quite a few years younger, and at that age several years mean the difference between two worlds: the world of boys, who chase after chickens, fish for trout in the stream, and catch lizards basking in the pricklegrass; and the world of men, who pull a plough because there's no ox, and haul timber out of the forest with the load pressing down on their shoulders and back, the rain-swollen ground swallowing their legs up to the knees. But that was nothing to agonize over. It'd always been like that, they said, from time immemorial, and so it would be until the calamitous Last Judgement.

Calamity soon came, and they called it the Second World War. And with it came armies with different uniforms, languages, objectives, strengths, and appetites.

The Germans and Ustashi came from the city, while the Partisans and Chetniks hid in the hills. The Germans went after the Partisans from time to time. On one such occasion they set fire to the nearby village where the Karavlasis lived, a Romany clan originally from Romania. The inhabitants were burned alive in their hovels or killed by bullets when they tried to flee the flames.

The Ustashi left a trail of fire in Orthodox villages, while the Chetniks killed Partisans, mainly by deceit, and pillaged and murdered in Muslim villages.

The Partisans were few in number, at least initially, and disturbed the others through their very presence more than any actual attacks.

In the spring of 1943, one Partisan brigade from Vojvodina was able to cross the Sava River and, before the Germans and Ustashi could stop them, linked up with the local Partisans, who by then had liberated much of the area adjoining the Sava region. Together they managed to free several more nearby villages in the plains and secluded valleys. After those successes, they were joined by a good part of the village youth, including Kasim. He was sixteen at the time.

In the face of an impending enemy offensive, the Partisans had to quickly withdraw toward the mountains in the interior of Bosnia, and Kasim went with them, singing the song he'd picked up:

When the men of Srem set out
from home in Fruška Gora
to aid their Bosnian brothers,
there was no braver warrior!

When the men of Srem now crossed
the swollen Sava River,
they saw proud Majevica,
its flanks of blue ashiver.

Proud beleaguered Bosnia,
o land of hill and vale,
the young sons of Srem have come,
our fight will never fail.

He wore a white jumper knitted from coarse wool and a small bag of the same. In it, he carried a piece of goat's cheese his stepmother had given him.

IV

THE SHOVELS HURRIEDLY piled the sodden, heavy earth and heaped it over Alija's remains at the bottom of the grave. I felt they were burying not only him, but also a never-told story.

1. *Dino and Nataša*

At the beginning of our alley, on the left-hand side, there was a green house. It glittered as if it'd been sprinkled with precious stones. Dino, my buddy who lived in that house, told me it was sand sparkling—there was sand in the plaster used for the façade. I didn't believe him and tried to persuade him that we should take out those precious stones so we could get rich. He didn't want to because it was his house, after all, and he was afraid of his grandfather too. His parents were also "officially" divorced, and his dad had moved back to his folks'. Dino and his mom lived with his grandfather and grandmother, who he called "Mother," just like I did my grandmother.

I was jealous of him because he played soccer better than me and because he was smaller and looked more like Bruce Lee. But what weevilled me most was that Nataša fell in love with him. While we were still little, a family from Srijem moved into the house next to Dino's. They had a daughter, Nataša, and a son, who we called Tot. Their dad was a goalkeeper and came to our town to play for Jedinstvo in the Second League.

Nataša was blonde and sweet and instantly fell in love with Dino. I wasn't so much fond of her as I resented her falling in love with him, of all boys. Dino teased her the whole time, pulled her hair, sang crude ditties, farted, burped, and did all sorts of other disgusting things, but she devoured him with her naïve little blue eyes. I tried to attract her attention by lying. I made up the most unlikely tales, but she'd only laugh at me. And then Dino would come, belch from the bottom of his stomach, and at the same time say "Knoooor," like in the ad for Knorr stock cubes. Nataša would just clap, pout her lips, say, "Ugh, you're so horrid!" and then go off after him.

Once I asked Nataša where her grandmother was, and she said she only had a deceased grandmother in Sremska Mitrovica. I was young then and didn't know what "deceased" meant. On one occasion I cursed her deceased grandmother. She started to cry and didn't want to talk to me anymore. I asked Suzana what "deceased" meant.

"That's when somebody has died, see?"

2. Pele and Liso

The boy who lived on the other side of the street, Pele, was blond and surly. You always had to be careful what you said in front of him because he'd easily get angry or, what was even worse, start to tease you. He could abuse you for days for saying something at the wrong place or time or start a fight with you for the most trivial little thing. He had a brother two years older, who every-body called Liso. I once told Dino that it was because he looked like a *lisica*, a fox—always ready to talk you into some nonsense and then laugh in your face when you realized you'd been duped. And all the others would laugh together with him. Still, he liked most of all to tease his brother Pele, and could hardly wait to tangle with him. They swore at each other constantly. But if anybody else swore at Pele, Liso would bash him up. Pele, on the other hand, didn't like his brother to defend him, and then he'd fight against both his brother and the one who'd sworn at him.

3. Soccer

Dino and Pele supported Partizan, while Liso and I were fans of Red Star Belgrade, and that was the cause of everlasting quarrels and squabbles: which club was better, which had more championship titles, who played better—Momčilo Vukotić or Vladimir Petrović Pižon? I was the worst player, and Liso the best. Liso and I always played against Pele and Dino.

Even back then, I realized that soccer brings out the worst in us. One of the main reasons for our fights, which often erupted into little bloody wars, was that we didn't have proper goals. We would make them of stones, tracksuit tops, or sticks thrust into the ground. It was simple if the ball went through the middle of the goal, but that never happened. It would always go right next to the goalpost, or rather the stone or piece of clothing. And even if the ball went through the middle of the goal, somebody would protest straightaway that it was too high, meaning it'd gone over the top of the goal. By tacit agreement, the imaginary crossbar was somewhere at knee level. The only problem was whose knees, because we were all different heights.

BEKIM SEJRANOVIĆ

Then we'd bicker: it was a goal—no it wasn't. We would swear by our mothers, fathers, dead grandfathers and grandmothers, but it didn't help. In the end, if nobody gave in, it'd all end in a fistfight. Whoever got beaten had to admit that the other was right.

The mildest swear word in situations like that was "dammit," or "darn it," and was used mainly in minor altercations. Next up in weight was "by my grandfather's grave" or "by my grandmother's grave," even if your grandparents were alive. And when you wanted to be deadly serious, you'd swear by Tito.

4. May Tito die stone dead

We were playing behind the technical college one Sunday. It was actually a parking lot for the teachers, an uneven concrete surface excellent for small-field soccer. As always, it was me and Liso against Pele and Dino. Or rather, it was Red Star vs. Partizan.

We had kit, too, for that Sunday match. Liso and Pele had proper jerseys from somewhere, Liso was Red Star, and Pele Partizan. They really looked genuine and had numbers on the back—Liso was number seven and Pele nine. The sleeves on Pele's jersey were so long that he was forever having to pull them up.

My jersey was a bit different than Liso's, though it was also Red Star. It was a present from my dad and didn't have a number on the back. Grandmother later sewed on a white number five for me, but it turned out a bit crooked and looked shabby.

It was actually the jersey of FC Kozara from Bosanska Gradiška, red with two white stripes on the front. I told Dad it didn't look exactly like the Red Star jersey because the two lines were thin, whereas the real Red Star jersey had red and white bars of equal width, evenly spaced. Dad frowned and said it didn't matter what the stripes were like.

"Is it red and white? It is. So there you go," he said, and gave me that look of his, after which I also had to believe it.

When it was 3-2 for Partizan, the ball somehow found its way to me. Only Dino was now between me and the goal, and he quickly planted himself in front of it to try and stop me from scoring. I'd never been good at dribbling, so I took a chance and shot at the goal. The ball hit Dino's leg, deflected diagonally, and a second later was over the goal line. Liso and I instantly screamed, "Goooaaal!" But the Partizan players went, "What goal? The ball hit the post and went out."

Our goalposts were two stones, and the ball went right over the left-hand one. Who could tell now if it'd hit the outer or inner side of the post? We all started swearing by our ancestors, be they living or dead.

Liso and Pele had living grandfathers, so Liso swore, "May Grandfather drop dead if that wasn't a goal!"

But Pele roared, "Grandfather and Grandmother can go to hell if that was a goal!"

It was now for me and Dino to decide things. We needed stronger arguments than our grandparents.

Dino raised the stakes, "If that was a goal, I don't love Tito. See?"

"Aah," I shouted. "You don't love Tito! Dino doesn't love Tito!"

"What rot! Who doesn't love Tito?" he bristled. "Swear then, if you dare!"

Liso and Pele started shouting, "C'mon, c'mon!"

Liso yelled, "Swear, dammit! It was a goal, in Tito's name, I saw it!"

Pele said, "A goal my ass! C'mon, let him swear by Tito if he dares!"

What could I do?

"It was a goal," I blurted, "on Tito's name, it was a goal!"

Dino squinted maliciously. "C'mon, if you dare. Say: May Tito drop dead if it wasn't a goal!"

I stopped for a moment. I wasn't *that* sure it was a goal, but what could I do?

"May Tito die stone dead right now if it wasn't a goal!"

The others fell silent. That was that. There was no oath or spell more powerful. You just needed the guts to say it.

"Alright then, 3-3, but now we're gonna knock the shit out of you," Pele hissed and looked at his brother, who bared a despicable grin.

5. *Tito's dead!*

Even today I'm not sure if it was a goal or not, and Tito didn't die right then, but seven days later.

Dino and I were playing "passes" in the alley, no goals, just kicking the ball back and forth. Suddenly I saw Dino's mom rushing toward us. Dino couldn't see her because he had his back to her. I saw her all aflush, running out into the alley like a forward into the penalty box. She was wearing a green terry dressing gown.

Dino's gonna cop it, I thought, and I felt sorry for him for a moment. Only for a moment.

Just as my momentary sympathy was turning to malicious glee, she shouted, "Dino, come inside! Tito's dead."

She spoke, turned, and marched back into the house. The ball I'd kicked rolled up to Dino, and he sat down on it, touching the ground with his knees. He looked at me in fear, as if waiting for an answer.

"She's lying," I said to him. "How could Tito die? C'mon, shoot!"

We stared at one another like that for several moments. I could feel we were both seized by a boyish excitement, like before an adventure, a prank, or a beating.

6. Tears for Tito

We both ran off home. At my place, Grandfather was sitting with Sakib the neighbor, an old man in his eighties but still hale and hearty. They sat, smoking and sighing.

Sakib lived in the house next to ours with his wife; he hadn't spoken to her for fifteen years and nobody knew her name. Everybody just called her "Sakib's wife."

"Old Friend has died," Sakib said.

"Yes, my good Sakib, he's died," Grandfather said with sincere sadness.

When I went into the kitchen, Grandmother was puttering around. I asked her what'd happened, and she answered that I should be quiet and that Tito had died.

"It's best that we both be quiet," she said.

Grandfather shouted, "Stop it with those pans, for God's sake! Didn't I tell you to stop the noise? Cut that damn clatter now!"

Then all of us sat in front of the TV. I was on the floor, hugging my knees with my arms and waiting to see what would happen next. The TV was playing solemn music, the screen was black, and it read, "Extraordinary News." I started to yawn a little from the music, and when I yawn it makes the tears run.

I often pretended like that at school to claim stomach pains or a bad headache—I just yawned a few times and my eyes filled with tears.

Grandmother felt pity and said, "Come here, don't cry.

I didn't want to be cuddled.

Then the news announced that at exactly 3:05 p.m. that day, May 4, 1980, the great heart of our beloved Comrade Tito had stopped beating. There was no denying it—it sounded terrible. And maybe it was terrible to some extent, but nobody knew to what extent. At least not yet.

7. *The pocketknife*

When I was on the way to school the next day, my dad's car appeared out of the blue. I was surprised to see him. The surprise then turned to a mild fear. He'd always turn up unexpectedly like that. I wouldn't see him for months, and then he'd pop up out of nowhere. First there'd be a round of faultfinding: why was I wearing those clothes or those shoes, why didn't I tuck in my T-shirt ('cos only assholes do that, Dad, I thought, but I didn't dare say it), why were my nails so filthy and my neck grimy, as if I hadn't washed for months? Afterward we'd go and have shish kebabs and a soft drink, or he'd take me shopping.

Once he took me into the department store and said, "Choose any trousers you like, and Dad'll buy them for you."

I ran straight to a pair of green woolen ones. I really liked them in green.

Dad cuffed me on the back of the head and hissed, "Why on earth those green ones, you hick?"

He bought me a pair of jeans with a thin white stripe down the seam at the sides. I thought they looked silly, and the back of my head hurt. But the worst thing was that he called me a hick. And that he'd promised I could choose any pair, but then he wouldn't let me. I wanted those green ones, though now I can't remember why.

When my dad turned up after Tito's death, he invited me to get into his car, a Polish Fiat, which people called a "Pole." I had a little sit inside, we chatted, and he gave me a blue pocketknife. I looked at it all the way to school. I liked the color.

8. *It was a goal*

When we arrived at school, the teacher informed us of every-thing again and said we wouldn't be having math and natural science that day but talking about Tito. She explained that there'd be seven days of mourning, which meant: no singing or whistling, no loud, boisterous behavior, and no laughing. But I saw lots of people laughing in the street and whistling, and one guy with a droopy moustache who rode by on a bike was even humming. I heard him. How could he, when it was a time of mourning? I didn't sing or whistle. The 7:15 evening cartoons weren't on either.

When Dino, Pele, and I were going home from school that Monday, they brought up the goal from our match a week ear-lier again.

"See what happens when you swear but you're lying," Pele said.

Dino could hardly wait—they'd obviously planned this in detail.

"We're gonna tell everybody what you said. You're really fucked now."

Then they started giving me a hard time and they weren't bad at it, I must admit.

I put up with it for a while, and then shouted, "Oh, go to hell both of you!"

I ran home and this time tears truly welled up in my eyes, not out of fear that they'd snitch on me but out of fury that I'd let them unnerve me like that. I knew Tito hadn't died because of me. He would've died one way or another. And it was a goal.

9. They called me Gyp

On that Tuesday we kept on talking about Tito, mainly all the good things.

A table was set up in front of the assembly hall, with a red tablecloth, and a black-and-white photo of Tito from the fifties was placed on it. A black ribbon was draped over the top left corner. Every ten minutes, two students would take turns at being guards of honor, and they had to be dressed properly: with a Partisan cap on their head and a red Pioneer scarf around their neck. I also had the honor, together with a boy called Mustafa. He was short, stocky, and very dark-skinned. Even darker than me, who they called Gyp, because they said I looked like a Gypsy. That annoyed me at first and once I came home in tears with a messed-up nose because I'd gotten into a fight with a boy called Osman, who teased me the whole time that I was a Romany.

Uncle Alija explained, "Romanies are people like the rest of us, kid, they're just not interested in soccer and politics. So soccer and politics ought to be banned. You get it?"

He gave me a sharp rap on the head and limped out of the courtyard like a savant of the East. I stood at the gate with my bloodied nose, rubbing the top of my head that still tingled from the whack of his middle finger.

I was standing at attention there guarding the memory of Tito with Muće, as we'd nicknamed Mustafa, each of us at his side of the table. He had hair that grew almost out of his forehead. He was a screwed-up guy, but in a stupid way—he didn't scare anybody, nor could he make anybody laugh. And you have to do one or the other, though nobody realized that at the time.

I noticed he was goggling at me strangely. I gave him a sign with my eyes: what's up, whaddaya want, huh?

"Well," he whispered, "was it really a goal?"

I pretended not to hear him, but inside I fumed and cursed him. And Pele and Dino too. Muće kept bothering me, and I started collecting saliva in my mouth. When I'd had enough, I went up and spat in his face. He wiped it off, came up to me, and we started shoving each other. Then the new guards of honor came and managed to separate us. When we went back to the classroom for the lesson, Muće suddenly said I'd spat at him for no reason.

The teacher gave me several smacks on the butt with a ruler, and she only sent Muće back to his place. She was manic, but more from fear than fury. After she'd thrashed me with the ruler, she said that only Gypsies spit.

10. *Our unhappy teacher*

Our teacher was a stunningly attractive, middle-aged blonde. Her husband owned a games hall where kids left all their cash, playing video games, foosball, pinball, and all that. Once I pinched a whole series of Grandfather's special-mint silver coins with Tito's image and spent them on games of Pac-Man. I used the silver coins with Tito instead of five-dinar coins and the machine accepted them without any trouble. I don't know

now if that's what made them rich, but they soon built a big house and opened some kind of private firm.

Her husband had his throat cut in the first days of the war, and she fled to Germany. She was very beautiful even as an old woman, but unhappy both young and old.

In her youth because she married for money, and in her old age because she was beautiful when she was young.

11. *Tito's funeral*

Tito's funeral was on Wednesday. They sent us home from school early so we could watch the broadcast on TV.

With us at our place were Suzana's mom, Sakib the neighbor, and Uncle Alija.

Everybody was solemn and mournful except Alija. He was sullen and unshaven. You got a fright when you looked at him, and you didn't know exactly why.

Hundreds of thousands of people were on the streets of Belgrade, and everybody was crying. The camera particularly loved tearful women and children.

I yawned as much as I could, but I wasn't satisfied with the quantity of tears compared to the people on the screen. Grandfather was serious. Grandmother, with a sad face, was probably thinking what she'd make for dinner the next day. Sakib the neighbor smoked and clenched his jaws with his false teeth.

When it was time for the coffin to be lowered into the marble-clad vault, Suzana's mom got up, crossed her arms below her belly, and started crying. Tears poured down her face. The others also stood up. Then Grandmother cried too. Even my tears began to flow, only I wasn't sure if the yawning had finally worked or if I'd really started to cry. It was hard to remain calm caught up in a scene like that.

Alija alone stayed sitting in stone-faced silence, smoking and rolling cigarettes with amazing speed. He had a lighter that smelled of gasoline and was a real delight to smell. Nobody spoke at all, and I wondered why he didn't get up like the others. I thought it might be because of his leg that he injured when they were blasting in the coal mine, but I didn't dare to ask aloud.

Especially not him, with eyebrows like that.

V

THE MEN AROUND Alija's grave slowly got up, went to within a foot or two, took a piece of earth, and gently dropped it in. The gravediggers took no notice. They swung their shovels like last admonishments and covered up the remains of a life.

Grandfather Kasim stood between me and Alija's son and cried like an abandoned child.

1. *Hero*

Kasim returned from the war with the rank of captain, twice wounded. He'd grown visibly thin, and he was also bald from the typhoid fever he'd picked up during an offensive in the craggy country between Bosnia and Montenegro. He marched into the city in a uniform pieced together from American pants and a German overcoat. He had a Schmeisser across his chest and a cocked Partisan cap.

Everybody in the village welcomed him as a hero, and his stepmother as a son who'd come back from the war alive.

After the war, Kasim chased Chetniks on the slopes of the Majevica mountain range for a time, and later he commanded one of the youth work brigades that built the first postwar Yugoslav railroad line from Brčko to Banovići.

He soon married a girl from a well-to-do family that lived on the outskirts of the city. They moved into the city, and within a short space of time his wife bore two large and healthy girls.

She delivered the first child after rolling around for hours on an iron bed, and the second one standing up, gripping the bars on the window.

Before the Brčko–Banovići railroad line was even properly finished, a second one was begun, from Šamac to Sarajevo. Kasim and his youth work brigade were transferred to the section near Doboj and continued their work.

They sang:

Brčko–Banovići
That is our bold goal
To build the railroad
So the route is whole.

One, two, three,
One, two, three,
Tito's youth makes history.
It's off to work, one and all
To reconstruction's call!

Later they just modified the first line. The song now began with "Šamac–Sarajevo." The new route was longer and more important, but everything else remained the same.

2. Brothers

Kasim's half-brothers, Ahmet and Alija, stayed in the village after the war. They lived together with their mother, Kasim's stepmother, in the house built by their late father Suljo, dubbed Šehaga.

Years followed years, and village life after the war was hard.

The land under orchards passed to the cooperative, and Ahmet went back to clearing the forest. He looked after his mother and his younger brother Alija.

Those who remember him from that time describe him as a broad-shouldered, sullen man with pale blue eyes. They say he was taciturn and hardworking.

Ahmet didn't marry for a long time, nor did he seem to contemplate tying the knot. And then unexpectedly, some said suddenly, he arranged a small and nondescript wedding.

His bride was known in the village for her beauty, poor background, and a speech impediment. She spoke nasally and slurred her words. That didn't prevent her from talking or being understood; on the contrary, she talked a lot, and always with a smile on her face.

Before nine months had passed after the wedding, she bore Ahmet a son, and just over a year later, a second one.

3. The youngest brother

Alija was no longer a boy at that time, but even less a man. People in the village said he was different and a bit of an oddball. Some saw his eccentricity as being in his unusual little moustache like nobody else in the village had after the war, others in him getting hold of a *saz* from somewhere and beginning to play it like nobody had before.

Soon no gathering was imaginable without that quiet and absorbed young man, and the village's idlers and inveterate alcoholics realized that Alija's hand plucked the *saz* with the plectrum even more finely and tenderly after a few small cups, *fildžans*, of mild *rakija*. Alija soon realized that too.

Alija was no shirker. He worked more than anybody, but only when he felt like it. And that was precisely the problem—you never knew when Alija felt like ploughing and sowing, picking the plums, or chopping wood, and when his thoughts were wandering who knows where, who knows to which parts of the country, beyond hills and valleys, toward the sea, which nobody in the village had ever seen.

He most liked to spend the days on the sunlit tops of the hills, where sea cliffs protruded below the gorges. These were remnants of the bed of the Pannonian Sea, which had once lapped its southern shore here eons before human memory. He'd take his flute and a woven bag, in which he would drop medicinal herbs he picked along the way. Old Hadži Murat—still alive, just even older—taught him to identify the herbs; which cured which illness, which was good if you were healthy or ill, which grew and flowered when, and how to dry and prepare them.

Alija would slowly follow his goats and look for herbs. He'd sit on one of the cliffs dappled with fossils of shells and get out his flute. He'd play for a long time and then often doze off. When he woke up, he'd roll some tobacco in paper and smoke, blinking at the sun. He felt the fumes irritate his throat, caress his lungs, and calm him.

I imagined him sitting on the grass and looking into the sky behind the tops of the hills, pondering something vague and indefinite, but great enough for his lungs to swell at the thought: something that made him restless and nervous, something neither happy nor sad, something that let him forget the goats and the fact that he lived in a house that'd been taken over by his elder brother, for whom he was now nothing but a nuisance.

It'd also help him forget that he lay awake at night, intently listening to the sounds from the main bedroom—the noises made by his elder brother Ahmet and his fertile wife. Every morning after a night like that, and there were many, especially in the winter, when Ahmet and his wife got up and she put on the first coffee, Alija fled. He ran outside, be it frost, snow, or rain. He ran into the barn, or into the hills on little trails through the snow, he ran where nobody else would've gone, only so as not to see them. So as not to watch Ahmet sipping his coffee with relish, exchanging smiles with his wife, and calling his sons with mock strictness. He ran so he wouldn't have to look his sister-in-law in the eyes and wouldn't have to see her buxom form, as if everything on her was about to burst: her chest, thighs, and rear. He ran so as not to hear her giggle and tell him through her nose that she'd slept like a log.

He ran so as not to think or—Allah forbid—blurt out, "Slept like a log? More like squealed like a hog!"

That's why he fled. And he would've run even farther if only somebody had shown him the way, told him of other paths and routes to go. He always ran like that to the top of the hills, to the old Pannonian cliffs, and gazed at the surrounding peaks.

He looked into the sky above them and dreamed he was a bird that could fly and discover what lay beyond.

4. The devil

The truth is that Alija had known such uneasiness from the beginning, but after his beautiful, smiling, and serene sister-in-law came into the house, he began to stay away for two or three days at a time, sometimes more. That didn't disturb Ahmet so much at the beginning, but after a while he too felt that his younger brother brought uneasiness into the house, without knowing exactly how.

He told his wife, who was the centerpiece of his simple but idyllic life, that something was eating away at him inside. He felt Alija's uneasiness was infecting him, he said, and his brother's eyes fled from him every time they met, and his silence that rankled them all day long bothered him more than when he came in through the gate in the morning drunk and humming a song that awakened the unhealthy urges in a person: the impulses that drive them first to crush and destroy themselves, then those closest to them, and finally everything they see.

That's how Ahmet spoke to his wife in their room at night as they lay pressed up against one another under the warm quilt. Ahmet's wife would listen and then answer in her nasal voice, which, however others may have found it, was still music to Ahmet's ears. She'd try to convince him to let Alija do what he liked because, after all, he didn't ask for bread and didn't disturb them. He shouldn't harm him because that was a sin and because the poor fellow had it hard. And then he shouldn't make the man's troubles any worse but should help his brother in any way he could, and if he couldn't, he should let him go with goodness and in the name of God.

Then she'd wrap herself around her husband and whisper to him coyly not to lay a finger on his brother. "Why would you drive your own brother out of the 'ouse? There'd be a scandal and the 'ouse and our children would be stained. Let Alija be, let 'im live, it'll pass, like everything passes. One day the fellow's alive and well, the next day 'e's gone and nowhere to be seen, like 'e never existed in this world. So don't 'arm your poor brother, you don't know what tomorrow and the time ahead will bring for you or 'im, we never know who'll need who, and when."

Ahmet heard out his wife every time, admiring how wisely she spoke. It seemed to him that she spoke more sensibly than any hodja or learned man, and certainly more than the Party Committee rep in the village, and that he had no choice but to take her advice.

The very next night, however, as soon as they went to bed, and the light went out early in that house, Ahmet would start his story again about the uneasiness Alija brought into the house, and his wife would soothe him again. The more he talked, the tighter she pressed her body up to him and tried to convince him to put such thoughts behind him. Then he'd quiet down, and for a while afterward nothing could be heard from their room except the pulsations of flesh, the rubbing of skin, and sighs, which Alija, lying afire in the second room, would think were the sounds of the devil incarnate, rending his body and soul.

VI

THE MEN DISPERSED, moving slowly toward the path that provided a way out of that charnel of human remains. As if by a command, they took out their cigarettes, lit up, greedily inhaled the smoke, and blew it away, throwing back their heads.

The gravediggers had finished covering Alija's last hideout and were now mercilessly beating down the mound of soil with their shovels.

1. My last visit

After Uncle Alija was buried, I went back to Oslo. I stayed for several months. Selma and I broke up.

Afterward I went away to the island of S. in the far north of Norway. I would've fled even farther, but there was nowhere else to go. Grandmother and Grandfather died while I sat in my room on that island and stared at the lowered shutters on the window. It was dark outside and nothing could be seen.

When I went back to Oslo from the island of S., I didn't know what to do next. I thought of calling Selma and saying something to her, anything, but I didn't.

Then I saw them one day in "our" park in St. Hanshaugen. Her and him. It was a white, Norwegian summer evening. They were pushing a buggy together.

She was saying something, and he was looking up and nodding in a fatherly way.

I stopped for a moment and tried frantically to wrench some kind of feeling from the abyss of my own being, but I didn't feel anything. I expected nausea, disgust, or, at best, hatred, but there was nothing. I wasn't even curious, I didn't feel even the most innocuous desire to see the child, which may have been mine. Or, if nothing else, I could at least have been generous, I could've sincerely wished them happiness. For Selma's sake, for the sake of our former love, or at least the child. I could've been moved a bit by that seemingly beautiful and optimistic image: a man and a woman out walking their progeny on a sunny Nordic evening. Like a scene from an IKEA ad. But I didn't feel anything. I watched them and knew they couldn't see me, because I was no longer there.

Several days afterward I traveled to Zagreb and wanted to go straight on to my native city in Bosnia, on the banks of the Sava. While I was in the hotel room in Zagreb, Goran called and told me, stuttering, that Kole was dead. The f-f-funeral would be in two days' time on the coast near Rijeka.

After Kole's funeral, I went from Rijeka to Brčko for the last time.

There was nobody left there whose funeral I could go to.

I stood at the entrance to the alley I'd once called mine. I tried to evoke some memory, but the pictures were blurred and elusive. Dino's house still stood there on the left-hand side. It was still greenish like before, but the "precious stones" in the walls no longer shimmered.

Dino fled to Germany during the war, got married, and had two children.

In 1997, he was struck by a car and killed while crossing the street.

2. Brotherhood and Unity Street

So there I was, after all that'd happened, walking along that street—the only one I'd once been able to call mine. But nothing was the same anymore, neither I nor the street. The street's name had been changed, and my name was the only thing about me that hadn't. Or maybe nothing had changed, maybe everything had always been just like this, maybe my memory resisted the truth. You don't know what causes you more pain: memory or the truth.

I don't believe memory, and I can't bear the truth.

I went past the elementary school I once attended. Its name had been changed too. The crosswalk was still there in front of the school, where I was hit by a light blue Fiat when I was six. Now I almost smiled. The driver of the baby Fiat came to visit me while I lay at home in bandages. You could see he genuinely felt sorry, and he didn't know what to say. I felt sorry for him, too. After several minutes of silence, he spoke.

"If only you'd managed to grab on to the windshield wipers when I hit you," he said in earnest, more to himself then me.

When the man left, I started cry. Grandmother asked me why I was crying, and I said it was because I hadn't grabbed on to the wipers.

After a short pause, Grandmother hissed, "Bah, to 'ell with 'is damn wipers!"

I walked on down what was formerly Brotherhood and Unity Street toward our alley. Men passed by, and young women and boys. I was glad not to recognize anybody. I was actually dying of fear that somebody would stop and say hello to me. I went past shops and the tinted windows of coffee bars. Now and again I cast a glance in the glass and saw my reflection.

I was surprised I still recognized that face.

3. *The alley*

I headed along the alley toward the house where we used to live. I counted my steps. From the beginning of the alley to our gate it'd been thirty-six of my steps and forty-two of Dino's. In width, the alley was five-and-a-half steps of mine, and six-and-a-quarter of his. I went halfway along the alley and counted ten steps. Something wasn't right. Either this was the wrong alley or maybe I wasn't me anymore. I looked at the house where I grew up. I didn't recognize it.

Then I realized that me having counted just ten steps and gone halfway along the alley had nothing to do with the length of my steps. Nor did the dilapidated, crooked house have anything to do with me not recognizing it. It simply wasn't that alley anymore, nor was it that house. Nor was I me.

Then again, everything was the same.

I turned and walked out of the alley. At Dino's, I headed right and continued down the street. The ice cream and pastry shop Vardar had once been right next to his house. Dino and I demolished our first *tulumbas* in syrup, whipped-cream pies, and ice creams there. And, less often, a custard slice.

Now there was a catering business in its place, with a different name, purpose, and meaning. A large tinted glass surface like the eye of a cyclops gaped at the street.

4. He's lying, you know, he's lying

Once, when I was still me and the street was called Brotherhood and Unity Street, and when the ice cream and pastry shop was still called Vardar, and Dino's house scintillated as if covered in gems, I hurried along that street, skipping, clenching a twenty-dinar bill in my hand and singing "Swear It, My Love" by the band Srebrna Krila. They stole the tune from Boney M, and my father said they were gay.

I'd wheedled the twenty dinars from Grandmother to buy Pad III. That was an art class kit for third grade. When I arrived at the kiosk, I saw the latest issue of Commander Mark in the display: "Ontario in Flames." I opened my mouth to ask for Pad III, but my mouth wouldn't obey me. It asked for Commander Mark. He was a freedom fighter from the region of Ontario who fought against British redcoats, together with his inseparable friends Sorrowful Owl (chief of four native American tribes), Mr. Bluff (a former Caribbean pirate), and his dog Flock (a skinny, flea-infested mongrel).

Commander Mark may not have been such a good comic strip, but we liked it because it didn't come out in instalments. Every issue contained a complete story, on exactly sixty-six pages. No more, no less. You could rely on Commander Mark for the number of pages.

After buying the comics, I headed back the same way, but not in such a hurry now. I had to come up with a story for Grandmother. I was peerless as a liar, maybe because I lied so impudently that Grandmother simply couldn't believe *her* grandchild could think up such falsehoods.

Once, when I went to Pele's birthday party across the road, Grandmother dressed me in my best blue woolen pants and a white shirt. She told me that if we went out to play after eating the birthday cake I absolutely must come home and get changed first. I didn't do as she said but went into the woods to play Partisans and Germans in my good clothes. I came home, in her words, "as filthy as a bull." I sold her the story that we'd gone for a walk from Pele's house to the stadium, and then soldiers had appeared out of nowhere and forced us to do exercises, to crawl, throw ourselves in the mud, and roll.

Grandmother looked at me puzzled and asked, "But why, for God's sake?"

"They told us: Don't ask, you'll need it in future!" I answered, and I believed it myself.

If you believe in something strongly enough, it's no longer a lie.

Grandmother fell silent, shook her head, and took off my muddy clothes. I was five at the time. Afterward she told the story to Grandfather, who cast a wily glance in my direction and said nothing.

Later she told it to Alija, who'd dropped by wearing a beret and with his moustache trimmed, and he went, "Bah, what soldiers? He's lying, you know!"

Grandmother then probably realized at last. She pulled me to her with her strong, heavy hand, but I laughed. She immediately gave me a whipping there in front of Alija, and he just kept saying, "He's lying, you know, he's lying!"

I cried and giggled hysterically. At the same time.

Another time, she left me alone at home because she had to go to the doctor. I was a bit bored, so I took her cigarettes—green "57s," the famous pack with the cigarettes upside down. I stood in front of the bedroom mirror and smoked, observing myself. Afterward I sat in the living room, watched Branko Kockica's children's program, and smoked. When Grandmother came home, the house was full of smoke.

"Who's been smoking 'ere?"

"Nobody."

"What's this smoke from then?"

"I don't know."

Then Grandmother went to the Kreka stove that was stoked with coal.

"Could it be from the Kreka?" Grandmother asked, inspecting the pipe that went up into the chimney.

"Yes, yes, it's from the Kreka," I said, quickly finding my feet.

Then Grandmother turned around and saw the ashtray full of cigarette butts.

"Kreka my foot, who smoked so many cigarettes 'ere? Not you, I 'ope?"

"It wasn't me, really, it wasn't me," I answered in a frightened voice. I didn't have any excuse ready, so the catastrophe was approaching. My mind worked feverishly, various combinations and permutations, plots, dramatic phrases—everything was at stake. I came up with the ruse that a woman had called, looking for Grandmother. And I'd told her that Grandmother would be back soon, so she waited and waited, and smoked and smoked, and in the end she left.

"What woman?"

"I don't know."

"'Ave you ever seen 'er before?"

"Maybe."

Then I had to describe her: what her eyes were like, how she was dressed, I had to imitate her speech, how she talked, and how she smoked. It was like Grandmother sat in the theater, and I was auditioning. My five-year-old butt was at stake.

But finally I got through. For days afterward, Grandmother kept asking herself who it could have been. When Grandfather came back from his trip, she attacked him with accusations that it must have been a lover of his, and he defended himself by saying he had no idea, he'd been on the road for a week through all of Bosnia and Montenegro. How should he know who it was. And why did she go and leave me alone at home? At the same time, he shot a few angry glances at me, but he didn't give me away. Who knows, maybe it would've been better if he had. Maybe I would've quit the habit of lying, though I doubt it. Maybe I wouldn't have bought Commander Mark instead of the art class kit, and I wouldn't have had to think up that story for Grandmother.

When I finally returned home that time, she asked where my art class kit was.

"Grandma, you know what happened?"

"What?" Grandmother gasped. Then she saw the comics in my hand.

"When I got to the kiosk and asked nicely, 'Have you got Pad III?', he said to me, 'No, we've just run out, but we've got the latest Commander Mark. And he gave it to me," I finished, shrugging my shoulders and widening my eyes.

And now, as I neared the place where that kiosk had once stood, I felt I could hear the whistling of Grandmother's cane as it descended toward my butt. I lied better when I was a boy, I thought. Better to myself and to others. Now I'm not even good at lying to myself. People don't mind when you lie to them, you just need to know how to do it. The truth is nothing other than a well-worded lie.

Truth is the lie you believe.

Truth is the lie you live for and die for.

5. *As if I wasn't there*

I stopped on the corner where I'd been "forced" to take Commander Mark, and expected something to happen. Behind where the kiosk had been was a ruined building, which before the war had housed a school for the mentally ill. Across the road there had been an old white mosque. It'd been bombed out in the war, and now a new concrete one was being built. People walked past me. High school boys with puss-filled pimples and vacuous looks, girls with trussed-up butts and unhealthy smiles. It was as if I wasn't there. I stood there like a ghost clutching "Ontario in Flames." I stood there like the kiosk that'd vanished, like the mosque reduced to rubble, like the defiled ice cream and pastry shop Vardar, like the gems that'd disappeared from Dino's house.

I crumbled like the demolished school for the mentally ill.

VII

WHEN THE OLDEST of the gravediggers beat down on the mound for the last time, Alija's son laid flowers at the wooden grave marker. He then said goodbye to us and started down the path toward the road. Grandfather stopped crying.

When Alija's son had gone a little way, Grandfather went up to the mound, noticeably dragging his left leg. He bent down with effort and took a flower from the bouquet. Then he couldn't get up, so I had to help him.

I watched for an endlessly long time as he walked along the path toward the other end of the graveyard. He came to a marble gravestone and laid the flower there. The name of his half-brother and Alija's brother, Ahmet, was carved in the stone.

1. Yes, my Ahmet

One day, Ahmet went to see Kasim in the city to complain about the unbearable situation at home.

"It can't go on like this," he said. "Somebody's gotta move out, either Alija or me. If you know what to do, and 'ow—good.

If you don't, may God 'elp us. No, dear Kasim, it can't go on like this. Yes, 'e's my brother and I love 'im and care for 'im like a brother, but it's not right . . . it can't go on."

Ahmet continued the lament he'd begun in bed with his wife. Kasim listened in silence and reflected. He would've helped, yes, he would've helped without a word, and it would've been his pleasure to be asked for help. To be asked to do something for somebody, to loan them money, to drive them to the hospital, to give them advice, anything, but he was never asked. Instead, he was now being asked to be a judge, to be a judge for his brothers who lived in a world he'd fled from when he was still a boy, and here was the proof that he still wasn't free of it. He sat and smoked, looked at the fildžan of Bosnian coffee in front of him, and listened as Ahmet listed his grievances and tried to convince him. He complained, begged, and threatened at the same time. If Kasim didn't help him, he didn't know how all this would end.

"It won't end well, because nothin' in this world can end well if it's not God's will, and livin' like we do is neither God's doing nor is it fit for people," Ahmet said.

"Yes, yes," Kasim said, sighing wearily at first, and then a bit nervously. "Yes, my Ahmet, yes."

But Ahmet harped on because he was used to talking about his troubles until his wife, in a quiet voice that only he could understand, started to assure him, calm him, and at the same time, inexplicably, lull him to sleep with her distinctive susurrations: "Ah, ah . . . ah, Ahmet, aaaah . . ."

When Ahmet arrived home, it was night. All the lights in the house were out. He slipped quietly through the gate and crossed the courtyard. He wondered for several moments whether it was best to knock on the window of their room, where his wife was doubtless sleeping, or unlock the door himself and sneak into his own house like a burglar. He decided in the end not to wake his wife, but to silently steal into the house, creep into the warm bed, and snuggle up to her, to inhale the smell of her skin and feel the fullness of that healthy body.

But when he lay down beside her, he felt the bed was somehow different—firm and cold. He dug his gnarled fingers into her flesh, but this time he didn't feel it submit to him. The flesh evaded him unfaithfully, twisted away, and melted like old snow.

2. Coffee

In the morning, Ahmet, his wife, and his mother were sitting, having coffee.

"Where's Alija?" he muttered, mainly to himself.

He was visibly sleep-deprived but had an air of satisfaction about him. He didn't find it strange that his brother wasn't there; he could turn up at the gate at any moment. And Ahmet felt he could see him staggering on wobbly legs, desperately clenching the saz under his arm and gaping dull-eyed into space.

His mother turned away, began adjusting her kerchief, untying it and tying it up, and then all over again. At the same time, she quietly mumbled the words of a chant or prayer. Every little while she spat toward Ahmet's wife. At one point Ahmet's wife spilled the coffee she was pouring for her husband, but his old mother went on with her incantations without even pausing to breathe.

Ahmet's wife dashed to get a rag to wipe up the coffee, while Ahmet stiffened and just sat there looking in amazement at his mother.

3. *Something warm and moist*

In the evening, when they went to bed, Ahmet began complaining to his wife again about Alija, like some absurd foreplay: he didn't come home all day, nobody knew where he roamed or where he slept, nor with whom and in what state he spent the nights, but that'd soon come to an end because he'd found a solution for that, too. He knew how he'd get the upper hand over his brother, that good-for-nothing. He went on and on like that, as if waiting for his wife to join in, snuggle up to him, begin to sweet-talk him, and convince him not to touch his brother, to leave the poor fellow in peace.

But this time she didn't, and Ahmet, after short pauses, in which he impatiently expected his wife to speak, droned on without end.

Her head lay on his chest, and at one point he felt something drip onto it and run on down, following the contours of his body. He raised himself up a bit and lifted his wife's head. Not much could be seen in the darkness, but when he turned her face toward him with both hands he felt something warm and moist drip onto his naked chest one more time.

VIII

AFTER HE BENT DOWN to lay the flower from Alija's bouquet on Ahmet's grave, Grandfather could no longer stand up. I heard him calling for help at the other end of the graveyard. I cursed and swore to myself as I once again lifted him up. He was crying again.

"Let's go home, Grandfather, let's go home," I said. "Oh do stop whining, that's enough."

He really started bawling then because he was ashamed to cry in front of me.

"Let's go home."

1. *Farewell, old house*

Now, a year and a half after Alija's funeral, I stood in the courtyard in front of the house where I grew up. I tried to sing Morrissey's "Late Night, Maudlin Street" in my head, but it sounded schmaltzy, even to me. I said goodbye to the house with that song. I bid it farewell, said *ciao*, *alahimanet*, *adios*, *au revoir*, but truly, I didn't feel I was parting with something very important to me. I didn't know if that was because I'd already parted with the house many times or because it was just a pile of bricks and plaster. Maybe both were true, but now I knew that this was the last time and knew that from now on the house was no longer mine—from now on it *really* was just a pile of bricks and plaster.

I didn't know what Morrissey wanted to say in his song, nor did it matter to me anymore. The difference between his and my feeling was probably like that between his Maudlin Street and my Brotherhood and Unity Street. Like the difference between that English house and my Bosnian one here. Between a cup of English tea and a fildžan of Bosnian coffee. Whiskey and slivovitz. Me and Uncle Alija.

There was a difference, but only the blind could see it.

This time I knew I was parting with the house forever and just wanted to satisfy the form of the separation. That's why I needed this scene, that's why I needed that song, that's why I tried to shape the moment. I'd planned everything in detail: I'd say goodbye to the house, go to graveyard, say my farewells to Grandmother and Grandfather, then walk down to the bank of the Sava, cast one last glance, and disappear forever.

2. Leaving

I stood and looked in through the non-existent windows.

I felt for a moment I could see somebody parting the old, white, holey curtains. I heard them opening a window and letting the morning air into the house.

Grandfather and Grandmother sat, drinking coffee and smoking. I lay on my tummy on the rug eating scrambled eggs and reading Commander Mark, The Great Blek, or Zagor. If we were alone at home, Grandfather and Grandmother let me eat on the floor. When Mom came to visit, I wasn't allowed to because she said you couldn't eat on the floor "like a dog."

"What's wrong with dogs?" I'd ask.

She never answered.

Grandfather lit two cigarettes and took one out of his mouth and put it in Grandmother's. Then they smoked like children, without inhaling the smoke into their lungs. They were silent and took occasional sips of coffee from their fildžans. When they drank like that, in silence, it meant Grandfather was going on another trip. Grandfather was a traveling salesman for the Izbor shoe factory. He traveled around with a suitcase full of shoes, which he showed to people in other cities. I felt sorry that Grandfather had to travel and would be away for several days, but at the same time I was glad because he always had something for me when he came back. He always brought something for Grandmother too, but she didn't like him traveling. She thought he had affairs on those trips, and once he was almost caught red-handed. Grandfather never admitted anything.

I don't know if Grandfather cheated on Grandmother, but he cheated me countless times. He told me all sorts of lies, too, but I loved him because of it. He cheated me and lied to me because I wanted him to. I don't know if Grandmother wanted it, but I needed it. Real life was worthless to me, I needed something more, something more beautiful and more exciting than normal life. I needed the Great Blek, Kit Teller, Commander Mark, or Tarzan. Sometimes, for days, I'd be Za-Gor Te-Nay, the spirit with the hatchet from Darkwood. Instead of a stone-bladed hatchet I used Grandmother's wooden meat tenderizer. When I was Tarzan, I'd go about the courtyard half naked for days. Later on, I took a brown piece of leather from Grandfather's suitcase of samples and made myself a loincloth like Johnny Weissmüller wore when he played Tarzan. Johnny went mad in his old age and died in a mental hospital, making Tarzan cries.

Once Grandfather brought me a cap from Belgrade like Commander Mark and the Great Blek wore, with a tail at the back. When my dad came to visit he said, "You look great in that Davy Crockett cap." He had no idea.

Uncle Alija dropped by and happened to see a comic strip. Every time he came after that, he'd ask, "'Ave you got any more of those great stories? I like the guy with the cap best."

And I always gave them to him, but Grandmother got angry because Alija never gave them back.

When I showed him the cap Grandfather had brought me from Belgrade, I could see the envy in his eyes. He asked me countless times to give it to him, to sell it or loan it, but I didn't want to. He offered me his fur hat in exchange, his beret, his lighter, cigarettes, everything, but that was the very reason I didn't want to relinquish it. Later I found the cap boring, but I still didn't want to give it to him. And maybe he only wanted it because I didn't want to give it to him.

Before I learned to read, my favorite thing was listening to Grandfather's stories from his days with the Partisans. They weren't of the sort: me alone against a hundred Germans. He told me about when they plundered a German food truck and everybody grabbed what they could. He got his hands on a slab of bacon, which he ate without bread, and then got the runs so bad that he shat for three days, nonstop. He told me they were so short of food that they ate beech leaves. Afterward I went out and ate lots of apricot leaves and also got diarrhea. He mentioned a guy from Dalmatia who ate a bellyful of prunes on an empty stomach and had the runs all the way from Foča to Višegrad. He told me how they used to move in single file and had to call out "Next man!" to each other in a muted whisper all the time so they wouldn't get lost at night in the forest. Once he misheard and thought the comrade in front of him said "Rest if you can," so he lay down in the mud and instantly fell asleep. He taught me the song "Bandiera Rossa." And then there were the Italians who ate an Orthodox priest's black cat near Kotor Varoš. Those were the kinds of stories Grandfather had. And he told them in such a way that I always laughed, though I'd already heard them a thousand times.

And then the Partisan movies ruined everything. Bata Živojinović—who killed half the Third Reich single-handedly—was to blame, along with my boyish intellect. The question had to come up sooner or later, with or without Živojinović: "Grandfather, how many Germans did you kill?"

He shook his head.

"Not one?"

"Not one."

"Well, did you at least wound one?"

"What are you goin' on about that for, bud? I don't know. I really don't know. They fired at me and I fired at them. Look, 'ere's a thousander, go and buy us each an ice cream, and get a move on. I want chocolate, go on, 'urry up, for Pete's sake."

I took the ten-dinar bill that Grandfather still called a "thousander," despite the revaluation, and looked at it with scorn.

As I left, I said, "You were wasting your bullets then."

To our mutual contentment, I soon discovered comics, so I forgot about the Germans, and my main enemies became the redcoats.

Neither existed anymore now, there was nobody. And this sentimental farewell to the house was really just a poor attempt to assure myself that I'd once existed, that I once used to run about this courtyard with Grandmother's wooden meat tenderizer and fight the enemy. The black fence at the bottom of the yard was a line of redcoats or a gang of nefarious gunslingers, and the apricot tree was their leader, an infamous bandit, who I'd hurl my stone-bladed hatchet at in the decisive moment with a cry of "Aaaaah!"

Now they were all gone: the apricot tree, the fence, the bumbling redcoats. Grandfather and Grandmother too. Now, in the courtyard, there was only a heap of trash and old iron, remnants of somebody's furniture, pieces of a smashed toilet bowl. As if somebody had vomited their chewed-up life and left it there to decay as a reminder.

I made a move at last, turned my back on the house, and headed down through the courtyard toward the garden. As I walked through the mud, I tried not to look at the dead trees, which I once used to climb. My gaze fell on the next-door garden that belonged to the late Hasan. I saw a moonscape of holes full of muddy water from the last rain. His wife Fikreta had been searching for him. He was killed at the beginning of the war, but his body was never found. Somebody lied to her that he was interred in the garden.

I left all that behind and went off down the path that, like salvation, led over the muddy ground and far away from the razed houses, withered fruit trees, and dug-up gardens.

IX

I HELD GRANDFATHER by the arm as we trudged toward the path that led out of the graveyard. The clouds that had been jostling above the valley ominously all day now finally released their rain. Grandfather couldn't go any faster.

1. *Rain*

Hard, remorseless rains leached the land that fall, like never before. People in the village said it was a right deluge. The swollen streams carried away everything in their path. Brown water poured down the hillsides, cutting new gullies.

How long it'd been since anything was heard of Alija, nobody could say for sure. His first disappearance was noticed by the idlers who gathered that summer by the river, a little way above the village. There they'd enjoy the breeze from the hills, cool off in the river, or refresh themselves with the rakija that stood all night in the mountain water. They weren't worried about Alija. They wouldn't even have remembered him if rakija hadn't stirred up the blood of one of them. The false strength and power of passion, such as only slivovitz can give, made the man's chest swell and his eyes widen. He would've hugged all the people around him, and embraced the river and the hills and the sky and the whole world, but he had trouble getting to his feet. And then a song welled up all by itself in that puffed-up chest: a song with a tremulous voice, difficult melody, and sad end. A song best accompanied by Alija's saz. Another of them sighed that it was no damn fun without a saz—he wouldn't even sing. Then they began to swear and harass Alija into playing, they promised him rakija and a snack, they threatened to throw him in the river, and the saz with him, if he didn't start playing that instant. But all that was in vain because Alija wasn't among them.

Only then did their alcohol-sapped, heavy, sluggish thoughts arrive at the conclusion, "'Ow can 'e play when he ain't 'ere?" Some began to swear by all that was holy that Alija had been with them just now and had played for them, undeniably, while others insisted that he hadn't been seen for almost a week, a month. He had, he hadn't—the quarreling and the circus basically went on as long as there was rakija; and there was a similar ruckus on the second day, and the third. On the fourth day, a man came from the next village, brought a saz, and thus the debate about Alija was ended. On the fifth day, nobody asked after him anymore.

Ahmet then noticed that his brother hadn't come home for two or three days, true, but he didn't worry. Alija will be Alija, he thought. He boozed at night, and during the day he probably holed up somewhere and slept. Besides, Ahmet had other concerns. Something was wrong with his mother. She nattered the whole time, speaking what might've been incantations without rhyme or reason. And spat at his wife. He didn't know what was up, what'd come over her—had she lost her mind, had some devil gotten into her? Who should he go to, a doctor or the hodja? He didn't rightly know, but he had a strange premonition that neither one would be of any help. And as if that wasn't enough for him already, his wife became conceited. She worked and obeyed him as before, but she no longer looked his way and didn't try to please his eye and ear. When he asked her anything, she just shrugged. When they went to bed in the evenings, she'd soon start crying.

Ahmet told Kasim about the thing with his mother, though he was heaven knows how far from being able to say what it was and what he'd do. Ahmet didn't mention his wife, and in terms of Alija he said only that he'd been gone for five or six days, that it was a disgrace that he drank so much, and that he was just waiting to have to carry him into the courtyard absolutely blotto. The neighbors would see it and laugh at him. Not only at him, but at all of them for letting the devil take Alija.

The sultry days were passing and everybody hoped for rain and a bracing change. Alija was still gone, Ahmet's mother didn't stop spitting, untying and tying up her kerchief, and whispering as if she was cursing somebody, and Ahmet's wife didn't become her old self again.

Kasim drove Ahmet and his stepmother to the hospital, the doctor examined her, and said the old lady was fine, as fit as a fiddle, would live to be a hundred.

"And about her being a bit . . . you know—that's just old age. People enter a second childhood, there's not much you can do about it."

"What can you do, that's 'ow it is," Ahmet repeated to himself as they were leaving the hospital.

Kasim drove Ahmet and his stepmother back to their village. They were silent in the car, and each of them had their own worries. What was there to say? It was as if they resented their mother being healthy. If she'd been ill, at least they'd have known what was wrong with her, but like this there was no illness and no cure.

It was cramped in Kasim's car, with no legroom, and the road was one pothole after another. They bumped along like that and were silent, only their mother jumped at every curve.

"Go right, Alija, right!" she'd scream.

"It's not Alija, mother. Kasim is driving. It's Kasim, mother," Ahmet explained.

"Left, Alija, left, left, left!"

He gave up explaining and their mother would keep on shouting at every bend.

"How is Alija, by the way?" Kasim asked all at once.

At that, their mother began untying and tying up her headscarf, whispering and spitting. Kasim and Ahmet looked at each other in the rearview mirror.

And so that long and sultry summer ended without the slightest transition. The sweltering heat gave way to rains that did not let up until winter. The leaves didn't have time to turn yellow but were torn from the branches by the wind and rain, together with the late fruit. After several weeks of rain there could be no thought of going out into the fields anymore—even on a horse you'd get bogged in all the mud and debris. Some begged Allah for the rain to stop, some asked the hodjas to find a prayer that might work, and others cursed the hodjas and the rain, both heaven and earth.

X

1. *Rakija, tamburitza, and shovel*

THE RAINY FALL passed, and after it a winter, dry and without snow.

Spring and summer passed, both Bairams too, and there was no sign of Alija. Ahmet didn't worry at first and thought, He'll come back when he's hungry or runs out of rakija. But Alija still didn't return. Ahmet asked around among the village drunks, but they too hadn't seen him for a long time, and if he saw Alija he should tell him to join them because nobody could play the saz like him, nope.

Afterward he went to see Kasim so they could go together and report his disappearance to the police, but Kasim told him not to worry, Alija was alive and well, working in a mine near the sea, and doing well there.

"Good on 'im, good luck to 'im then," Ahmet said and went home. He had more important things to do.

Years passed, and news about Alija was always sparse and unreliable. It was known that he'd worked at the Raša opencut coal mine, and once he wrote from the mine in Trbovlje, near Ljubljana. He got himself into a big mess there—some said he drank himself silly and smashed up the miners' canteen, others claimed he smacked the shift boss in the mug for a reason known to them alone. Afterward all trace of him was lost for a time and it was hard to establish where and how he'd spent that year or two. First the rumor spread that he'd been in jail, which later turned out to be untrue. People also said that he'd joined up with some Romany musicians and traveled around with them, earning his bread with the tamburitza. After that period, he came back to Bosnia and stayed for a while at Kasim's before wandering off again, God knows where to.

There followed a period where Alija came and disappeared again at regular intervals. With the first fall rains, he'd turn up in Kasim's courtyard, spend a while at his place, and then go away to work at one of the coal mines. Sometime in the spring he'd turn up at Kasim's again, but only for a day or two. He'd leave some things there, take the saz and the tamburitza, and vanish again. Nobody knew where he went then. People said all sorts of things, but the supposition closest to the truth was probably that he roamed around, playing for money, rakija, or fun in good company.

It's hard to say what kind of terms he and Kasim were on in that period, but it isn't hard to imagine. He didn't see his brother Ahmet.

Kasim found Alija's unexpected comings and goings difficult, but it was his dramatic materializations at the gate in the dead of night that upset him most.

My mother, the elder of Kasim's two daughters, used to tell the tale of one such appearance. She was fond of her Uncle Alija, though that affection wasn't the result of any great attention on Alija's part. Alija wasn't particularly attached to her, or to anybody for that matter (except for rakija, the tamburitza, and the shovel, Grandfather Kasim would say).

2. Runt

Everybody called my mother Zada because she didn't like being called by her real name, and she didn't like Grandfather to call her "daughter." Least of all did she like me to call her "mom."

I didn't see her often after she and my father separated because she went to Rijeka to study math and physics. When she came to visit us, I'd sneak into the room where the adults were having coffee or snacking and silently eavesdrop on their conversations. Now and then they'd catch me, and Zada would say, with venom in her voice, "Look at him! Look at those eyes, he picks up everything with them. Nothing escapes him!"

And her girlfriend, the neighbor Fikreta, who twenty years later would search for the bones of her husband Hasan in the garden, added, "You've got rid of the one, but there's still your runt. You can't get rid of him."

The two of them would laugh, and although I had no idea what they were on about I started to cry and threatened that I'd tell Grandfather what she said. Afterward she and her girlfriends called me Runt.

3. Borneo

Zada told me about one of Alija's visits when I was seeing her off, before she boarded the train that'd take her out of my life forever. We sat, drank, and smoked all night, and then she suddenly remembered Alija and started to talk.

She told me that Uncle Alija was a frequent topic of conversation back then. And that they didn't measure happiness in terms of wealth because they didn't have much, just enough to survive. And if they'd had even less, it still would've been okay.

"'Ave or an 'ave-not, it all still comes out your ass," she quoted Alija.

Whenever a family member had some business to attend to in town, they'd drop by to see Grandfather and Grandmother, and rather often they stayed the night.

She told me that she and Aunty Zika fell asleep on a bed many times but woke up outside the door with Grandfather's old coat over them. Grandmother got angry and told Grandfather it couldn't go on—they weren't an inn where anyone who liked could drop in.

We didn't look each other in the eyes. We sat in a hotel room, Zada and I, waiting for the morning that would mean our parting. Through the small window we could see the empty, mute night falling. There was a wartime blackout in the city, people were shrouded in darkness, and everybody was seeking to escape.

Nanna Hata, Grandfather's stepmother, was already a bit loopy then. Nobody knew what was wrong with her. She had lucid moments now and again, but they never lasted long. When Grandfather Kasim managed to get her land back, because the cooperatives were being disbanded, she divided it into equal parts and gave one to each of the brothers. Then Alija appeared.

"He arrived unexpectedly at our gate one morning," Zada continued. "It was a sunny and slightly chilly morning. We'd just got up, when we heard a hullabaloo, music, and shrill cries. 'What's up now?' Grandfather worried. We went to the gate, and there was a sight to see. Alija had led a parade to the front of the house. The neighbors came out and people who happened to be passing by in the street began to stop and gather. And Alija... He'd grown a moustache like Charlie Chaplin, but you know how it is here. Everybody gave him a hard time and said he was Hitler, and he'd snap back, 'Hitler fucked your mother.'

He explained that it was a Charlie Chaplin moustache, and that Chaplin had had a moustache like that before Hitler. The moustache suited him well and went with his whole image.

"Alija was done up from head to foot," Zada said with a wry smile. "Suit, shoes, tie, beret—the whole kit and caboodle. He had badges with Arafat, Tito, Che Guevara, and Gaddafi on one lapel."

She said that his greatest pride was the pocket watch; its chain rattled against the hem of his blazer. He never took it out to see what the time was, and only when he wanted to say something profound would he get out the watch and gaze at it, and then he'd raise his eyes as if looking out to the endless open sea and come out with a wild idea he'd formulated who knows when and was just waiting for the opportunity to present.

If he had Gaddafi, maybe he imagined he was looking into the desert, I said to Zada in my thoughts, but I didn't have the strength to say anything. All of a sudden a scene from a geography lesson in grade eight came back to me. It was during the war between America and Libya, when I was living with my father for the first and last time. That one single school year.

I didn't have a clue about the conflict, of course, nor had I ever heard of Colonel Muammar el-Gaddafi before. But it was the first war my boyish mind was able to follow. I found Libya in the atlas and saw it was a big country, and I was quite surprised when I read that it had just three million inhabitants. And then I got angry about the Americans. Such a world power, and they go and pick on a small country with just a bit of sand and a camel or two. Then Zoki, the biggest geek in the class, started bullshitting and holding speeches about international politics, which I didn't exactly know much about. But I could tell he was doing it to show off to Samra, who at least half the boys at the school were in love with. Then Samra also said that colonel should be taught a lesson because he was rotten: "Why doesn't he give the Americans oil?" I didn't know why he didn't give them oil, but I figured that Zoki was feeding her with capitalist propaganda. She also said she'd heard that Gaddafi was totally mad, allegedly, that he'd abolished money, torn down the jails, and let out the prisoners. Then Zoki burst in and said that the madman had even banned soccer, I mean, hey, who ever heard of anything so crazy? I was fed up with it all by then, so I became Gaddafi. I didn't play soccer in P. E. anymore, which didn't spoil the quality of our class's game, on the contrary. I made myself an identity card by cutting Muammar's photo out of the newspaper and gluing it to a piece of the cardboard cover of Pad V. His given name, surname, and signature were given beneath the photo in "Arabic."

And so, in those days at school, I pretended to be the Libyan colonel who went to war with America.

Then the geography teacher called me up in front of the map for a little test. We were doing Yugoslavia: its macro and microregions, bifurcation, the Adriatic Sea, the Aegean and Black Sea drainage basins, the Vardarac wind, the Nerodimka River that flows into two different seas, one of Europe's only primeval forests, Perućica, the central-Bosnian coal basin, the Julian Alps, and the climatic characteristics of the Dinaric Alps. Although I'd actually done that in grade seven, recently I'd been reading about nothing but Libya.

Since I knew nothing about the economy of the region between the rivers Mura and Drava, I asked permission to answer about Libya instead. The teacher looked at me perplexed and told me to get serious. I was dead serious and said to him that I was Colonel Muammar el-Gaddafi, in the flesh. The malicious ones in the class burst out laughing and started to shout, "Yes,

yes, he's Gaddafi!" They giggled wickedly, sensing an unhappy end for me. The teacher was flabbergasted and told me he'd be giving me an F. I went up to his desk and held my ID card under his nose. Look now, see? Am I or am I not?

Anyway, I got an F, and later my father gave me a good beating after being called in to see the teacher.

As he was thrashing me with his leather belt, he repeated, "I'll show you damn Muammar el-Gaddafi, you little shit."

I was the strong, silent male at first, then I cried a bit, and at the end I screamed, "Better him than you!"

He gave me a very hard slap and went to have a shower.

Zada raised her head, fell silent for a moment, and looked up, as if she wanted to show me how Alija would gaze out to sea, or, as I believed, into the desert.

"When he was drunk, you could see Alija from a mile away," she hurried to continue. "He stood there in front of the gate with his legs wide apart, with a black umbrella over his arm, singing. There's no denying it, he really could sing beautifully, at least when he wasn't too drunk. But this time he was really blotto."

She went on to tell me that Alija arrived late in the evening by train and spent the whole night drinking in the nearby pub with his tippler buddies from the railroad station. In the morning he found a porter, and also some Romany guy with an accordion, and then he and his company traipsed through the whole city to Grandfather's house and stood out front. The porter took Alija's two small leather bags off his handcart and wanted to be paid so he could go. Alija started pestering him to drink, and the man had a nip of rakija from the bottle that was going around, but he insisted on being paid so he could go—he had work to do and no time to waste. Alija asked the porter how much he owed him. When he said the amount, Alija paid and even gave him a tip. The man, a wretched fellow, short and prematurely toil-worn, didn't show any great joy. Alija then turned around toward Grandmother, who was standing a little behind Grandfather, and exclaimed, "Wow, sister, is it cheap here!" Then he got out his cigar case, offered one to Grandfather, and when he declined, to the others. He took out a white holder, fitted a cigar into it, and lit up like some Ottoman gentleman. In the end, they had a hard time dragging him into the house and dispersing the gathered drunks and idle folk.

Grandfather was dejected for days afterward, and Grandmother took malicious delight in babbling as she revolved on her eternal orbit from the range to the fridge, and the kitchen to the living room.

"I knew it, I knew it. I knew Alija and 'is mines'd come back and 'it us in the face. 'Kasim,' I says, 'Don't go getting mixed up in things that are none of your business. But this time he went too far '."

Grandfather held his tongue for a while, and then he up and shouted, "That's enough from you, for God's sake. Not a single word more!"

And so it ended. Alija stayed at Grandfather's for several days and then vanished again. Zada said, finally, that what surprised her most was that he took the umbrella with him, though there was no rain at all.

She fell silent and looked into space for a long time. The morning was drawing near, and with it our last farewell.

She died two years later, at the end of 1994, in a refugee camp for Bosnians in the middle of the jungle in the Malaysian province of Sarawak, on the island of Borneo. She fell asleep one night and didn't wake up again. When they told me, I was already in Kristiansand, in Norway. I opened the atlas and looked for a long time at Borneo, but that didn't make it any easier for me.

XI

GRANDFATHER FLAGGED AS we were walking down the path through the graveyard. We stopped and waited. It drizzled and I held him by the arm. I turned around, looking for something to pin my eyes to.

1. *The Sava*

Grandmother and Grandfather died one after another in the space of a month. It was less than a year after Alija's death, at the very beginning of the new millennium. I couldn't go to their funeral because I was staying on the island of S. in the far north of Norway, which I'll tell you about later. When I returned from the island, I spent some time in Oslo, and then traveled first to Zagreb, later to Rijeka, and, finally, to Brčko. There I walked streets I didn't recognize and thought back to the past. I came to the old house where I grew up and said goodbye to it, singing Morrissey's song in my head.

Afterward I went to the graveyard where Grandmother and Grandfather were buried. I stood for a while and looked at their names on the wooden grave markers. When I judged I'd stood there respectfully long, I headed for the Sava.

I walked through the poplar forest toward the former recreation area on the river, called Ficibajer, a name from the Austrian period. It was October, and the air was cold and still. Darkness began to fall and silence took hold of the land. A few withered leaves hung on the branches, and shaggy nests and big black birds could clearly be seen in the tops of the trees. I stopped under them and listened: the silence was broken by the cries of the crows. And it stirred something inside. It always did. I wouldn't feel better when I went down to the riverbank. All at once the birds became silent, the view opened up, and I saw the great water, murky and mighty, flowing before my eyes. At any given time it carried branches, rotten tree trunks, plastic bags of pig offal, often whole carcasses, and even bloated human corpses. There was the same kind of forest on the other side of the river, with the same kind of birds. The shadows from both forests lengthened and the darkness thickened over the river. Its black surface fumed, as if the river was expiring.

2. *The Sava, II*

I stood on the bank and watched the river flowing like a weary giant. I tried to think of something pleasant, an experience here by the river as a child that, in a spell of enthusiasm, I could call a fond reminiscence. But memory is deceptive and follows the mood of the moment, I concluded again. I knew that I'd probably experienced some happy moments here, but I couldn't evoke them. Instead, other scenes came to the surface.

I saw the blind puppies that Dino and I threw into the river to drown. We stood on the muddy bank, it was a day like this

BEKIM SEJRANOVIĆ

one, and we giggled as we threw the little dogs into the Sava. A well-preserved old man also emerged from my memory, who offered me and two friends ten dinars if we showed him our dicks. The three of us got undressed in the forest a hundred yards or so upriver from the Ficibajer swimming area, hid our clothes in the bushes, and jumped into the water to swim to the other side of the Sava. The old man was still standing on the bank; he'd watched us undress and now offered twenty dinars for every dick. We swam toward the opposite bank, cursing the pervert with the foulest language we knew.

3. Master dredger

The Sava in my memory also evoked my father. He captained one of riverboats that extracted sand and gravel from it. To tell the truth, I wasn't sure if he really had the title of captain because the crew called him *bagermajstor*, "master dredger." That was because sand and gravel used to be extracted with dredges that were anchored in the river. Sand was dumped into barges that were towed by tugs. Sometime in the early eighties they started using special-purpose boats that had big sucker tubes on either side, like elephant trunks. These were lowered to the riverbed and the boat would suck up sand or gravel with them. So they weren't dredges anymore, but the term "master dredger" remained for the skipper of the vessel for extracting sand from the river. When I was small, people would often ask me what my parents did, and I always found it hard to answer. When I'd say my father was a master dredger, nobody knew what that was, so I had to explain. When they asked me about my mother, I'd say she was a student, and then they wondered even more.

4. Fathers, sons, and mothers

I find it hard to speak about my father. I tried to become closer with him, as he did with me, but for some reason it didn't work out. As I grew up, I got to know him better. I even began to understand him, but at the same time we began to drift apart. I started to feel how similar we were, and I didn't like that at first. I hated it. But now, when I think of it, I just smile wearily. Still, I don't believe anything between us could've been different. Can it ever be, between fathers and sons?

My father was born in Šabac. I don't know why, but the name of that city always sounded strangely cheerful to me. Maybe because of the big fair there, or Radio Šabac that played rural pop and Romany music day and night, who knows.

His father was a confectioner from the Bosnian part of the Sava region, and his mother was from Banja Koviljača, a spa town on the Drina River.

It's hard to know how life could weave a love story between those two, but like every such love—great, tempestuous, impossible—this one was also short-lived.

My father returned to Bosnia with his father before his second birthday, while his mother went away to Belgrade, where she housekept for a woman, a celebrated painter. When she grew old, she had a nervous breakdown and withdrew into the seclusion of her old shack in Banja Koviljača. She had a phobia about food, spending money, and her first and only husband. She didn't have a fridge in the house, or a TV, a washing machine, or anything. She kept food in the shaft for the water meter, and one dark, airless room contained nothing but dolls and dummies of different shapes, sizes, and origins. The room was full of them. Some sat rigidly on a sofa, others leaned back in dark corners in their rustling dresses, their glass eyes staring into space. The other room had a mass of paintings and photographs. One picture frame on the wall was filled with the heads of people cut out of old family photos. There were the faces of her parents, uncles, cousins, and my father. She'd talk and quarrel with those cut-out portraits. Sometimes one of the faces would fall from grace and she'd remove it from that mosaic of chopped-off heads. Only her husband's picture was never put in the frame.

During the last war, one of the Serbian paramilitary groups returning from their forays into Bosnia broke into her house and took all her savings buried in the basement. She was crushed by the loss and died three days later. I only saw her once in my life.

5. My child, my child . . .

It was the beginning of summer, just before the end of fourth grade, when Pele and I went fishing by the Sava. Pele usually fished from his old man's boat, but he'd been told he could forget about the boat until he improved his grade in math. We arrived at Ficibajer and followed the path through the forest a hundred yards upriver, a bit farther than the spot where Dino and I had thrown in the puppies. We cast out our lines with sinkers, rested the rods on forked branches, and waited.

After a while I thought I heard somebody calling my name. I told Pele. He listened and his eyes roamed, and then he shrugged. After a while, the calling came again. This time louder, as if coming closer. I went up the path and saw a grizzled, elderly woman and Uncle Alija. When they noticed me, Alija began to wave with his umbrella. I walked over to them.

"This is your grandmother," he said. "She's come from Serbia to see you."

The woman then began to hug and kiss me, and sighed over and over again, "My child, my child . . ."

I looked at Alija, confused. He smiled with satisfaction and lit a cigarette in his cigarette holder.

"She's your father's mother, kid," he said, almost sneering.

The woman kept hugging me and repeating, "My child, my child . . ."

I didn't understand; my father's mother had thrown herself into the Sava last fall. I went to her funeral. Alija said that was his stepmother.

"But nobody wanted to tell you. They thought, like people do, that because you're young—," he explained, inhaling smoke through his white cigarette holder.

I watched the Sava over the shoulder of the woman who clutched me as if she was drowning and I was her last chance. First I was overcome by a lifeless sorrow, but then I started to pull away, screaming and convulsing my head like I was mental. Alija came up and tried to quiet me and keep me in that embrace, but I managed to break loose and run off into the forest.

Shortly afterward I sat leaning against a tree. I listened to my ragged breathing, and at the same time I heard Alija's alcohol-eroded voice calling me, like a drowning man. As it moved away, my breathing gradually slowed down. Finally his voice died out completely and I could breathe easy.

6. Mom and Dad

My father's old man got married again, built a house, and had three more sons. My father was often at loggerheads with him and his stepmother, who later drowned herself in the Sava. He was intolerant of his half-brothers too, they say. His father threw him out of the house before he even turned sixteen, and he left for Belgrade. There he went to vocational school for sailors. To support himself, he carried coal into people's houses, mixed cement, and unloaded trucks. He was a fairly talented center halfback and played for FC Voždovac. His mother helped him as best she could with her weak nerves.

It seems he came to Bosnia to see his father on occasion, because it was there, shortly before his military service, that he fell in love with Zada, my mother. I don't know how they actually met because neither of them told me. They didn't mention one another. Who knows, if it hadn't been just before my father did his military service, it mightn't have lasted, because infatuation passes quickly unless something gets in the way. Great love demands suffering.

Sometime in the middle of his service on the Bulgarian border, when the men had started counting the days, a letter came from Zada telling him it was over. This news plunged my father into a deep depression, and he soon fled the barracks. When he returned, he was court martialed and had to spend three months in the lockup. But after all that happened, it was clear that their bond wasn't just love but a *great* love, as all those who are in love think is true of theirs.

After completing his military service, my father returned to Bosnia, Brčko, and Zada. They lived in the outkitchen in Grandfather Kasim's courtyard. I was born eight months into their marriage, and they divorced two years later. Differences had emerged back when Zada was pregnant. My father went away and didn't show up for a few months, and she sat on a hot tile in the hope that it'd lead to a spontaneous abortion.

After they finally divorced, my father went to Belgrade, and my mother to Rijeka. I stayed with Grandmother and Grandfather.

There followed a time where my parents visited me alternately.

I didn't like their comings, or goings.

As far as Zada's visits were concerned, I looked forward to them at first, but only until I realized that each one meant she'd be leaving again. She usually came at three in the morning. I'd always wake up, and I was happiest when she brought me a can of Coke from Trieste. We drank them sparingly and on special occasions. Later we'd go to the supermarket and buy Coke in a glass liter bottle, which we then poured into empty cans and drank out of them.

But I'll carry her departures with me for the rest of my life. It's because of them that I torment all the women I meet.

One evening, Grandfather, Zada, and I got into the green Zastava 101 and Grandmother waved to us from the steps. We drove to Vinkovci, where Zada was to board the Učka express train to Rijeka. I sat in the back in silence while the two of them talked. The atmosphere was tense and strained. Later on, when we were returning home in the car, just Grandfather and me, we didn't talk at all. He was silent and drove through the night, the road was endlessly flat and screened on both sides by the immense Pannonian forest. From time to time, he patted me on the head. I said nothing and sometimes sighed. Grandfather thought I was sad, but really I was furious.

My father, on the other hand, would appear unexpectedly and always had some complaint about my appearance. Either my clothes would be dirty and creased or my neck, legs, or feet would be grimy. *Look at your fingernails!* I'd never be good enough for him. That was tiresome, of course, but even then it didn't surprise me at all. Because just as every dream is much better than reality, just as every love is more beautiful while it's still desire, so too our children are probably dearer to us until they're born.

His disappointment left me insecure, afraid, and paranoid.

The only interesting thing in it all is that, under the influence of my mother's departures, I began to resemble my father more, while his pressure and carping made me more like her.

7. *The Sava, III*

I was still standing by the Sava, lost in thought and watching it flow, and all at once I began to recall that the river once nearly took away my life.

It was the first time my father brought me with him to "the boat," as he called his fifteen-day shifts on the floating dredge. He came to pick me up at Grandmother and Grandfather's and told me to get ready. The boat lay at anchor near Bosanska Rača in the region of Semberija, where the Drina enters the Sava. On the way there we stopped in Bijeljina and Dad bought me a T-shirt with the smiling face of Heidi, the heroine of the book of the same name, which was popular at the time, and was later made into a cartoon. He also bought me a green book, *The Flying Caravan*, which described the ordeals of a flock of wild geese on their journey southward. The main hero was a gander by the name of Gak.

The boat had cabins for the crew, a galley, and a mess. It was interesting to sit among the sailors and listen to their stories. They'd mainly rehash their sexual escapades, youthful drinking sprees, or anecdotes from their time in the army. In the evenings they'd play cards, and sometimes I was allowed to join in. There I learned to play "Stich," blackjack, and poker.

Once, the sailors arranged to play soccer on the meadow above the gravel depot one hour after lunch. I went up there with them, but I soon became bored watching them run about. It was unbearable to watch them sweat, take off their shirts to reveal faded Yugoslav People's Army tattoos and the occasional badly etched anchor, and bulging bellies, and to also have to listen to their foul language. I wanted to go to the cabin to read about Gak the gander. I told that to my father and he sent me to the cabin with two bunches of keys. One for the cabin and the other for the car. I clenched the keys tight as I walked across the board that was the gangway from the shore to the boat, and I imagined what it'd be like if I dropped them into the river. It's the same thought as when you stand on a balcony on the eleventh floor and imagine what it'd be like to jump. The thought makes you feel queasy, and your legs go shaky, but something still makes you ponder it. I raised both bunches of keys into the air and shook them over the river. They jangled in symphony, and I went up the short gangway onto the boat and walked along the railing. Since nothing had happened when I crossed the gangway, a brassy courage grew in me and I began to rattle the keys even more. Now I stopped, leaned over the railing, stuck my arm out over the river, and waved the keys violently. In the end, both bunches splashed into the water. I was petrified, first with shock, then with fear. Fear of my father, which made me realize that my fear of him was unnaturally large, larger even than the fear of death. That isn't really strange because children aren't afraid of death, and that's what makes them children. Children are afraid of their parents. When fear of our parents is displaced by the fear of death, it means we've grown up.

I ran back over the gangway to the bank and waded into the muddy river. It was more than three yards between the bank and the boat. I waded in to above my knees, bent down, and groped about in the mud, but the keys weren't there, of course. They'd fallen straight down from the side of the boat, so I had to go in deeper.

I gradually came closer to the spot. But the water was already above my waist and it was harder and harder to reach the bottom with my hand. At one point I lost my footing and fell full into the river. The current carried me under a pontoon vessel, and the whole time I didn't dare to shout.

The cook Slobodan, who the crew made fun of by calling him Sloppy Dan, happened to come along and saw me struggling and panicking in silence, trying not to be pulled under the boat.

That was how I felt now as I stood on the bank of the Sava. I felt the pull of the heavy, sluggish water. This time I wasn't afraid, this time there was no panic and no fear, neither of the water nor of my father.

XII

GRANDFATHER AND I stood on the trampled muddy path of the village graveyard. We'd stopped halfway down the hillside and were waiting. I looked down at the road, while he turned to look back up the hill, toward Alija's grave. If I'd know more about life, maybe I would've looked that way too.

A year and a half after Alija's funeral, I traveled from Norway to Zagreb. Before going to Brčko and saying goodbye to myself, I went to Rijeka for Kole's funeral.

1. *Kole's funeral*

It was late summer and the funeral procession trudged and wheezed up the path toward the cemetery high above the coastal town. It seemed everybody was pretending not to see the grave gaping voraciously at the coffin in which Kole lay with a hole in his right temple. The coffin rested on a kitschy white cart pushed by four figures in black suits. A corpulent priest waddled in front of them, lethargically and with visible reluctance. He'd finally agreed to come to the funeral, but by virtue of his faith in canon law he refused to hold a service for somebody who'd committed suicide.

Kole's mother reeled along behind the cart, medicated with sedatives. She was virtually carried by Kole's elder brother and Kole's young cousin, who held her by the arms while she stepped in her black shoes on the sticky summer asphalt. Lena, Kole's de facto wife, shuffled beside them stiffly and mechanically. She'd come back from work and found him on the couch in the living room with his gory head. A shrimp of a man with a trumpet—probably a member of the local volunteer fire brigade's brass band—darted about beside the procession; he ran on a little way ahead and stopped. He took a deep breath, pursed his thin, lifeless lips, and started to play Frank Sinatra's "My Way"—or the Sex Pistols', depending on your take on things. When the procession moved past him, he did another run-up and scuttled twenty yards out in front of the procession, took another breath, and mopped his wrinkled, worried brow with his hankie, because the slope was steep and the day was hot. When the cart with the coffin came closer, he closed his eyes, drew a deep breath again, and started to play the same melody, and the screech of the brass instrument told of how life in this world is transitory and worthless.

I met Kole in that old town, Bakar, situated on a beautiful bay reminiscent of a Nordic fjord. Of course, humans made it ugly, with a cokery replete with the eyesore of a massive, almost 800-foot smokestack. The cokery isn't there anymore, only its chimney remains as witness to a troubled past and the fine, black dust that blighted our dreams of a brighter future.

The town was home to the maritime college I was to attend, be it due to a twist of fate or parental toying with my fate. When Zada finally returned from her studies in Rijeka to our city on the bank of the Sava, she neither knew what to do with me, nor did I know what to do with her. She tried as best she could, but the fury that'd built up in me over all those years when Grandfather and I would drive back through the foggy Pannonian nights had only grown, becoming stronger, and it seemed to have no intention of releasing me from its hard, cruel claws. In the end, she gave up.

When I finished seventh grade, she decided to send me to my father for him to "put me in order," "teach me what's what," and "knock some sense into me," depending on the occasion and the seriousness of our discord. At that time, I'd fallen in love with a girl three years older than me. Zada taught her math at the technical school. She knew with the certainty of a jealous woman that the girl was a manipulative social climber. I shouted around the house, threatened that I'd run away into the wide world with Sandra the "social climber," and that Zada would never hear from me again, not even on her deathbed. Maybe Zada was right, as jealous women usually are, but instead of letting the matter pass by itself, as every infatuation does, the two of them—driven by strong motherly and elemental female possessiveness, no doubt—only disquieted, distressed, and, in the end, devastated me more than that ludicrous love ever could have, even in a worst-case scenario.

Then again, can it ever be different between mothers and sons?

Sandra was the first girl I kissed on the mouth. Without tongue-kissing, admittedly, because I didn't know about that yet. She tried to teach me, but just when I was almost ready, my mother packed my things in a bag and sent me off to my father like a living parcel.

I looked at Grandfather and Grandmother beseechingly, without a sound, begging them not to let me go because I was theirs, after all, but they only shrugged, hid their eyes in the corners of our house, and repeated, "You have a mother, you have a father, it's for them to decide."

Sandra and her bleating laugh stayed in the city on the Sava. She soon became rundown and got hooked on heroin in the early nineties. In the war, she donned a camouflage uniform, tagged along with the grotesque figures that called themselves soldiers, and would sell herself for a fix. Death caught up with her just before the end of the war, like the long-awaited liberation.

Kole's funeral procession, too, was reminiscent of a march of liberators filing victoriously through a jubilant crowd. Except, instead of smiling young women throwing flowers, this column was met by staring gravestones with the occasional photo of a weary, elderly face. And chrysanthemums, that cheapest symbol of death, burnt in the sun like expended human souls cast onto a trash heap. There wasn't a single cloud in the sky, the sun moved slowly west toward Mount Učka, and the sea was calm and blue. The sea and sky were as blue as they ever can be as I went up the hill in the funeral procession and made my way through the appallingly tacky tombstones. I made my way to the hole in the ground where they were going to bury my former friend and asked myself what he might've been thinking the moment before he demolished his brain, and I fearfully tried to discern whether I felt sorry for him or envied him.

The four figures in black, well coordinated like a string quartet, lowered the coffin into the ground. The embarrassed priest stood to the side, as if weighing up for the last time what was more important for him: ecclesiastical discipline or Kole's soul. He gave a forced cough and signaled with his eyes to a little old man to come up and make a speech. The old man tried to say something, but he stammered and his eyes called for help first from the priest, and then, looking into the sky in desperation, from God Himself. He took a pair of thick-lensed glasses from his breast pocket and a piece of paper from the back pocket of his pants. The silence pressed in from all sides as the old man adjusted his glasses for an inconceivably long time, turned the piece of creased paper over from all sides, repeated "Oh, God, oh, God," looked into the sky again, and at the priest; one and the other pretended not to see or hear him.

Like that poor man with the face of a prematurely aged child, I too tried to give the story of Kole a new beginning.

2. *Coke*

We can imagine it beginning on the first day of college, the first Monday of September in 1985. That was the day I arrived in the coastal town of Bakar, near Rijeka, where I'd spend the next four years of my life. My father and I were taken there by Bato the driver in the dirty old gray van of Sava Water Management, the firm from Bosanska Gradiška where my father worked as master dredger.

We bumped along the whole night in that van, its cabin filled with the intoxicatingly pleasant smell of diesel, and arrived in Bakar in the morning. Bato dropped us off in front of the student dormitory, honked twice, and vanished in a cloud of sooty smoke down the Bakar road lit up by the morning sun and covered in black coke dust.

The dormitory of the Tomislav Hero Maritime College was in a once pleasant location, a grove on the edge of the Bay of Bakar. The dormitory was built in the sixties, but fifteen years later the cokery, with its smokestack, was built just a hundred yards along the shore. Workers' barracks were planted there later for the poor who came from Bosnia and toiled away their lives there.

The banded smokestack, the cokery, and the mountains of fine coal dominated the area. There was also a dirty yellow metal pipe that went through the courtyard of the dorm—a pipe through which a conveyor belt ran day and night, carrying coke. In front of the maritime college it turned into a concrete tunnel that snaked along the seabed to the other side of the bay, where there was a terminal for bulk carriers. How to describe that rotten-egg stench in the smoke that poured from a low, wide installation adorned with metal bars regularly, every fifteen minutes? How to evoke the fine black coke dust, which got into every crack and crevice, every opening of the body, into the lungs, bronchia, the small and large intestines, into the urinary tract, hair, nails, clothes, shoes, and in the end even filled the human soul with its wash of black?

One winter in Bakar, by some miracle, it snowed. We went to class in the morning, all of us were happy because snow isn't a common event on the coast, and the whole of Bakar looked like a sea of young brides, festive and white. We didn't feel that dry rubbing of the dust underfoot, our hands didn't sting from dryness, our eyelids didn't hurt from the accumulated layers of coke. But within half an hour, the snow turned black and the whole bay looked like a cancerous tumor in the lungs of a seventy-year-old chronic smoker, Uncle Alija.

3. *The dorm*

I arrived in Bakar that sunny September morning and was shown to my accommodation—a room with four iron beds. My father said goodbye to the director; his surname was Luburić and he taught Marxism.

My father told him to call if there were any problems, and added, "I wanted to enroll him in military academy, but he's flat-footed and they didn't accept him."

I looked at my shoes and could feel the new orthopedic liners in them. I felt the blisters in the middle of my feet and a pressure in my throat and my scrotum. It was like a cold snake climbing up my spine, and the back of my head. I felt I could cry, but not with sadness, and not for fear of being left there, no, that wasn't why. It was all because of the shame at being there, at having been sent there in the first place, because of standing there and watching my father blathering enthusiastically, because of the essentially worthless heap of banknotes he gave me as pocket money and that I now clenched nervously in my sweaty palm in my pocket, and because of his insufferable remark that he hoped there'd be no problems with me being a Bosnista, to which the director declared that he was from Herzegovina himself and that it was no problem at all.

I was also ashamed when my father said goodbye to me with a cold, affected resolve and spoke phrases like "and now pull your socks up," when he went back toward the van, in which Bato the driver was blowing the horn, and when he waved to me like some Ottoman gentleman as he disappeared behind the bend toward the Adriatic highway.

I wasn't ashamed of what I was, because of my roots, origin, accent, vocabulary, or the clothes I wore, but because of my forsakenness, a feeling of inadequacy, and not belonging to anybody or anything.

After that I went to the college. We gathered in groups in the courtyard, the day was windy and sunny, a cold northeaster blew the black dust into our eyes, the teachers called out names, and all of us students lined up. We went into the classroom, I didn't speak to anybody, I looked at the floor and wondered where to spit the sooty dust of unknown origin that was suddenly in my mouth.

BEKIM SEJRANOVIĆ

Then the teacher called out everybody's name in turn, and we had to stand up and say where'd we gone to high school and what our grades were. Almost everybody was from Rijeka, and I was the only one staying at the dorm. When it was my turn, I thought up a new identity on the spur of the moment. Bosnia wasn't so cool, so I did my best to put on a Belgrade accent and pretend I was from there. I kept up the act for the next four years. By the end they blew my cover and mocked me for lying, but I laughed because I'd duped them for so long. As if anybody cared at all who I was, where I was from, and why I'd come there. That's why my lie survived for so long. Only for that reason, and maybe to a small extent because, by coincidence, I shared a room in the dorm with two brothers from Belgrade and a complete nutcase from somewhere near Kragujevac in Serbia, who we all called "Saint Sava." I learned from them to speak with a mock Belgrade accent and kept up my impersonation campaign, without any reason or sense. I simply wanted to be somebody else, a different me, a bigger me.

I also found it fun, to be honest.

Actually, when I look back on it, many—at least the slightly brighter ones—probably soon realized I wasn't from Belgrade, but I simply didn't want to give up the story, and I constantly thought up more new details: gathered information from the brothers from the suburb of Zvezdara; learned the parts of the city, the main roads and side streets; made up buddies and girlfriends; invented events; life histories of my imaginary neighbors, their faults, the habits of their pets, the tits of their lovers; and I told and retold all that with an ever more convincing Belgrade accent. I noticed sometimes that they laughed in my face, but I didn't give up. Why should I? There was no reason to lie, but no reason to speak the truth. There was no point in living, and none in dying either.

There were fifty or so students in the dorm, who could be divided into two groups: those who were from the surroundings of Rijeka and stayed there from Monday evening to Friday morning, and those who came from more distant areas and only went home when the dorm closed for the winter and summer vacations.

You name it, we had it at the dorm: brutal fights, bullying of the young and weak, practical jokes, snitching, and malice, but also drinking sprees, sniffing glue, sharing food, helping each other study, and genuine friendship. A new director came to replace Luburić, and I christened him The Terminator because he trained in all existing martial arts and practiced them on us. Later people said he began dealing in weapons early in the war. He stepped on a mine in the rugged, contested region of Lika and lost a leg. I don't remember which one.

4. *Paranoya*

It's hard to say when you've really gotten to know someone who you've become close with, who you have some special connection with. It's also hard to say what it actually is that connects you. The latter probably becomes a bit clearer if a person close to you dies, if you watch as their coffin is buried, and if you search for the sorrow you can't excavate from yourself on the faces of the people throwing clumps of earth into the grave.

I don't know exactly when and how I got to know Kole, but we started hanging around together when he joined our class. He was three years older than me because he'd had to repeat two years, and I started school a year early. What connected us was punk.

When I finished seventh grade, I moved to live with my father and started at a new school. One day, somebody spray-painted "PUNK" and "A" in red on the school building, and our homeroom teacher Milica, with a pointy nose and tiny, malicious eyes walked stiffly in her high boots over the school's parquet flooring with her crooked, rickety legs and explained to us that the school had been targeted by anti-Yugoslav separatists. The tags "PUNK" and "A" had appeared on the wall of the school. Did we have any idea what that meant? I wanted to say a few words and show off, so I raised my hand. I mentioned the Pistols, but I was stopped abruptly by her icy gaze and her thin, bloodless lips twisted into a smile full of pity.

"How naive you are, children. PUNK means, 'Power to the Unbeatable Nation of Kosovo!' And the 'A' is for Albania."

One girl and I glanced at each other and smiled. For a number of reasons. Bandy-legged Milica looked at us with wide-open eyes, her pointy face white with righteous rage.

In the early nineties, she donned a uniform together with her daughter, a cadet at the military academy in Sarajevo, and joined the decisive struggle against PUNK, without realizing that it was long since dead.

Her daughter was killed shortly before the end of the war. Milica fell into bed soon afterward and lay ill for a time, unable to use her legs. She died of arterial calcification. The elementary school in Bosanska Gradiška is still standing, though it no longer bears the Partisan name "Ivo Lola Ribar." Even today, especially in sunny weather, you can see the word "PUNK" in faded red letters on the wall.

Kole and I connected through the Pistols and punk. Or maybe it'd be more accurate to say we were connected by unhealthy exhibitionism, a desire for self-assertion in any way, a feeling of inadequacy and dissatisfaction entwined with abrupt bouts of self-love. Back in that classroom with Milica I'd been guilty of that.

One evening, as we were coming back drunk from a concert, we decided in the bus to form a band. The only problem was that neither he nor I played an instrument. Kole decided he'd be the singer, and that it'd be best for me to play bass. I agreed, a little reluctantly to be sure, but I could never say no to Kole.

Several days later I stole the brand-new cowboy boots of a boy at the dorm and sold them at the flea market for a hundred marks. Kole and I then went to see some guys from his neighborhood, who also had a band, and I bought a bass guitar from them. I felt a bit ashamed when I was meant to try it out in front of them because I couldn't play anything at all. Only "Smoke on the Water," and a punk like me with Mohawk a bit smaller than Wattie's from The Exploited wouldn't be caught dead playing that. Especially not in front of Kole.

Kole soon put together the rest of the band. He found the drummer Zoki, the guitarist Đuro, and another bass player, Goran. Of all of us, only Đuro knew how to play, and he was pretty good. But what did we care for minutiae like that.

Our first differences arose because we couldn't agree on the band's name. We hadn't had a single practice or written a song, and I hadn't learned to tune my bass, yet we quarreled about the name for days. The ideas were many and varied. I searched through an encyclopedia and tried to find something in Latin, Goran raved in German, and Kole came up with a plethora of terms mostly for various mental illnesses. Đuro wanted something in English, preferably American, while Zoki got hooked on the name "Off the Leash" and just couldn't let it go.

One day—I don't remember exactly when or where, nor do I know for sure whose idea it was, because each of us later claimed rock solid that he'd thought it up, especially Kole—the word

"Paranoya" popped up, and everybody seemed satisfied. Everybody, that was, except perhaps Kole's mother, who just shook her head in wonder. She'd ladle gnocchi and goulash onto our plates and ask herself more than us, "Why do handsome boys like you need an awful name like that? What's it supposed to mean anyhow?" Why couldn't we be "The Gulls" or "The Sea" or, if we really wanted something wilder, what was wrong with "The Squalls"?

Kole and I made sour faces and stuck two fingers down our throats, like when you want to make yourself vomit.

Kole's mother was whisked away from the funeral as soon as the coffin was in the ground. After that, people stood over the grave, threw in a few clumps of earth, and hurried off. I threw in a tiny stone without looking. Several minutes later it was all over and people were strolling down the hill, talking and laughing.

We had our first practice at Đuro's, in the shared laundry room of his new apartment building in the Rijeka suburb of Škurinje. We rehearsed five songs. We had a few problems with the lyrics, but all in all things were ready. Just before the end of the session, Đuro's mom brought us sandwiches with Podravka chicken pâté. We wanted to put on a concert in gratitude, but Đuro was embarrassed to play in front of his mom. It was a crying shame.

At the second practice, Đuro's neighbor Boško, who was a city bus driver, burst in and wanted to smash Goran's amplifier with an ax. After that, we moved to a garage, a makeshift sheetmetal construction wedged in between the workers' barracks in Bakar, not 200 yards from the cokery. There was an angry mutt on a thick chain by the garage, and three yards further was a pigsty with two fat hogs. Zoki practiced drums by rapping his drumsticks on their thick, meaty heads. We made our first demo tape there on an old cassette recorder. The recordings were particularly rich because the dog's chain could be heard rattling the whole time, and the dog barking like a wounded animal. The feedback seemed to cause it acute pain and it vented its rage and distress through howling.

It was then that we first recorded our greatest hit, "Your Meat." Goran wrote the music, while everybody thought I wrote the lyrics. But I must tell the truth once and for all. The lyrics were by Rale, my best friend from Brčko. I only started to hang around with him when I left the city, or rather when my mother sent me to my father in Bosanska Gradiška, and we continued to meet after I went away to Rijeka. Whenever I visited Grandmother and Grandfather during vacations, I'd hang around with Rale and a handful of other punks. We'd gather in the outkitchen, where I'd once lived with my parents, and listen to punk and hardcore, write songs, discuss literature, philosophy, girls, life and death, and drink ourselves into a stupor. Once Rale came there holding a sheet of paper with a set of lyrics written and corrected in pencil in one hand, and a bottle of Foal's Blood wine in the other. I didn't recognize the value of the lyrics straightaway, but I still showed them to Kole when I returned to Rijeka, and he liked them. I lied that they were mine and he was full of admiration. Later on he asked me to write a few more songs, and I tried my very hardest, but without any great success. When I played Rale the recordings from the garage in Bakar or from one of the concerts where we performed the song, he was visibly satisfied. I never told him that I stole his song and adorned myself with his plumes.

Paranoya didn't last long. It was the late eighties, and there were dozens of bands playing in Rijeka. The band would play a few concerts and then fall apart. Then it'd reform, and there'd be another concert or two at the Ivo Lola Ribar Youth Club, better known by the name Palach. The greatest achievement would've been to win the Gitarijada competition or the famous Ri Rock Festival, but that was the limit, and we had no such aspirations anyway. We performed at the Gitarijada in 1989, of course, and expected to win. But we came in twenty-first out of twenty-four bands. We were mentioned in the young people's paper *Val*, which wrote that we were the surprise of the evening, whatever that meant. We saved that short article for months, reading and re-reading it, and showing it to would-be groupies while we tirelessly drank bottles of wine in the Krimeja bocce court near the port.

Once I thought I could write a whole novel about those years, but now only a few images are left, blurred and unreal. Kole drank three raw eggs before the first concert to try and make his voice velvet, Ðuro spilled a bottle of homemade white wine over his amplifier and caused a fuse to blow, blacking out the whole joint, a dump on the island of Krk. Then the winter night spent at a bus station in Istria after a gig at the Cultural Center in Nedeščina. When the bus to Rijeka finally came in the morning, we got in frozen and hungover—under the weather. We couldn't even say where we wanted to go, but the driver took pity on us and didn't make us buy tickets.

Now Goran and I were heading down the same path we'd climbed half an hour earlier in the funeral procession. A man came up to us and started talking as if we knew each other. Several minutes later I realized it was the drummer Zoki. At the bottom of the hill we met Ðuro, who was still the same—time had stood still for him. We stood there, looked at each other, and spoke a few words.

Kole was dead, and Rale too: he stayed in the city on the Sava throughout the war, and then one evening in the coffee bar with the fatuous name Bolero a shot was heard. The bullet ended up in Rale's head, and the circumstances of the incident long remained obscure. Some claimed he'd been playing Russian roulette at the table, others that it was an accident, others still that he killed himself out of pure spite. Maybe everything got cleared up afterward, but what good is that now? There was a lot of speculation concerning Kole's death too, but that's not important anymore either.

The essential facts are: Rale wrote the song "Your Meat," which I gave to Kole to sing and pretended I'd written it myself. The two of them never met. Both ended up with a bullet in the head. Both are under the ground. Both of them were my friends.

And as we stood there at the bottom of the path to the graveyard, I felt that all of us were dead too. The man here next to me wasn't Zoki—the Zoki I knew was long since dead. Đuro's real name wasn't actually Đuro. Đuro was his old man's name; he'd been killed in a fistfight in Novi Sad during the war when he left Croatia with his family. The real Đuro was dead, and these here were only his embalmed remains. And I was dead too, just waiting for somebody to hammer the nails into the lid of my coffin or to wrap me in a sheet and put me on a bier.

Only Goran was left. I looked at him distrustfully and tried to find some trace of death on him.

Sometimes I see it all differently. Zoki isn't dead, but the man has changed. He works as a cook on a cruise liner, sails from continent to continent, sleeps with whores in the ports of the world, and sends money home for his wife, who cheats on him innocently and transcendentally with a youthful yoga instructor, and for their daughter, who can hardly wait for her dad to go to sea again when the summer's over.

Đuro is alive, has a band that plays what he says are Dixie blues, and works at construction sites, mostly off the books— sometimes legally. He has an understanding wife and a son who doesn't understand why his dad drinks and doesn't come home on Fridays or around the first of the month when, with a bit of luck, he gets paid.

Maybe they've just changed, I reflect, maybe they've grown up, matured, or whatever it's called, and it's really just me who's got snagged along the way. I'm the only one lugging memories behind me like a sack of old bones. Time seems to have stopped, I just don't know when. Once again: I don't believe memory, and I can't bear the truth. Maybe I could if it existed. You can't even believe facts, I fear. Every truth depends on your choice of facts, and that choice depends on the mood of the moment, coincidence, and the time. Because facts could also say that Rale, beginning sometime in elementary school, became obsessed with blood, death, war, and a monstrous and all-encompassing apocalypse. With Kole, on the other hand, his face would often go as pale as death, his pupils would dilate unhealthily, and he'd be seized by a madness that manifested itself in violence and sadism. Later, Rale got hooked on nationalism, and Kole on heroin. Heroin gives you a better kick, but nationalism is cheaper and legal.

Now both of them are dead, and the song that the former wrote and the latter sang doesn't mean anything to me.

XIII

1. *Andrić*

A FORTNIGHT HAD passed since Kole's funeral, and still I couldn't make up my mind to leave for Bosnia. I stayed at the Continental Hotel and spent the days in my room there smoking hash. The whole time I was afraid of somebody knocking at the door, though I didn't know who could knock. Nobody knew I was in Rijeka, nor did I call anybody. I sat on the bed, crumbled hash and mixed it with tobacco on the cover of *Signs by the Roadside* by Ivo Andrić, rolled joints, smoked, and then read the book. One of the thoughts Andrić recorded there was: "Dissatisfaction with myself, first of all, and afterward with everybody else in the world, has always been the basis of my mental being, regardless of passing moods and any momentary thoughts I may have had and managed to express."

2. *Kamov*

I couldn't sleep at night, so I'd go out and stroll the empty city. As I walked, I sometimes reflected on the last year on the icy island of S., on what took me there, and what brought me back here, to this city I once thought was mine. This was the city where I fell in love for the first time, got drunk for the first time, smoked a joint for the first time, had sex for the first time, wrote my first poem, first performed in a band. It was also the city where I was first asked for my identity card, arrested, thrown out of university, harassed, and beaten up. It was the city I had to flee from with my tail between my legs, like a hyena. And yet now it was just a desert, icier and more lifeless than the white wastes on the island of S.

One night I left the hotel and went to the generous, wide bridge over the Rječina River. Here was once the border between Italy and the Kingdom of Yugoslavia, the city was divided here into a western and an eastern part, Fiume and Sušak. That division looked strange and unnatural now, but it was probably different once. Just like we learned in the first years of school that the south Slavic lands and peoples had once been divided and warred among each other, and that fact sounded distant and archaic. But people get used to everything, it seems. People endure, survive, and supersede everything; they get on top of it all somehow, and then again, thank God, they die.

I made for the statue of Janko Polić Kamov, the rebellious modernist writer who died in Spain but grew up in Rijeka. Kamov leaned nonchalantly against the railing of the bridge as if he was waiting just for me. And I leaned against the railing next to him, took out a cigarette, lit up, and puffed the smoke into Kamov's oversized face. He was silent and looked away to the side. As if he was ashamed to know me, as if I'd disturbed him on that still September night. Below us flowed the amazingly clear river, carrying dreams, fragments of hope, shattered destinies, crushed lives, untimely and anonymous deaths abroad. It hummed with unfinished verses, violated rhymes, poems painfully broken off, novels published too late and never understood, underestimated short stories. Beneath the bridge, the Rječina bore Kamov's flames of resistance and black rosy kisses.

3. Milo the Bighead

Then a policeman came along and asked for my identity card. His face was young, younger than mine, freckled, and smooth like the bronze of Kamov's statue. Before I could give him an answer, a vague, nameless fear was aroused in me. Fifteen years earlier, not far from that spot, I hurried to "the Cont," as we used to call the concrete area in front of the Continental Hotel, where I was supposed to meet Kole. At that time, the Cont was the place where young people gathered, the starting point of all of our nights out and drunken sprees. The endpoint was usually the Palach.

I hurried, leading a blonde and smiling girl by the hand, and I had a crest of hair on the top of my head made with the help of оно glue, and at the sides I was freshly shaven. A few passersby turned around to look at us, and it wasn't clear if it was because of me or her. They probably wondered what such an attractive young woman was doing with a bum in hobnailed boots. At the crosswalk opposite the Continental we were stopped by a policeman of ill repute at the time, Milo the Bighead. He got his nickname for his huge head, with a sheepskin hat atop it like a nesting hen. Others claimed he was given it for the "head" of his dick. People said he liked to abuse boys and young men. Bighead and dickhead though he was, he was afraid of real, hardened criminals. Everybody knew the story about when he fled from Gajo, a local hood known for his soft heart and hard fist. Milo bolted in the middle of the day in his uniform, with a nightstick and a pistol at his belt, and holding his hat in one hand. Gajo caught up with him and gave him a thump and two kicks in the ass. Milo called for help, but nobody wanted to help him. From then on, whenever Milo saw Gajo, he ran to the other side of the street, and if he couldn't, he greeted him, bowing obsequiously to the sidewalk.

But he treated kids differently. He'd slap them around, take away their identity cards, write their names in a notebook, and threaten them, looking them in the face with his alcohol-pitted nose, like how the cartoon antihero Superhik blew his booze-rich breath into the faces of the unfortunates he'd stop to ask for their ID. I must have seemed the perfect victim for him, and when it turned out that I didn't even have an ID card, wasn't from Rijeka, and certainly wasn't the son of some fatass, or, heaven forbid, Gajo's younger brother, he thwacked me without any further explanation. Then he pushed me up against the wall of the En Passant coffee bar and searched my pockets. Several worthless dinar coins tinkled to the sidewalk, and he took me by the crest and forced me down on my knees to pick them up. My girl was shocked and tried to intervene. At that, Milo shoved her away and shouted, "Whaddaya want? Does your papa know who you're runnin' round with? Vamoose, girly, or I'll fuck the livin' daylights outa ya! Don't let me . . ."

He pushed her again, she began to cry, and he pushed her once more and chased her down the street. I stood in front of him with tear-filled eyes and my jaw clenched, ashamed and furious because of my helplessness and cowardice. The people who gathered stood and watched calmly, nobody raised a single word of protest, nobody asked what was going on; all they saw was a thickset, bigheaded policeman reprimanding a scruffy delinquent. He was sure to have done something wrong, stolen, or shouted something illegal, and just look at the scarecrow!

I hated those spineless figures, those gray faces dulled from not thinking, those fake, artificial smiles with welfare dentures. Back then already, maybe even from birth, I hated that petty-bourgeoisie rabble whose xenophobia stank from their mouths, from under their armpits, and thundered in waves from their hemorrhoid-ridden asses. I hated them more than Milo the Bighead himself, because Milo was just a product of them.

But, to tell the truth, that didn't seem so worrying to me just then. Because after Milo finally let me go I went to the Cont, where I met Kole—my girl soon arrived too—and we rehashed the unpleasant experience for him, exaggerated and distorted things, laid on the irony, and laughed about Milo, me, her, and we all laughed together. We went to a store, bought wine, drank on a bench, and devised plans for the band, for world tours, and unfulfilled dreams. We went to the Palach, met friends, listened to music, danced, hopped, shoved each other, hugged each other, fought each other, pissed, vomited, and tottered back to our homes.

The young policeman was still waiting for me to give him my identity card. I explained that I didn't have one, that I wasn't from there, that I was staying at the hotel—he could check—and that I'd come out to have a cigarette and talk with Kamov.

"With who?" he asked full of hope, probably thinking he could ask him for his ID card too.

XIV

1. *Landlady Silvija*

OCTOBER WAS DRAWING near, the chestnut trees in front of the Continental Hotel were slowly losing their leaves, and I lay on the bed, staring at the ceiling and calculating how much money I had left, how many more days I could loaf around in that expensive hotel room and mess with my brain cells, be it with cannabis, be it with wise and depressive Brother Ivo Andrić. Truly, I could've spent eternity like that, nothing induced me to move on, and I had nowhere to go. I realized, and finally admitted to myself, that it was completely irrelevant to me whether I was in my little room in Oslo, in a cabin on the island of S., in Rijeka, Bakar, or Brčko, in a ship's berth or a prison cell, because the emptiness in me was the same, the loneliness the same.

It was similar back in the early nineties when I was in my room above the market in Rijeka. I didn't have anywhere to go then either, but that changed. The war and all that accompanied it came loudly and abrasively, without asking if you wanted to join in the pseudo-intellectual jabber about origin and faith, blood and soil, graves with the bones of ancestors, to participate in mass-meetings where people cheered national leaders who looked like bad guys from the Alan Ford comics.

The landlady had an apartment with a kitchen and two rooms. She lived in one of them, and I in the other. She glided around from the kitchen to the bathroom and from her room to the balcony, soundlessly, with her long, dense, black hair combed back, always in the same worn, black silk robe with red roses that bled like her former beauty and youth. Sometimes, maybe a bit too often, on hungover mornings, I'd imagine her as a youthful, luxurious Italian courtesan, an elusive queen of the night, saucy and licentious, or maybe transparently and falsely chaste. I'd imagine who could've had her: naval officers, political functionaries, high-ranking dignitaries, or maybe even their ritzy and preserved wives, agents, spies and spooks, soldiers. Who had her? Nobody. Nobody had Silvija, my landlady. They had her once, but now she was mine, I concluded stupidly. I was the one who stayed with her in the end. She made herbal tea for me when I was sick, washed my clothes and hung them out on the balcony to dry, and hid me from the police when they searched for me; I'd go to the store for her to get groceries, liquor, and cigarettes. I'd also go to the market for grapes or tomatoes, and she'd usually lie in bed all day, smoking slims and drinking martinis with a defiant melancholy, listening to Edith Piaf and browsing old Italian fashion magazines. There wasn't a single picture hanging on the wall of her room, nor a photo of anyone dear to her pinned to her chest of drawers.

2. Problems, doldrums, disasters . . .

I stayed with her for a year and then abruptly left for Norway, without at all having planned to. Let me go into some of the problems I encountered due to not having the right papers in those poxy times.

In a nutshell, Croatia had become an independent state, and, according to the documents I had, I was from Bosnia. I applied for a six-month alien's residence permit on the basis of being a student, and I also worked at a daily newspaper. I submitted an application and they told me to come back in two weeks, which I did, but it still wasn't ready. It wasn't ready two weeks later either. Or four months later. My case was being processed, they said.

My case? As if I was Josef K., I thought. After five and a half months, they said I had to reapply because the use-by date of the application had expired. You apply for a six-month residence permit, they let you wait five and a half, and then they tell you: please reapply. There was no point in doing that because if they'd really wanted to resolve my "case" they'd already have done so. The troubles that resulted from this were manifold, and I'll mention just a few.

One of the main operative methods of the police in our part of the world was—and still is—random identity checks on passersby. They seemed to particularly like my mug. One young woman also told me that she'd stop me if she met me on the street.

The troubles involved with having to produce identification weren't so serious at first, but as the war gathered momentum refugees came in ever-greater numbers. Particularly after the war between Croats and Bosniaks in Bosnia became ever bloodier, the police started to arrest pedestrians and detain them at the station for a check. For a time, I got myself out of trouble with a press card. I'd tell them I'd forgotten my ID card, but that I was a journalist on assignment, and look, I had a press card. It usually worked, though not always.

An absurd situation arose at the newspaper I worked for when they wanted to extend my employment contract, but they couldn't because I had neither a work nor a residence permit, and the police authority said it couldn't give me any such permit because my employment contract had expired.

At the university, in turn, they said that if I wanted to enroll for the following year I'd either have to show proof of Croatian citizenship or pay 5,000 marks a year. I had neither one nor the other. I took my matriculation book and went to see the dean. He received me politely, he was always smiling and prepared to help, at least with a friendly face. He explained to me that as a foreign citizen I had to pay for my studies, which was the normal state of affairs everywhere in the world. True, but I asked him how it could be that people who gave their ethnicity as Croatian, but came from the same country as me, Bosnia, could study without paying a fee.

"Because they're Croats, logically," he replied.

I took out my matriculation book in front for him. Until 1991 it'd said: Yugoslav. Since the word "Yugoslav" was equated with "Chetnik" at that time, in 1991 I added a hyphen and wrote "Muslim." As if anybody cared for the difference at all. So I asked the dean if I could borrow his ballpoint pen for a moment. He gave it to me and I made another hyphen in front of his very eyes and added "Croatian." His pen left a mark darker than the one that'd written "Muslim," and especially "Yugoslav."

The dean looked at me, still with an endearing smile, and obviously didn't understand a thing. To be honest, I hadn't understood a thing for several years either. They drove you to take a position, label yourself, put yourself in a box, choose sides, support the cause, respond when called upon, obey, and fear. I felt as if I was filling in a form but there were no boxes on offer, nothing to tick, no options that suited me, but I had no choice, they forced me to write something. Now I'd made a box myself, I reflected in self-love, like a crackpot genius.

BEKIM SEJRANOVIĆ

"So does this mean I can continue studying now?" I said haughtily.

He looked at me and took his glasses from his nose. "Er, what? What's the meaning of this, young man?"

"For one, it means I'm now also a Croat. Can I enroll now?"

"But you can't do it like that, you can't do it just like that."

"How then?"

"You can't declare yourself a Croat just like that," he said smiling.

"Why not?"

"That's not how you become a Croat."

"Then please tell me, how does one become a Croat?"

"Listen young man, I don't have time for trading shots like this," he said, wiping the nice-old-grandfather smile off his face.

I went then, of course, since I had no intention of being forced to become a Croat, just as I'd simply never cared if I was supposed to declare myself a Yugoslav, Muslim, Romany, Albanian, Serb, or even a Norwegian. But for others that was obviously important. For others it meant absolutely everything. All the Balkans' legal-administrative-cultural imbroglios to do with ethnicity, citizenship, right of residence, and the definition of the national language and identity were simply a bold farce designed for the ignorant, intimidated, and maddened masses of the population by shrewd and greedy politicians, enterprising and arrogant criminals, and narrow-minded quasi intellectuals. Unfortunately the farce grew into a tragic war. The price was paid by the masses, while the beneficiaries were politicians, criminals, and quasi intellectuals.

In the summer of 1991, armed clashes flared up in Croatia, and I went to Brčko to visit Grandfather, Grandmother, and Zada. Just then, a notice came demanding that I report for service in the Yugoslav People's Army. It was short of troops for the war in Croatia, so it started gathering young men in Bosnia. I fled back to Rijeka. In the meantime, war began in Bosnia too, and conscription letters came for me from the Croatian Defense Council, the Army of Bosnia-Herzegovina, and even the Army of Republika Srpska. While I was trying to organize a certificate of citizenship in Croatia, I was told that I could get papers if I volunteered for the Croatian Army and went to the front.

After Brčko fell into the hands of Serbian forces, a large part of the population was expelled and imprisoned in concentration camps, and many were killed. Zada, Grandfather, and Grandmother fled to Croatia, but even there things became difficult after a while due to the clashes between Croats and Bosniaks back in Bosnia. My mother went to Malaysia as a refugee and stayed there forever.

My father, on the other hand, lived in Bosanska Gradiška and was captured by one of the Serbian militias. They interned him for six months in the concentration camp in Stara Gradiška. He was saved from possible death by my stepmother, his wife, who was a Serb. After his release from the camp, he was hospitalized in intensive care for a while. Later he made it to Croatia, where he was arrested and interrogated by the Croatian secret service under suspicion of being a spy. His place of birth, Šabac, was particularly suspicious to them, as was his youth spent in Belgrade. Finally they let him go with the order to get his ass out of Croatia within twenty-four hours, otherwise "the darkness would swallow him." Those were their actual words. Instead, he was swallowed by the red dust of the Australian state of Victoria, where he went after five years in Germany spent slaving away on construction sites and drifting drunkenly like an old cat with a wrecked spine. I don't know exactly where his grave is, nor does it interest me.

3. Scratching

When I rang at landlady Silvija's door the first time, it was cold and I was hungover. I'd just been thrown out of my last room for "unseemly behavior." She took me in straightaway, without superfluous talk. She poured me a local grappa and made herself a martini, lit a cigarette, and asked, "Can you pay up front?"

I answered that I could, but I'd need a few days.

"Excellent!" she said, thrusting her open hand between my legs, gently cupping my balls, and slowly scratching the root of my penis with her fingertips. She looked me straight in the eyes, coldly and without any expression. She blew her smoke away to the side, drew back her hand, got up, and went to bring me my bed linen.

I explained that there might be problems with the police when she went to register me as a lodger because I didn't have a residence permit. She told me not to worry, she'd go there personally and sort it all out.

When she came back from the police station the next day and took off her—what seemed to me—rather expensive fur coat in the hall, she sighed and said she hadn't gotten anywhere. I feared for a moment she'd throw me out and find somebody else's balls to scratch. She came up close. She was a head shorter than me and skinny, even gaunt. She looked at me again with her dark, dour expression, scratched me on the balls, this time faster but more lightly.

"Why should you give a fuck?" she said.

But not everything went so smoothly. Police checks, raids, deportations, and people disappearing became common occurrences. It was mainly Serbs who disappeared, but they also expelled Bosniaks who didn't have valid papers. I tried to move about as little as possible, but sometimes I really had to go out and have a drink. On one such occasion I managed to get involved in a punch-up while awfully drunk. I was actually trying to calm people so they wouldn't fight. I was just explaining to one of them that it was better we drink another bottle of wine instead of arguing, when he smashed a beer bottle and jabbed its neck into mine. Not too deep, fortunately, but enough for me to look like I'd been butchered. The police arrived, bundled the few of us who were still at the scene into a Black Maria, and drove us to the station. There, after a short talk, they let everybody go except me. I was taken to the workers' barracks in the Rijeka neighborhood of Rastočine. There was a police guard at the entrance. They led me into one of the barracks and a policeman opened the door of a room and told me to go in and sleep. I was still drunk, I didn't understand what was happening, and it didn't matter to me at all. In the darkness, I realized after several moments that the floor was covered with sleeping bodies. I found a small bit of space and fell asleep like falling into an abyss.

Sharp, unpleasant shouts made me open my eyes. Two mustachioed policemen were standing at the door and trying their hardest to seem strict and threatening, and the people got up off the floor unwillingly and sluggish, like sleepy children: there were eight men, two young women, and three boys aged from three to seven. Some of the men were wearing blue tracksuit pants, white singlets, and had blue-and-white plastic scuffs. We were led out of the room and made to line up in a queue that stretched to an old bus. Policemen with Kalashnikovs stood on either side. The morning was sunny and warm, and the warbling of tiny birds filled the air. Two police officers stood at the front of the queue, right at the door of the bus, handing out bags with dry food: a quarter of a loaf of bread, a wedge of Zdenka cheese, and a boiled egg. Then they told you to get in.

BEKIM SEJRANOVIĆ

When the bus was full, the driver started the motor and muttered something under his breath like why did he have to transport this riffraff, and it'd be best just to chuck 'em all in the sea. A young police officer in plain clothes told him to cut the crap and just drive. The remaining people, myself included, were mostly young men but also a number of women and children, had to stay and wait for the next bus. I looked at the young plainclothes policeman, who was dressed in black bermudas and a black Lacoste jersey with short sleeves. Probably an imitation, judging by the way it'd stretched and faded in the wash. My head was throbbing from the hangover. I didn't understand at all where I was or what was going on. I looked at my T-shirt and expected to read "Red Hot Chili Peppers—Blood Sugar Sex Magik," but I saw it was covered in blood, my pants were bloody too, and blood slowly crawled down my neck; I smelled the cheese and the rotten boiled egg, I saw the imitation green crocodile coming up to me, the concrete below also came up to meet me, what sort of stupid joke is this, I thought, and fell unconscious.

The police drove me to the hospital, kept me there for several hours, and then took me back to the barracks, where another bus had come and collected the remaining unfortunates. They were Bosniaks who'd lived at the workers' barracks for years and worked at the shipyards or the docks. They were taken by bus to the ferry, by ferry to Split, and from Split to Mostar, where they were handed over to the Croatian Defense Council. What happened to them after that, I don't know. The inspector in the black jersey threw a glance at me and told me to scram.

"You know what you look like?"

"Yep."

I walked down through Rastočine toward the city center, the insolent sun beat straight in my eyes, the sutures on my neck felt like creeping wiry caterpillars, and tears of self-pity rolled down my alcohol-creased face.

When I got home, I fell into a fever that lasted almost three days. The face of landlady Silvija hovered over me, like an evil fairy or a good witch. She applied compresses and blew her cigarette smoke away above her head. And I just wanted her to scratch my balls.

XV

From nowhere to nowhere

FOR TWO DAYS I'd been trying to leave Room 414 of the Continental Hotel in Rijeka. I was prevented by an inexplicable fear of going out among people, in the daylight, but I was driven by an anxiety that's hard to describe, a wish for change, a thirst for something different, maybe even a death drive. I waited patiently for that anxiety to overcome my fear. I looked at my rucksack and imagined leaving, going down to reception and paying the bill, striding out of the hotel, crossing Rijeka's paseo for the last time, arriving at the bus station, and getting on the bus to Zagreb, afterward one to Brčko, and then . . .

Everything was reminiscent of my departure eight years earlier. Only the rucksack I now carried was somewhat bigger. The feeling was similar, but this time more conscious: the farewell to the city's streets; breaking the bond with something I thought had been part of me; expecting novelty and change, uncertainty; the wish for it all to end, for you to be rid of your bones, your skin, the hair on your chest, for your goggle eyes to drop out of their sockets; the wish to forget the desperate need for love, that damn hunger for love that destroys, for a love that costs and demands more than you can imagine, and which in the end crushes you and turns you into a worm. Then again, if you're not prepared for love like that, it's not even worth living.

Instead of going straight to the bus station, I found myself at the market in Rijeka's main square. It was a cloudy morning on the first day of October, people were moving about slowly, chatting, babbling, haggling, quarreling, scamming. A small group of chewed-up and spat-out, unshaven, middle-aged men were devotedly drinking their first morning bottle of wine. Everything was the same, as if I'd never left, as if I'd never been there. I stopped in front of a stand selling apples, pears, and grapes. A sullen man with a large moustache and a big belly was hustling his produce. Next to his stand was a Romany couple—the man small and stocky, the woman beautiful, with large, brown eyes and voluptuous round breasts. They yelled as loudly as their vocal cords were able and the eardrums of the customers could stand, offering nighties, superglue, and rice-crispy chocolate. Above their heads on the fifth floor was the balcony of my former landlady Silvija. It looked lifeless and deserted.

I was on that balcony for the last time on July 31, 1993. A day earlier Aunty Zika, my mother's sister, had called and told me to come to Zagreb. She worked for a humanitarian organization and was the only person who could possibly help me. She helped Zada go to Malaysia. She'd offered that I could go to Germany, but I didn't want to, or rather, I didn't have the courage to. I didn't want to go anywhere, but after my last arrest it was obvious I couldn't stay anymore. I went out to the balcony to get my clothes that were now dry, but I only took my boxers and a T-shirt. I still didn't believe that going to Zagreb really meant *going away*. Naively, I hoped to spend a few days in Zagreb until my aunt arranged papers for me—maybe some kind of residence permit, proof of Croatian citizenship, or at least Bosnian papers, anything, just so that I had something to show when the police stopped me. Nor could I tell Silvija that I was going away for good because I didn't have the money for the next month's rent, and I still owed her for July. Everything looked even more unreal because I'd spent the previous week in Jadranovo, a small coastal town about twenty miles south of Rijeka, with two buddies, Saša and Hamid. All those problems seemed far away there. The summer sun and sea didn't ask about papers, proof of descent, or religion.

Saša was a writer, had a big nose, and I'm not sure he ever had anything published. He was half Serb, half Croat, and at that time was hiding from the military police so they wouldn't conscript him and send him to the front. First he stopped eating meat, afterward eggs and cheese. Later he stopped eating vegetables too. Back then, in that last week of July 1993, which we spent in the house of a girlfriend of ours, swimming and sunbathing, he only ate blueberries, currants, and blackberries. Later he stopped eating entirely. He died in the hospital in the late nineties of anorexia.

Hamid was half Croatian, half Sudanese. His father had come to Yugoslavia to study, got married, had him, got divorced, and went back to Sudan. Hamid stayed and treated his identity crisis with alcohol and ill-fated affairs. He spoke with a real Dalmatian drawl, drank wine diluted with water like the locals, and didn't believe in God. In the mid-nineties he went to Sudan on several occasions, and every time he returned even unhappier, skinnier, and drunker.

That morning, I went into my landlady's room for the last time to tell her I was going to Zagreb for a few days. She was sitting on the bed, leaning on two large pillows, with a towel around her head because she'd just had a shower. She smoked and looked morosely the other way, out the window.

"You won't be coming back."

She said it in such a way that I believed her. Then she turned toward me and demanded that I pay her for the last month. No problem, I answered. Of course I'd be back, I was leaving all my things there. She turned her head away again and said nothing more.

I left her room, took my rucksack with a T-shirt, boxers, a walkman with a cassette of *The Queen is Dead* by The Smiths, and also a book, and left. I never paid her for July 1993.

Now I stood at the entrance of her building and wondered whether I should go up to the fifth floor and ring at the door. What if I heard steps, what if Silvija opened the door? I also tried to grasp why I'd want to do that in the first place. To pay a debt eight years old? Nonsense, as if she was the only one I owed a debt, as if I believed in things like that. I just wanted to see the remorselessness of time toward the female body, to feel the punishment for a boyhood dream. I felt that if I saw it I might be able to get over it all more easily. But what if the same Silvija opened the door in the same faded robe, with that same icy look, maybe even a few years younger? And then grabbed me by the balls and squeezed so hard that I howled and started crying?

I didn't go up the stairs, of course. Instead, I went up to the beautiful, chesty Romany woman and bought three tubes of glue and two rice-crispy chocolate bars. Her beauty had just reached its apex and now slowly, but irreversibly, would disappear—the ephemeral value of beauty.

At the bus station, somebody grabbed me by the shoulder from behind and began to shout with glee. It was Hamid, terribly skinny and missing one of his top front teeth. He was with a guy we called Dalton. Once we'd worked together at the paper, I as a writer and he as a photographer. When I'd left for Norway, he fled to the Czech Republic. He'd been a volunteer in the Croatian Army and even had the rank of sergeant or something.

Once he threw a grenade at a window where a Serbian soldier was, hit the frame, and the grenade rebounded and wounded half his platoon, including himself. But it saved the life of the enemy soldier. After the shrapnel was removed and he'd recovered, Dalton was to be mobilized again, but he'd had enough of war. He said he'd already put his ass on the line for Croatia, so he went to Prague. He got married there, opened a photo studio, had two sons, got divorced, and had now returned to Rijeka.

Both of them had obviously been drunk for several days. They were glad to see me, but I couldn't drink with them. Hamid said he'd just come back from Sudan, where he'd spent the last two years. He'd worked in some warehouse, counting sacks. I don't know what was in the sacks. Dalton had tried to open a photo studio in Rijeka, but they didn't let him because he didn't have the necessary papers. Both of them said in one voice that they were going back—Hamid to Sudan, and Dalton to the Czech Republic.

Hamid complained about losing his tooth, worried that he was too skinny, and feared he'd end up like Saša. "I took shish kebabs to the hospital for him while he was dying of anorexia. I think that's what killed him."

I gave them the chocolate and glue I'd bought from the Romany woman. I told Hamid he'd gain at least two pounds if he stuck his tooth back in. All three of us laughed. Then we went to the station pub and drank beer. To the lousy olden times, the mangy present, and the wormy future.

I boarded the bus and left. From nowhere to nowhere.

XVI

GRANDFATHER FINALLY BEGAN walking again. He turned toward me and looked at me pleadingly. He said that Aunty Zika had bought a burial plot. For him and Grandmother. I turned my eyes the other way and read the names on the gravestones. I worked out how old people were when they died.

"You'll come and visit my grave, won't you?" He started to cry again. "There's nobody else to come."

I calmed him angrily like he was a small child afraid of the dark. I made a stupid attempt at a joke, saying that you never know who'll visit whose grave. At that, he stopped for a moment, glanced at me, and then began to cry even more. I rolled my eyes and pulled him furiously by the arm.

1. *The reindeer*

A year and a half after Alija's funeral I stood on the eighth-floor balcony of the student hostel Sogn in Oslo. I was going to visit Grandfather's grave.

BEKIM SEJRANOVIĆ

I watched the torn clouds in the west. In the east, the insolent sun was already up, though it was only four o'clock in the morning. In Zagreb, I was certain, it was still dark. Due to the degree of latitude. The plane to Zagreb didn't leave until seven, but I got up early because I could no longer sleep. I rolled a joint before the trip to calm me down. But it didn't really work for me anymore, it actually now forced me to meditate, making images, sounds, smells, and feelings come back. Often it gave me a hard-on. The chattering of birds began at the crack of dawn. First songbirds, then the magpies, crows, and gulls. Two dirty gray gulls were deviously tugging a plastic bag from a dumpster. "Rema 1000," it said on the bag—the name of a no-frills supermarket.

Slowly, like a bad premonition, the picture of a dark Norwegian fall afternoon rose before me. I was making my way through the gloom, carrying the same kind of plastic bags full of groceries. I hurried toward a ramshackle little wooden house, which stood completely alone on a flat-topped, bare hill ringed by forest. Mist sprawled over the surrounding swampy fields lined by sparse, deaf-mute birches. The rain seeped tiredly from low, leaden clouds. I looked in front of me as I squelched along the wet path. Sara and her two-and-a-half year-old son Jon were waiting for me in the little house. They'd lived there since Sara's husband found out about the two of us and threw them out. Nobody in the village pointed a finger at her, but you could feel the whisperings that followed her like a cold drop of water running down your back. In the small, pious village of L., scattered over the granite hills of southern Norway, they hadn't heard or seen anything like that before. Yes, it happened there too, like in distant and libertine Oslo, that couples got divorced, that they cheated on each other. But a woman—with a small child—living with two men? When her husband went to work on an oil platform in the North Sea another man had moved into the house with her; a foreigner, moreover, as dark as a Gypsy, almost black, heaven forbid, probably a Muslim too, a refugee from some war in the south of Europe, or maybe the east (who knows, they're all the same bad lot), with less than honorable motivations and, people said, a huge, uncircumcised penis. And how could they not be ashamed in front of the child, if not before God? How would their modest wooden chapel withstand such a disgrace?

The previous Sunday, the plump priest had threatened with his protestant God, a God who dislikes false pleasures, ornamented altars, and kitschy frescos, a God who demands quiet, devoted work, self-control, abstinence, and who promises no rewards, not even in heaven.

All at once, as I was walking along that path carrying those bags, whose contents would nourish our sinful bodies, my eye caught a gray, horned creature stalking on cloven hooves across the sodden fields. For a moment, the apparition was lost in the mist, but soon it reappeared near the path, jumped over the barbed-wire fence, and halted in the middle of the way, just twenty yards ahead of me. For an instant I thought of the devil and imagined he was appearing now as a reminder of the ruddy priest's warning. But it was only a magnificent specimen of a male reindeer. He stood and watched me calmly. I was frightened at first, and then marveled, and then was frightened again. Although reindeer aren't usually dangerous, this was a huge animal, almost six feet tall. If it wanted to be dangerous, it could be. It was the hunting season, so it had probably evaded a hunt and lost its way. There were quite a few of them in the surrounding forests, and every fall a certain number were allowed to be shot.

BEKIM SEJRANOVIĆ

We stared at each other like that for several moments, two intruders in the village. Two beings earmarked for culling, two beasts who, for the time being, had escaped the hunt.

Then he calmly and elegantly leaped over the barbed wire on the other side of the path and trotted away into the forest.

Now I was still looking from the eighth-floor balcony at the enticing concrete sixty feet down. The two gulls tore apart the Rema 1000 bag, each of them greedily grabbed a piece of something I couldn't identify and flew off. The clouds covered the whole horizon in the west, sailed to above the very building on whose balcony I was standing, and released a hard and irrepressible stream of rain. Like the tears of an abandoned wife.

2. *Ulysses*

I met Sara in December 1993, several months after arriving in Norway. It was then that I first went by ship from Kristiansand to Denmark. People traveled on that ship for two reasons: to shop and to get drunk. The ship was huge and could take on cars, buses, and even trains. It had space for several thousand people, who spent their time in several bars, discos, casinos, a movie theater, numerous stores selling all sorts of things, and cabins. The highlight was that after leaving port in Norway the whole ship became a duty-free zone, meaning that alcoholic drinks were markedly cheaper. And really, within fifteen minutes everybody was wasted. Young and old alike, male and female.

I liked it, and in a way I can say "I found myself there." The ship would sail at seven in the evening, within four hours it arrived at the Danish coast, and then waited for morning. People drank, tottered about, vomited, and gambled. Some danced and yelled in the disco, where a Bulgarian band played a repertoire from Boney M to AC/DC, and sometimes a few couples would end up in cabins having bad sex.

That's where I got to know her, the red-headed Norwegian with whom I'd spend more or less the next five years of my life. I noticed her the moment I boarded the ship. She was dressed in a totally outmoded white suit, had a Prince Valiant haircut and Pippi Longstocking freckles. I went up to her much later, after at least a pint of the cheapest whiskey. We spoke English, or rather I put on my best imitation of Irish English. I told her that my father was Irish, had been a member of the IRA, and had fled because he'd done some terrible things, maybe even killed somebody, so he went to Yugoslavia, where he married my mother. Then I recited translations of my own poems for her, intoned with my "Irish" accent. Later I riddled her with lofty, invented quotes from Joyce, Yeats, and Shane Mac-Gowan. I ran the movie *In the Name of the Father* in my head and tried to imitate the facial expressions and movements of Daniel Day-Lewis. I really was an Irishman that evening. Sara believed that preposterous story for five more years.

Once, when I'd long forgotten everything, she started telling it all in front of me to one of her girlfriends. I burst out laughing and said I'd never heard such rubbish. She looked at me perplexed and said she remembered me telling her that—I'd told her several times, in fact. She started to enumerate details I didn't remember at all. I'd embellished my story, thought up figures, details, names of villages, surnames of families we were related to, surnames of other families we were in a centennial feud with, listed and mentioned uncles who were members of the IRA, quoted imaginary poets and revolutionaries. Because a lie, like a good story, and art in general, is nothing other than the craft of making up details. The art of connecting incompatible

BEKIM SEJRANOVIĆ

concepts. The harder the concepts are to combine, the finer but also stronger the bond required. You have to devise a thread as delicate as a cobweb that can bear five hundred tons.

"But that was a hundred years ago," I said to Sara.

The Irish phase was long past. I told her that only a fool could believe stuff like that. She started to cry, and her girlfriend left.

Sara shuffled about the house for several days teary-eyed, and I kept trying to appease her by calling myself the foulest names I could think of in Norwegian.

I soon left on a long-planned trip to Bosnia to visit Grandmother and Grandfather. When I returned, I tormented her for several more weeks before she threw me out of the apartment.

3. A good dog

I avidly inhaled the last smoke through my joint's cardboard filter, stubbed it out, and threw the butt from the balcony of the student hostel. I aimed at the dumpster where magpies had now come in place of the gulls. Then I left the balcony and walked down the long, narrow corridor. On the right were three doors of rooms and a shared bathroom, and on the left another three doors and a shared kitchen. I entered my room, the last on the left, immediately next to the bathroom, took my rucksack, checked that my passport and plane ticket were there, looked around the room one more time, and was gone. A box of books was all that I left behind. The other things belonged to the actual tenant of the room, a student from the north of Norway who'd gone home for the summer vacation. It was common for students to rent out their rooms to tourists, seasonal workers, or other students. I locked the door, went out through the left wing of the eighth floor, and left the key in the fusebox as agreed. After I pressed the button to call the elevator, I heard the dull sound of its movement. And as I listened to it rising, that familiar feeling of emptiness and inadequacy crept over me. A life spent in temporary accommodation, hostels, reception centers, bachelor hostels, and semiprivate rooms. Eternal moves with one box of books and one bag of clothes. Languishing in rooms never larger than ten feet by ten, running from back rent, excuses for late payment, paranoid of somebody knocking at the door, inventing identities, insecure when asked questions like: who are you, what do you do, where are you from, where do you live? I admitted to myself sometimes that my identity consisted of a mass of half-truths, fancifully told lies, and distorted relationships with women. There was nothing more than that, nor need there be.

Sickened, I left the building and headed for the bus station where the airport shuttle would collect me. I went past the magpies and stamped loudly on the asphalt to scare them away, but they didn't care in the slightest. One of them tilted its head a little so as to better captivate me with its evil eye and uttered a drawn-out, sharp screech. What a send-off from Norway after eight years, I thought superstitiously and with pathos. The policewoman at the Zagreb airport had shrieked with a related, congenital ill-temper when I'd left Croatia eight years earlier. I'd arrived in Zagreb two days before. Bosnian refugees were being picked up around the city like stray dogs that had escaped from the pound, only to be sent back. They were gathered up all over the place, but most of all at the station (those who'd just arrived from Herzegovina), in front of the mosque (those who got through the station and were now sleeping rough or waiting for humanitarian aid around the mosque), in front of the embassy of Bosnia-Herzegovina (people who were waiting for papers so as to be able to flee somewhere), and, the most

BEKIM SEJRANOVIĆ

unfortunate, at the airport (those who'd managed to avoid all the stress already mentioned and were on the verge of leaving). I hid for two days in the apartment of a Malaysian humanitarian aid organizer, and on the third day Aunty Zika came, brought me a passport, a ticket to Norway, and gave me 400 marks.

"This is it. Today you're going to Norway," she said.

Norway was the last country in Europe that was still accepting refugees from Bosnia-Herzegovina. I stared at the pile of vitally important papers in my sinewy hands and didn't say a word. I didn't feel like a refugee from Bosnia-Herzegovina, but, fuck, I obviously wasn't from Croatia either. I hoped I'd perhaps count as a Norwegian one day. Yeah.

At the airport I had to show my passport, and the angry policewoman asked me if I had a permit from the military authorities for leaving the country. My aunt had a confirmation that I worked for the Malaysian humanitarian organization, but she couldn't give me the document because there were several more names on it. She was at the entrance to the security zone. I waved to her to come up so she could show the document, but she didn't understand what I wanted and just waved off. The queue behind me was getting impatient, the policewoman began to yelp aggressively. With a frantic energy hard to describe convincingly, accompanied by threatening glances from the police and a few curses, my aunt forced her way through the throng, while rummaging in her bag for the fake piece of paper. When she made it to the counter, where the exasperated policewoman had risen to her feet, she shook out the contents of her handbag in front of her in panic. The policewoman went pale, screamed, shook her head neurotically, and flared her nostrils. I almost felt sorry for her for a minute.

It was my first time on a plane. It was full of refugees, mainly people recently expelled from Herzegovina and the area around

Mostar. My flight went first to Frankfurt, then on to Copenhagen, and finally Kristiansand. I'd heard of that city in southern Norway only hours earlier. During the flight I got to know a guy my age from Mostar. He told me he'd been expelled and only made it to Zagreb by the skin of his teeth. He'd been able to stay with some acquaintances of his parents. They told him he could sleep at their place for a while until he arranged papers for leaving. They had a large apartment in the city center and a policeman was always standing at the entrance of the building because a government minister lived there. They told him he needn't be afraid of the police anymore because he was under their protection now. In return, he sometimes walked their dog, the labrador Alfie. At first he was afraid of the police, but when they stopped him here and there he'd tell them where he was staying and that he was looking after their dog. And every time, to his great surprise, everything would be okay. He asked himself in the end who was minding who: he Alfie, or Alfie him?

Once, when he took the dog out and let him play in Opatovina Park, Alfie shot straight toward a man, jumped at him, knocked him to the ground, and started to bark in his face. The guy from Mostar tried to restrain him and drag him back, but the dog was merciless. Then two police officers appeared out of nowhere and came running up, rescued the unfortunate man, and then Alfie calmed down. The guy from Mostar now imagined himself in jail, in a deportation bus, prison camp, or a nameless, cheerless, dimly lit cell. But the policemen busied themselves with Alfie's victim. They checked his identity and searched him, and they found a small amount of heroin hidden in his socks. They then went up to the guy from Mostar and looked at the dog again.

"My God, is that Alfie?" one of them said.

They explained to him that Alfie had once been the best police sniffer dog for narcotics. The whole police force knew him. The guy from Mostar now realized that his host must be a senior police inspector.

While he talked, we flew over the monotonous plains of Germany. As if somebody had spread out a rug with a multicolored, symmetrical pattern.

The guy from Mostar looked out the window wistfully and said, "He really was a good dog."

4. *The mousetrap*

When we arrived in Norway, we were picked up by the Norwegian police and delivered to a refugee reception center. Medical examinations, vaccination, and police questioning followed over the next few days; my photograph was taken *en face* and in profile, as well as the fingerprints of both hands.

Several weeks later, they helped me and three families move into a suburban house rented by the Social Welfare Office as temporary accommodation for refugees. My room was in the basement, next to the building's supply of fire wood, and full of mice. Jamil, a young man with a broad, white smile, who came from Bangladesh and was employed by the Integration Section of the Norwegian Aliens Department, gave me four rather vicious-looking mousetraps to place around the basement. I put them by the wood, but I didn't set them.

Sara and I had sex for the first time in that basement. She'd told me on the first evening, when we met on the ship to Denmark, that she had a husband and a small son, one and a half years old. Nothing happened between us on the ship, at least not physically. I sent her a well-worded letter a week later, and she answered quickly. In her letter, she described herself as being behind bars. That's how she felt in the house her husband had recently bought with the money earned on the oil platform. After that, we spoke on the phone and arranged a meeting. She drove to Kristiansand, with her son, in her husband's Mercedes. As we strolled through town, I pushed the buggy in which little Jon was sleeping; he looked like Sara. Afterward we went to my room in the basement and five minutes later were fucking on the floor. I was underneath. She rode me with her eyes closed as her son hopped up and down at her back, pulling her hair, calling, and crying. Later, when I lay on top of her, he squealed furiously and rapped me on the head. We stopped and she took him out of the room and shut him in the room with the wood. When she came back inside, I saw that blood was dripping from her vagina. I asked if she had her period; she said no. I asked with a good dose of sarcasm if she was perhaps still a virgin.

"Maybe," she replied, as if she wished it was true.

Jon wasn't making any noise, so we kept on fucking. When we were done, we both rushed out of the room to see what the kid was doing. He was sitting in the corner, teary-eyed but calm. He was holding a mousetrap in his hand and examining it with curiosity. When he saw us, he started to cry again.

Sara and I kept up our affair in secret for six months more. She claimed she didn't have sex with her husband. I didn't believe her and would go mad at the thought of her sleeping with him. Maybe that's why we stayed together. And also because of little red-haired, freckled Jon, who I really took to. Soon the whole village knew what was going on. Her husband would leave for the oil platform for several weeks, and I'd then move in, usually the same morning. When he was due to return, I'd go back to Kristiansand, to my basement with the unset mousetraps. Her husband was the only one oblivious. Until one day. Then he threw her out of the house.

She stayed in her village for some time more in a crooked little house for outcasts, where a guy they called Kjelvis had just died. (His name was Kjell, and he made a living as an Elvis Presley impersonator.) Then she, Jon, and I moved to Oslo together. I worked nightshifts in a bakery, sometimes illegally on building sites, and tried to study whenever I could. She was a nurse at a hospital. Our relationship soon fell into various clichéd ruts and we broke up many times, even for months at a time. I tried to leave her and find some other woman, to fall in love, but I was too attached to Jon, and he to me.

It would've been better for all of us if I'd been more resolute and left. It probably would've been best if we'd never met at all.

5. Abandoned wives

Sara's mother hated me and made no attempt to conceal it. She always said that our relationship had no future, that Sara was just wasting her time with me, and that we were both selfish, especially me, and that we should think of the child. She was right, of course, but I didn't like her mug, so I firmly resolved to prove her wrong.

Sara was born three years before me in New York, where her parents had gone in the early sixties in search of a better life. She was three, and her sister one, when their father was diagnosed with cancer and given, at best, six months left to live. He didn't want to die abroad, so the whole family moved back to Norway, to his native village of L. But the cancer withdrew thanks to the therapy, Sara's father gained new strength and he built a large house with his own hands. His condition soon worsened again, and the cancer metastasized, passing from his internal organs to his right leg. There were numerous treatments again, chemotherapy, and long and frequent stays at the national *Radium-hospitalet* in Oslo. And he was better again, but only for a while, because the illness moved to other parts of his body. All in all, instead of the predicted six months, Thomas Eirik Pedersen lived another eighteen years. He was more sick than healthy in those eighteen years, but his caring wife Ragnhild was always by his side. Two years before his death, he announced to her that he'd been in a relationship with a young nurse for several years, that he loved her and intended to spend what little time he had left in the world with her. He was leaving the house to her, his wife, and to their daughters, Sara and Anita, who'd now come of age. He thanked Ragnhild for all the years she'd been by his side and hoped she'd find the love she deserved. He realized the situation was awkward, but what could he do? He loved the nurse.

Long after his departure, Ragnhild still drew compassionate glances, which are harder to get rid of than the mange. Some said it would've been better for her if he'd died back in America. Shortly before his death, Sara got married. She tried to get pregnant as soon as possible because she believed it'd make her father happy. It only worked after a year and a half, and her father never saw his grandson—he died when Sara was four months pregnant with Jon. At the funeral, all eyes were on Ragnhild, who saw off her husband without a single tear. The woman he spent the last two years of his life with wasn't there. Everybody thought it was better that way because she would've spoiled the solemnity of the last farewell. The plump and energetic priest, who tried in vain to comb back his hair to cover his balding pate, and who saw the work of the devil all around him and invoked God's punishment as the only remedy for all our misfortunes, was also glad. It was actually Sara who went to see the woman, only a few years older than herself, and begged her not to attend the funeral.

I thought about that woman, whose name I never heard, as the bus drove me to Gardermoen Airport, where the plane to Zagreb was waiting. I wondered if anybody thought about her as she mourned in the solitude of her room for the man who died in her arms. I pictured her coming to the graveyard after the funeral, alone, soundlessly like a ghost, yet followed by the invisible, piercing gazes of the stern and hypocritically pious village. I heard the whisper of the south-Norwegian dialect—reminiscent of a death rattle—trying for the umpteenth time to stifle and disparage her love. Her shoulders gently shuddered, tears welled up slowly and rolled down her face to fall on the fresh mound of earth covered by artlessly colorful bouquets of flowers.

XVII

1. Hoka hey

THE SCANDINAVIAN SAS plane rose above Oslo and slowly gained altitude, circling and making its way through ever bigger and thicker pillows of cloud. I cast one more glance at the city where I'd been dissipating the debris of my life for years. It shot through my mind that I was perhaps seeing it for the last time, and I didn't find that tragic.

Before the aircraft stabbed its nose into a thick layer of cloud, I had a wonderful view of the whole of the Oslofjord with its many little islands. And then, when the whole fuselage was engulfed in milky white, I closed my eyes, and a mosaic of the past flickered under my eyelids, made up of little islands, boats, and a dirty white parrot.

That was my most carefree summer in Oslo. Only whispers of Sara remained—pleasant ones, I'd say. Several months after we'd laid our long-departed love to rest forever, she returned to her village in the south of Norway. At the beginning of that summer, six months after her leaving, the rumor came that she was living with her husband again and was many months pregnant. One acquaintance, a Bosnian who lived in Kristiansand, minced those words over the phone discreetly, as if to spare me. His words brought me a vague and slightly deceptive sense of relief, though it was painful at first, to tell the truth. I felt betrayed in a way, but I didn't know why, just the usual male vanity. But after a short time I finally started to feel light and carefree. I didn't ask myself anymore if I should've tried to make up with Sara and make some change in our empty lives. And so Sara passed into legend. Our love was entombed, and I was still alive.

It was a hot summer, like they sometimes are in Norway. Oslo was graced by tall, tanned blondes who, scantily dressed and unhealthily trussed up, showed the world their curves as they strutted like peacocks cooped up in small cages. I played the guitar and sang in the underground station at the National Theater. I seized the eyes of passersby and tried to hypnotize them so they might throw a few crowns into my guitar case. It flashed through my mind that it was good to be free again. Soon not even stray thoughts of Sara. It was better that way.

Although I earned relatively good money as a busker, it wasn't enough for a decent life. And I found it boring to play every single day. So I set about searching for some temporary work. I'd work a bit and play a bit when I felt like it. Life would be laid back and sweet, I thought.

I soon started work on a small ship that ferried people to and fro around the Oslofjord. The boat started out from Oslo and transported passengers from island to island, and our route included Hovedøya, Lindøya, and Gressholmen. There were weekend cottages, beaches, and a few small restaurants on those little islands. My job was mainly to sell tickets. I wore a white uniform, dark glasses, and smiled at the girls in their bathing suits. And now and then at their moms.

My co-worker was Lars, a short and stocky Swede who was a jack-of-all-trades on the ship. Sometimes he'd sell tickets with me, sometimes scrub the deck, putter around at the motor, or stand at the wheel; in a word, he knew and did everything on the vessel better even than the captain, an eternally grumpy old man. But Lars and I didn't pay him any mind.

At first I thought Lars was maybe just a few years older than me, and I was more than a bit surprised when he told me he was over forty. He shaved his head every few days, but judging by his beard his hair was bright carrot red. Multiple tattoos showed from under the sleeves of his shirt. They were mainly motifs from Viking mythology: swords, huge grim fuckers with axes and helmets like Hägar the Horrible and Conan. Later, when we went for a swim, I saw that he was covered in tattoos, on his back, chest, and even on his thighs.

When we tallied the takings at the end of that first day working together, it turned out there was a surplus in the till. No huge amount, just enough for a few beers. I asked Lars what we should do with the money.

"What do you think?" he said with a laugh. "Fifty-fifty?"

We didn't work the same shift except in that first week when Lars taught me the ropes. One of us would work the morning shift, the other in the afternoon, but there were several hours of overlap when it was busiest and we would work together. One day he asked me to fill in for him for a bit because he had to take his parrot to the vet. It'd broken its leg, he explained with concern. It was a bit hard to imagine that tattooed, bald Viking taking a parrot to have its leg put in plaster. I thought he was making fun of me and started to laugh, but he really looked concerned for his pet.

Lars and I had a surplus in the till the whole summer, so in the evenings we'd drink beer together. We didn't just hang around in the evenings with insipid Norwegian beer but also went on outings, to concerts, and sometimes, when it was raining, to the movies. I even started bringing him books and had a

BEKIM SEJRANOVIĆ

hard job convincing him that they were worth reading. He liked some of them, while others he just handed back with a contemptuous smile. A few times he also brought me books he'd read, but I didn't like his, though I always had to tell him that in a roundabout way. They were cheap historical novels with sword, ax, and bare male biceps as the protagonists. He mostly read magazines about weapons, and he knew every rifle and knife, not to mention warplanes.

Once we went on a bicycle trip to the forested, hilly area called Nordmark, which stretched for over a hundred square miles north of Oslo. We came to Lake Bjørnsjøen, where we rented a canoe and rowed out to a little island with a pine forest. There we pitched camp and spent the night. Lars got sunburned that day and I teased him about looking like the last Mohican. He didn't get my sense of humor, but I found it hilarious that the formidable Viking that covered his whole back had also turned red. Now and then I'd toss a "woah, Chief" at him, which he didn't understand and I couldn't explain. I told him that in my country Indians in comics used that word in every sentence. I once also said "hoka hey" to him, and was able to explain it. In the language of the Sioux it means, "It's a good day to die." He liked that expression and afterward often shouted it, both at appropriate and inappropriate moments.

One evening after work we went into the city together for a real pub crawl, with countless beers. Each time we toasted, we'd shout "Hoookaaa heeey!" and then laugh long and drunkenly. In one place we came across a girl who was quite tipsy. She was sitting and drinking alone at the table next to ours, and then all at once she started talking with us. Something seemed to be preying on her mind, but I couldn't tell what. Lars threw himself at her like a hungry tiger and made no effort to hide his intentions. The girl wasn't the headturner kind that makes men drool, but I don't know what type of girl would voluntarily come up to the two of us—a swarthy foreigner in tattered boots and a tattooed, sunburned lunatic.

The three of us changed venues a few times. We drank, danced, and seemed to be having a good time. Lars became ever more aggressive and started going for her thighs and ass, hugging and pulling at her. I found it sickening to watch, and she was too drunk to defend herself. In the last pub, when the girl went off to the toilet, Lars suggested we take her to his place after this beer and give her a good pummeling. He had some cocaine too, so we'd really have a fling. I thought of the day after. I thought of that skinny girl and her body being kneaded by Lars's giant hands. And mine. First I felt like crying, probably from the alcohol, then I wanted to whack him over the head with the beer bottle and run away with the girl. I'd give her something to eat and let her fall asleep on my lap while I fondled her hair. Instead, I told him it was a stupid idea. When the girl sobered up and saw who she'd ended up with, she'd call the police and say we raped her. Which wouldn't be far from the truth.

"What the fuck," Lars said, shaking his head. "Nobody's forcing her to be with us."

He kept trying to persuade me, but I remained firm. Then he flew into a rage, called me a cowardly twat, and said he just wanted a bang. He went off to the toilet when she came back, leaving me alone with her. I slipped her a hundred-crown bill under the table. I told her it was for a taxi and that she should scram because she'd had quite a bit to drink. She answered that she was feeling fine and wanted to have a bit more fun. I tried to explain it to her again, but she was too drunk to understand anything. Then Lars came back. I saw straightaway that he knew what I'd told her. He blew his top. He started to scream at me, threatened me with his fist under my nose, and put his strong calloused hands on my neck. I had a full view of the veins that stood out on his skull. Our eyes connected and sparks flew. He really did look like an Indian. One of those who harry and kill when the palefaces sell them firewater.

I shouted at him too, but bloodlessly. Intimidated. I really don't know this man, I thought. The girl looked at us and gave a ribald laugh. Then she took Lars by the hand and pulled him out of the joint. I headed after them several moments later but just managed to see them get into a taxi and vanish down the street.

2. *Lars*

Once, when he returned some books I'd loaned him, Lars said he was considering writing a book about his life and thought it could be a good read. I answered haughtily, as if talking to a child, that it's not so important what you write about, but how you write it. Lars sneered.

In the course of that summer, Lars told me his life story, off and on, during breaks at work, in smoky dives sticky from beer, on one of the islands while we fished for cod. He grew up as an only child, without his mother, in a small village in central Sweden on the shore of one of the big lakes that divide the country into two parts. He spent his childhood fishing with his father, who first worked as a lumberjack, but after an accident that crushed his left leg he retired on a disability pension. They went after freshwater fish, mainly perch and rudd, and the greatest success in angling was to land a pike.

After Lars's mother left them, his father became an even more devoted drinker of illegally distilled alcohol, which in Scandinavia is mixed with coffee and called *karsjk*. When Lars was sixteen, they received word that his mother had passed away in

Stockholm. He never managed to finish secondary school. For a time he did all sorts of jobs, but he couldn't settle down or find a suitable occupation. Then he fell in love with a local girl, and after several months they decided to get married. His old man sold their family house and bought himself an apartment, and a modest house for Lars and his wife, where they lived together for a few years. After the first idyllic months, Lars said, sarcastically emphasizing the word "idyllic," he got himself into the company of bikers. They were okay guys, he said. There were lots of parties and girls, beer flowed freely, and to be honest, he admitted reluctantly, there were also drugs, so they had problems with the police. He lost one job after another, and after three years of marriage his wife left him because of his drinking and hot-tempered nature and went to seek her own happiness. A few years later, Lars was sick of it all—the bikes, the bearded and tattooed scapegraces, the run-ins with the law—so he sold the house and set off on a trip around the world. He sold the house for chicken feed because a panic seized him. He couldn't imagine staying in that village, he was fed up with the same jerks acting out the American dream in the backwoods of Sweden. He'd had enough of farting around on motorcycles, and, worst of all, the alternative was to watch himself turning into his old man chainsawing the pine forest, guzzling karsjk, and waiting for the pike of his life to swallow his bait.

First he went to Brazil, traveled around for a time, and, later in Salvador da Bahia, he fell in love with an exceptionally beautiful black woman. He spent six months with her, full of cocaine and sex (that word made his eyebrows dance). She was the most fuckable woman he'd ever had, Lars sighed melancholically like a decrepit old man for whom an erection is just a distant memory. One day she vanished, leaving a heart-wrenching farewell letter in poor English and three damp flecks on the paper that were supposed to be tears. After that, he traveled to Thailand, tried to replace his dark-skinned lover and cocaine with prostitutes and opium, but it wasn't the same thing, he snorted disappointedly. Later he went to the Philippines, stayed there for a while, and then traveled all around Asia, even making it to Japan, but there it was too expensive for any of his typical interests. Finally he went to Amsterdam, and, after a short time spent there, when his money began to run out, he joined the crew of a cargo ship sailing under the Panamanian flag. He was at sea for thirteen years, changed dozens of ships, sailed around the world multiple times, passed through every harbor pub from India to South America, slept with a suspiciously large number of whores, and when he was sick and tired of it all he went back to Sweden, to his village, with a little bit of money, rented an apartment, and began hanging around with the same group again. He soon ended up in jail for reasons he didn't want to explain, and, after finishing his sentence of a year and a bit, there was nowhere for him to go. He had neither money, nor a job, nor an apartment. He stayed for a while with his senile, alcohol-wrecked, sick father, and then left again. He traveled around Sweden, worked where he could, and lived a modest and solitary life. He arrived in Norway several months before we met. He had no idea how long he'd stay, and he didn't care. The only thing he cared about was his large parrot, which had broken its leg that summer, and he didn't know how.

3. My future, former wife

Once, in the middle of that summer, Lars said he was going to Sweden briefly to visit his father. He was gone for a couple of weeks, and during that time I had to look after his parrot, which had recently had the plaster removed from its leg. It was a large, white parrot, but it looked strangely shabby and spent. It could only say "Hasta la vista . . . hasta la vista, baby," but its voice was awfully shrill and it took you a while to distinguish that. Need I mention that the parrot was called Terminator?

While Lars was away, I got to know Selma, my future wife. My future former wife and mother of the child that's perhaps mine. We'd noticed one another before because she took the 12:15 boat almost every day from the city to the island of Gressholmen, which was overrun by rabbits. You couldn't take a step without treading on rabbit shit. Hordes of children came and fed the already obese rodents for days on end. Their parents, during that time, would be drinking thick, bedewed mugs of beer in the nearby pub, where Selma worked as a waitress. She'd return late in the evening, but not always. Sometimes, it seemed, she slept on the island. Selma was tall, almost taller than me, with a bony, square face and pageboy hair. Everything about her was reminiscent of a precocious fifteen-year-old with gangly legs and little bulges on her chest. Her eyes were brown and totally round, with pronounced eyebrow ridges. When she was serious she made a drained, even tormented impression, and for a few moments maybe even a bit threatening, but when she laughed she did it with her whole face, eyes, and body. Her laugh was too loud, bleating, and obtrusive, and in time that neurotic laughter began to cause fear in me like the explosive tittering of a wooden harlequin. But at the beginning, at the very beginning, I found her smile and that pursy, impossibly wide mouth attractive. And, of course, her perfect, small, firm, almost nonexistent ass.

First we simply started to say hello to one another, and sometimes we just nodded. I'd smile, and she'd reply in kind, but sometimes she'd ignore me. Then she'd purse her lips, cross

BEKIM SEJRANOVIĆ

her legs, and try to look cold and eminently fuckable at the same time. Sometimes she'd even scowl, knit her boyish eyebrows, and a dark blue vein would stretch across her forehead.

One day, straight after Lars left for Sweden, we struck up a conversation. Soon we were talking all kinds of rubbish, she laughed loudly and slapped me on the leg overbearingly like we were old friends. I asked her if she wanted to go out for a drink that evening. She fell silent. I told her we could meet some other day, whenever it suited her. She suddenly frowned and gave me a little warning slap, like one might a cheeky child, light but crisp. She told me never to ask her that again. The next few days we didn't even say hello. And then she came up to me one day smiling, cheerful, and loud like an overjoyed child, or a hysterical woman, it was hard to tell which. She invited me to come to the pub for a drink when I finished work.

I didn't knock off until ten that evening because I had to do Lars's shift as well, and on the last leg I got out to Gressholmen. I drove the hordes of rabbits before me—the shameless critters crept up out of every bush like a plague—and made it to the terrace of the pub where she worked. As soon as she saw me, she took off her apron and found a table for us in the corner. Then she went to the bar and poured us two beers. Her boss would appear every now and then to serve customers. He was between fifty and sixty, tall, thin, and rather young-looking. With a Sean Connery beard. He obviously didn't like her sitting with me, and at one point he came up and told her with an air of paternal authority that she should be helping him because he had to prepare the meals, and somebody had to serve the guests.

"Bug off, old man, can't you see I've got a visitor?" she said to him quite intimately.

I felt a bit uneasy and started saying it'd be better if I went, seeing as there was work to do.

"Where will you go? How do you think you'll get to the city? Sigi will drop us off later with his speedboat, right Sigi?" she addressed him nonchalantly and then laughed bleatingly and provocatively.

Sigi puffed helplessly and returned to the kitchen. She shouted to him imperiously to bring us two more beers and something to eat.

Just before sunset, shortly before midnight, the owner of the pub, or Sigi, if I may call him that, because otherwise only Selma called him that—his real name was Harald—took us to the city in his speedboat. Selma and I were already drunk and supported one another when we got out of the boat. I thanked Harald, and Selma took me under the arm and pulled me along the boardwalk. Harald, or Sigi, disappeared back toward the island, cutting the peaceful surface of the water. I turned around and saw the sun setting and vanishing into the sea like my guilty conscience. I felt Selma's step synchronize with mine and knew everything was set now.

We hurriedly downed several tequilas at an outdoor bar on the Aker Brygge boardwalk. I told her I had to go home to feed the parrot and said she could come with me. When we went into my room, she sneered that the parrot had food and water for at least a week. She talked me into letting the bird out of the cage. Terminator flew out of his cage and started to nosedive our heads like a kamikaze. His metallically shrill voice filled the room between the bare walls: "Hasta la vista, baby, hasta la vista, baby, hasta . . ." We had to chase him for ages. Since we were clumsy about it, I must have squeezed his legs too hard. When I put him back in the cage, the parrot stood on just one leg, and when he stood on the other, he'd limp conspicuously. We took Terminator to veterinary first aid, where they X-rayed the leg and concluded nothing was wrong. The mustachioed vet in the white coat said with a serious mien that his leg probably still hurt a bit from having been in plaster until recently. He told us in a threatening voice to take more care in the future. As we were leaving the vet, Selma kissed me for the first time. I could've broken both legs of the parrot.

4. *Fuck the action, Lars*

Lars arrived from Sweden just in time for the afternoon shift. He looked sleepy and wasted. His pupils were tiny, almost invisible. I wanted to tell him about my new love and bypass the business with the parrot, but he was in no condition to listen to me.

Over the next several weeks, things repeated themselves. Lars would come to work with pinpoint pupils and sit indifferently at the stern. Sometimes he'd close his eyes for a few moments, his head would roll onto his chest, he'd wake up, look around him, and then switch off again. From time to time he'd light a cigarette, come to me at the bow, and launch into a conversation without beginning or end, and with even less meaning. At one point his knees would visibly start to buckle, so he'd go back to sit at the stern. His white uniform became ever dirtier. He began to take more and more money from the till, without issuing tickets. We'd done that before, but always within limits. We didn't go out for beer together anymore. He didn't call me, and I spent most of my free time with Selma.

One rainy day, after I'd finished my shift and began hurrying along the Vippetangen pier, Lars shouted from behind and caught up with me. We continued walking along the breakwater, under the porch made for passengers waiting for our boat. He laid his arm over my shoulders, leaned toward my ear, and asked quietly, in a conspiratorial tone, if I was game for some action.

"What sort of action?" I asked thick-headedly.

"Action that'll bring us love, you get me? That sort of action."

I stopped, pushed his arm away from my shoulder, and said, as I walked away from him into the summer rain, "Fuck the action, Lars."

5. Next time you'll be out on your ass

Lars didn't give up trying to involve me in some "action." When I told him in the middle of the short Nordic fall that Selma and I were getting ready for a trip to the Balkans after our wedding, he came up with a new idea on the spur of the moment. He asked me if there were still weapons there. I realized then that he was completely cracked. I told him I really had no idea.

"Pussy!" burst out of him.

I explained to him, as if he were a child, that it wasn't my thing at all. It had nothing to do with him. I simply didn't want to end up in jail again. But the idea itself wasn't bad, I tried to convince him with pretend earnestness. If I did anything stupid again they'd throw me out of the country, I added.

A few years earlier, when I was still with Sara, I technically lived in a room in a student hostel. I had a job in a small factory, packing software CDs. I stole about fifty CDs with multimedia programs for learning foreign languages. I stuck up ads all around the university offering the CDs for a third of the retail price, and I gave my name and phone number. It turned out that the creators of those programs were university lecturers, and they saw the ads, of course, because it was impossible to go through the campus without noticing them. They found it suspicious because the CDs hadn't gone on sale yet. They called the firm where I worked, and the firm informed the police, who set a trap for me, and so I was netted. I'd only sold three CDS. Then five police officers—the two plainclothes who set the trap for me, plus three uniformed cops—searched my 130-square-foot room and found the remaining CDS and some hash. The policewoman wasn't overly attractive, but in her uniform like that she looked quite enticing. She found porn magazines, heaps of them, and not of the tamest sort. She cast a superficial glance and quickly returned them to the wardrobe drawer. Afterward, as they were driving me in the Black Maria, the policewoman sat with me in the back. She said my idea with the CDS was good.

"You'd make a good trader," she said with a smile.

And you a porn star, I thought maliciously. Yes, in a summer uniform.

The paunchy, gray-haired policeman who registered me when I was processed was more than a little surprised when I answered that this was the first time I'd been arrested.

"Never fear," he added with a wry smile as he typed on the keyboard with two fingers, "I'm sure it won't be the last. Next time you'll be out on your ass."

When I told this to Lars, he had a good laugh. He said I was too mixed-up for things like that, anybody could see it straightaway. I asked myself why he suggested "action" to me so much, but I didn't want to say anything to him. You're not exactly a world champion in the art of living either, I thought compassionately.

Whenever I tried to get Lars to tell me his jail story, he'd just wave and say it was nothing. He was imprisoned for disturbing the peace and assaulting a public official, but none of that was true. He hadn't done anything that they had to put him away for. I laughed and prodded him to at least tell me some tidbit, but he was implacable in his silence.

"I'm innocent, totally innocent," he said.

I looked at those constricted pupils of his and didn't believe them. I imagined I was Karađoz, the prison governor in Ivo Andrić's *The Damned Yard*. Nobody is innocent.

The face of Uncle Alija emerged in my thoughts, and what Grandmother told me: "He was in prison for nothin', God knows it's true."

6. Damned Alija

One late afternoon, some men were returning from the hunt and came down from the forest into the village near Alija's place. Alija had a watchdog and it started to bark at them. The hunters, maybe as a prank or because they hadn't bagged anything that day or even fired their rifles—basically out of pure audacity—shot Alija's dog. When Alija ran out of his hovel, it was all over. Their rifles smoked, and the dog just twitched, bleeding out. Alija, by nature an impetuous man, lunged at them, but they pushed him away and leveled their rifles at him. In his helplessness, Alija began to curse and swear at them as tears of fury rained from his eyes. The father of one of the hunters was called Kito, or rather that's what they nicknamed him in the village because his surname was Kitić. Alija cursed Kito several times, and the group of men went off over the stream and down through the village, guffawing and whooping. When Alija went to the police station to report what'd happened, he was arrested on a charge of cursing Tito. Kito's son had denounced him.

"Alija declared that 'e didn't curse Tito, but *Kito*, that wretched no-gooder, but it didn't 'elp," Grandmother told me. "That didn't interest the police. It's much worse when somebody curses Tito than when they kill somebody's dog. Alija said 'e 'adn't, the so-called 'unters said 'e 'ad, and the police beat 'im.

Did you? No! They beat 'im again. Did you? No! They beat 'im a third time. Did you? Alright, I did. Fuck Tito and fuck you all! And 'e got six months' prison with 'ard labor. There's no jokin' with the police, my child."

"Cursed Tito my foot! You're makin' up stories, woman," Grandfather said. "It's true they killed 'is guard dog, but Alija wasn't 'ome at the time. But when 'e found out who killed his dog, 'e found them one after another and gave 'em a good beatin'. 'E beat up one of 'em, Kito's son, who they also called Kito, at the café Kod Agana. 'E ended up in hospital, and Alija in the cooler.

"They killed his dog 'cos it attacked them," Grandfather explained. "They got a fright and fired out of fear. There, that's the whole story. Tito, what nonsense!"

7. Hasta la vista, Lars

When Selma and I came back from the Balkans, Lars was gone. The grumpy boss looked at me suspiciously and said there was no place on the ship for guys like Lars. I agreed. Lars had come to work sleep-deprived and with a hangover, he said, and had helped himself at the till when selling tickets. They sacked him and even threatened to call the police.

"Who knows," he bitched maliciously, "maybe he was also using drugs."

"Maybe," I said.

I never found out where Lars ended up. First I called his cell phone, but it was off. The next day I took the underground to the suburb of Lysaker. Lars had a first-floor apartment in the house of an eternally stoned couple, Vidar and Heidi, who I occasionally bought hash from. I rang at their door, they opened up for me, we went in, sat down, and lit a joint before we did any talking. They said they hadn't seen Lars for several days, but truly, they didn't know exactly how many. The last time he'd been at their place was when he had an attack of vomiting, Heidi said with a cough and passed me the narghile.

No, they hadn't knocked on his door; he'd let them know one way or another that he was there. The three of us went down to his apartment. Vidar had a key, but the door was unlocked. It was dark and stuffy inside—and deserted. Suddenly we heard an ominous screech, "Hasta la vista, baby, hasta la vista, baby." The parrot was standing on top of the cupboard on one leg, watching us with an icy gaze. Something was hanging on the cage. It was a photograph, but in the gloom I couldn't make out what it was of. I took it and went to the door. It was a photo I took the time Lars and I rented a canoe and camped on the little island in Lake Bjørnsjøen. But Lars had been cut out of it. I turned the ruined photo. On the back it said: "Hoka hey."

XVIII

I DRAGGED GRANDFATHER down the path through the graveyard. He tried to keep up and sniffled ruefully. I swore and shook
my head. I accused him of upsetting me with his nonsense every time I came to visit. He only talked about death. Fuck death.

"Just die first, okay? Then I'll come and visit your grave!" I
shouted. "Why are you pissing me off with this?"

The next day I left for Norway, and a few months later I went
to the island of S.

1. *The island*

I spent a year on the northernmost Norwegian island, where
the concepts of "day" and "night" are replaced by the names of
the seasons. The island of S. isn't a harsh and terrible place in
itself, but it was the kind of place I deserved. In a great wasteland like that, all you have are your own thoughts, fragments of
memories ruthlessly wrested from oblivion, verses of forgotten origin and meaning, and juicy expletives in your native language, whose meanings you analyze in the endless polar night.

I sat on the bed in my room and stared at the sturdy wooden shutters on the window. There was no point opening them. There was nothing to see. We were into the second month of night, and, as they told me, it'd last at least another two months. Not that I didn't know that when I arrived on that island at the end of the world, but everything became different from dusk to dusk after the last raylets of the October sun gradually sank into the Barents Sea, which glistered in the peaceful cold. I waited for it for several days more, but it didn't come back. Sometimes a light could be glimpsed in the clear sky that dissipated on the horizon and whose cold colors created projections like hallucinogenic visions.

As soon as I arrived on the island of S., the head of the culture section welcomed me in her office and said there was a man who she thought came from the same country as me, whose name was Aljoša, and who worked as an electrician at the mine.

There were only two settlements on the whole island. Around 1,200 people lived in the first. If we exclude several Swedes and Danes, one Finn, who I'd later become friends with, and several Englishmen, everybody apart from me and Aljoša was Norwegian. The second settlement, over forty miles from ours, had been founded by the Russians in the time of the Soviet Union, and two thousand people lived in it.

Both colonies were there for the extraction of coal, which the island was rich with. A hundred million years ago it had been on the equator, but over time it drifted to within ten degrees of the North Pole. Once the island belonged to the dinosaurs and giant ferns, but now it officially belonged to the Kingdom of Norway, though special laws applied there. The real rulers of this archipelago were actually the polar bears, which there were at least three times more of than people, and when they got hungry they'd come down to the settlement in search of food. They'd sometimes also break into a cabin outside the settlement.

The first days on the island passed by in quite a rush. I spent the time with the head, a vigorous and energetic fifty-year-old woman without the slightest sense of humor who introduced me to what was ostensibly my job. I was to work at the library and organize a literature course, in which the people who enrolled would read certain books and later discuss with me what they'd read, and occasionally write an essay on a set topic. Sometimes a writer or poet would come from the mainland and read their stories monotonously or, conversely, recite their rhymed verses loftily and often drunkenly. Only a few people attended the course, mainly married women in their late thirties, whose husbands had no time for discussions about Anna Karenina's inner emotional and psychological split. I also launched an experimental school of creative writing, which didn't exactly generate any response, if we exclude the four high school students who'd just formed a hardcore trash-metal band and needed help with lyrics.

In our settlement, the name of which translated as The Longyear Town, there were no permanent inhabitants. The family with the longest stay had been there for nine years. The others came mostly for a year or two, and the occasional person for three. Many of them came on a seasonal basis, during the short summer, when there was work in the tourist industry. There were also those who, like me, had gotten an employment contract for one year, starting in September. These were mainly young men and the occasional young woman, who'd fled from Oslo or another large Norwegian city for this or that reason. They'd come to the island and stay for a year, and then they went back to civilization, pudgy from vodka. For them, it was like an exotic vacation. "I've come to see and experience something new," they'd say.

Thanks to people like that I was now sitting in my room and staring at the shutters on the window. And because of Aljoša. And Selma. And the child in her womb. And, to be fair, most of all because of myself and my cowardice.

I couldn't stay in Oslo, not after all that'd happened. I tried, but it was impossible to watch them walking together in our park. And then her belly became ever bigger, and his beard ever longer.

2. Aljoša

Although the head of the Cultural Center mentioned Aljoša at our first meeting, it was a long time before I met him. We saw each other for the first time at the annual party thrown on the last day before the sun finally vanishes from our lives and the long polar night sets in. A party that turned into an unbridled orgy before the end of the world. I stood at the bar in the Cultural Center with my alcohol-riddled consciousness and looked dully now at the head, who was downing vodkas like a Siberian bear, now at two Russians who were lifting glasses in their teeth and pouring the contents straight down their gullets. In that avalanche of unfamiliar drunken faces I thought for a moment that I caught sight of one that was surprisingly and uncomfortably familiar. I made my way past the sleazy Russians, who afterward would probably skin the she-bear, and made my way into the throng to find the evil spirit who'd unsettled me. And then we saw each other. I recognized him instantly, and he me. We stood there and looked at one another for a few drunken moments. I went up to him and we exchanged a few stiff, courteous words.

In the weeks that followed, I'd bump into him now and then in one of the bars. The Longyear Town had the most bars in the world per capita, and they served the cheapest booze in Norway. Aljoša and I avoided each other, as if by arrangement. He sometimes had a rifle over his shoulder, which was a common prop because of the wicked bears, especially if you wanted to go more than fifty yards outside the settlement. Some wore Smith & Wesson revolvers on their belts, like cowboys.

I was sitting, like I said, in my cramped room on the island, frantically shifting my gaze from the wall to the ceiling, from the ceiling to the boarded-up window, behind which darkness ruled the icy wasteland, and I struggled to explain to myself why Aljoša's presence gnawed at me like an insidious disease. He was, after all, only one of the many ghosts of the past, from the time I worked as an interpreter for the UDI, the Norwegian Aliens Department.

That had been several years earlier, in the mid and late nineties. I was an interpreter at the interrogations—"interviews" was the sanitized term—of asylum seekers from the territory of the former Yugoslavia. The interviews could last up to six or seven hours.

I don't know how many interviews I interpreted at, maybe hundreds, but I realized after the very first that it wasn't the work for me. At that first one, a middle-aged woman, stony faced and with her head in a kerchief, told of how soldiers had raped her and her daughter in front of her husband and son, who they afterward took out and shot in front of the house. Later on, the soldiers returned and raped them again. The female public servant who was conducting the interview and taking notes asked her about the details, and the woman spoke tersely and with unbearable precision. The public servant asked if she'd prefer a female interpreter, but she shrugged her shoulders, gave a deep sigh, and glanced through the window, just as big flakes of wet snow were starting to fall; then her gaze wandered back to me, and to the blonde interviewer with her big, trussed-up chest and conspicuously bulging nipples, and she said she didn't care.

The next day, I interpreted for a swarthy forty-year-old man, visibly shaken, who told of how he'd been expelled from his house, and the aggressors trampled his onions and heads of lettuce, and smashed all his windows. As he was speaking, he began to cry, crack his fingers, and wipe the tears from his cheeks with his thick farmer's thumbs. He told us with sincere grief that they killed his Mitsko on the doorstep. The blonde interviewer's tits strained through her thin, light blue shirt, but the nipples weren't to be seen that day. She asked who that was . . . Mee-tz-co.

"My cat . . . my cat Mitsko . . . they killed Mitsko," the man replied, choking on his tears.

There was a phase where we were doing two or three interviews every day, which altogether would often last ten to twelve hours, and more. I began to see myself in every one and simply couldn't avoid the impression that each of those confessions could've been mine. I knew how they felt, I knew what it was like to sit on the other side of a table, look into the indifferent faces of bureaucrats, and hope that the size of your misfortune was sufficient for them not to send you back to where you'd been expelled from. I tried not to remember what the people said, not to look into their bewildered faces and creased brows, not to listen as their cramped hands scratched the table. You tried to interpret coldly and cleanly as they voiced their tearful prayers and ominous curses.

After that I'd go home, where Sara was waiting and would tell me about the dying hundred-year-old ladies at the hospital where she worked. I couldn't speak, be it because of mental exhaustion or the physical pain I'd feel in my jaw after ten hours

BEKIM SEJRANOVIĆ

plus of uninterrupted talking. Everything that Sara, or Jon, said or I'd hear on TV—I'd automatically translate it into my language.

It finally all turned into an insurmountable guilty conscience because of my fortune, which seemed happy compared to theirs, because of my inability to help them, and because of their suspicion, which I had to put up with every day. All the asylum seekers asked me to introduce myself and say who I was and where I was from, but we had a so-called protected identity. Only a number and nothing more. As if a two-digit number could protect a person.

"Sorry," I answered, "but I'm not allowed to tell you anything about myself, we interpreters have a protected identity."

"Protected? But where are you from, sonny?"

"I'm sorry, I can't tell you that either."

But they told me everything. Trying to structure their jumbled thoughts and explain their suffering and the injustice that'd been done, they bared themselves to public servants, who, with a few honorable exceptions, didn't care much about all that. Nor did they pretend to care. I realized later, too late, that that was the only way you can do such a job and go home afterward, eat your warmed-up dinner in peace, and go to sleep without hash. Except I wasn't a newly fledged Norwegian lawyer who was using this position as a stepping-stone in an ambitious career.

True, there were also some asylum seekers who exaggerated their suffering, while being totally blind to the misfortune of others. There were some who lied shamelessly and blatantly, some who did it out of despair, others wantonly, others again because they truly believed what they were saying. The hardest thing was to endure the monologues of semiliterate local politicians who, without exception, considered themselves and

their role in the Balkan conflicts to have been of historical sig-
nificance for their people, their faith, and humanity in general.

I even understood them. I understood them all because I
could've been any one of them myself. I could've been Aljoša.

3. *The interview*

We were in the sterile, bare interview room. A middle-aged
female public servant from the Aliens Department sat on the
other side of the table behind a computer, across from Aljoša.
I, as interpreter, sat at the side. I didn't look them in the face
but stared at the empty space in front of me. There was paper
on the table for me to write notes, but I used it much more often for drawing neurotic squiggles. I imagined I was a machine,
attempting to exclude any feelings. The two of them played a
game of rapid chess, and I was the clock. I just heard voices
passing through me in both directions. I gave them form and
content.

These interviewers asked standardized, prepared questions,
filling in empty boxes on the computer.

"Given name and surname?"

"Aljoša Kovačević."

"Citizenship?"

"Bosnia-Herzegovina."

"Date of birth?"

"5.13.1960."

"Place of birth?"

"Sarajevo."

When asked about his ethnicity, Aljoša said he was from a
mixed marriage; his father was a Serb and his mother a Muslim. He said he'd declared himself a Yugoslav until the war,

but afterward . . . The form that blinked on the screen took no wishy-washy answers, and the interviewer repeated impassively, "Ethnicity. Please, you have to say something."

Aljoša said she should write that he was Bosnian.

The interviewer filled in the box with a mixture of boredom and satisfaction and then, monotonously, like a washing machine after a short pause for soaking, continued the washing cycle on this human life.

"Religion?"

"Atheist."

"Can you give all your places of residence, from birth until you came to Norway?"

"Sure I can," Aljoša said.

The interviewer waited several moments and then raised her eyebrows with a slight dose of irritation. "Well?"

Aljoša was startled, as if he'd drifted off, and then replied gruffly, "Aah, why didn't you ask me to list them straightaway?"

He glanced at me and said, "She asked if I can give all my addresses. Of course I can, pal. What sort of question is that?"

I looked through the window with a blank expression. I interpreted everything, including the "pal."

Then Aljoša said he'd lived in Sarajevo from his birth until 1992. After that, he lived in Sweden.

The interviewer asked him why, after all those years in Sweden, he'd now come to Norway to seek asylum, and he replied that he'd been deported.

"Why?" the public servant asked him icily, now fully certain of the futility of the interview. Because an asylum seeker who arrives from a third country, rather than their country of origin, was to be returned to the country where they first arrived. In Aljoša's case, that meant they'd send him back to Sweden as soon as possible. And Sweden would deport him.

Aljoša heaved a sigh and answered that he'd been deported from Sweden because of a two-year prison sentence, and after he'd served it he was ordered to leave the country. Having nowhere else to go, he came to Norway.

"What were you convicted of?" the interviewer asked, pausing in her typing.

Reluctantly, and choosing euphemisms, Aljoša said he'd been convicted of physical violence.

"Violence against whom?"

Aljoša said it'd been against his former wife. She'd provoked him.

"You were convicted of raping your former wife," the interviewer stated mercilessly, obviously well acquainted with his case.

Aljoša held his tongue. He clenched his jaws and didn't know where to look. After several moments he spoke again, in a low voice. "I hit her, yes. I hit her several times. But I didn't rape her, I didn't, by the name of my child, I didn't, I swear by..."

"But you were convicted of rape?"

He said nothing and just nodded. She told him he couldn't nod. He had to answer yes or no. He looked straight in front of him in silence, then he raised his head and said, "Yes."

"Marital status?"

"What do you mean marital status?"

"Are you married, divorced, a widower?"

"I've married twice."

"To start with, please tell me about the first marriage. When did it begin and when did it end?"

"1988 to 1993."

"Did you divorce?"

The silence in the interview room became heavy before Aljoša said that his first wife was dead.

"Widower," she concluded, satisfied that she'd filled in another box.

"What was your first wife's name?"

After a short pause for reflection he said, "Dženana."

The interviewer wasn't sure how to write the name, so she asked me to do it for her on my notepad. I wrote, "Dženana." My handwriting was rather illegible, and she enunciated "Tz-e-e-nana—," then she looked at him and asked, "Tzenana?"

He nodded slowly, then he probably remembered that nodding didn't count and said, "Dž, Dženana."

"Do you have children?"

"I had a daughter. Until '93."

She stopped for a moment, not understanding straightaway and probably not wanting to fill in the form with such imprecise answers.

He anticipated her. "Deceased."

There was obviously nothing more to say about that as it was no longer related to his current asylum application.

"And where were you at that time?"

For a long, painful while he said nothing, and the interviewer was silent too. I didn't look at either of them, but I could feel his face grimacing and contorting, and I expected him to start crying or to scream, to jump up and try to strangle us straightaway, to tear out her throat and my tongue.

Instead, he calmly told us—as if he'd repeated and honed the story inside for a long time, and told and retold it to himself thousands of times in the endless Nordic nights—that after a bitter quarrel he and his wife had finally managed to agree that *he* leave Sarajevo, not she and their small daughter, and that they'd come after him as soon as they possibly could. That was at the very beginning of the war, when everybody thought the situation would sort itself out. His wife had elderly parents and didn't want to leave them behind, and they didn't want to go under any circumstances. He wanted to at least take his daughter straightaway, but she was small, not even three years old, and his wife said he should go ahead and ensure there was accommodation, and they'd follow him. He left directly for Sweden because he had a cousin in Malmö who'd been living there since 1985 and was married to a Swedish woman. Then the war broke out abruptly and the telephone lines were cut. He tried all kinds of ways of arranging for his wife and daughter to leave Sarajevo, but nothing worked. They spoke to each other via a ham radio operator and then his wife told him she didn't want to leave the city. She sounded bitter and was full of spite. She told him that if he ever wanted to see them again, he should come back. He begged her to calm down, to at least think of the child, but she hissed that he was a traitor and the relationship was over. He reflected for several days, wrote several letters to try and convince her that it was best for her to leave, he'd sort it out somehow, he'd find the money and pay. He tried to contact her, but without success. Later he decided to go to Sarajevo himself and collect them. But that was difficult because he no longer had a passport. They'd taken it off him when he applied for asylum and given him a document for asylum seekers, which was no good for traveling. He went to the Swedish authorities to explain the situation. They told him his asylum application was still being processed, but he could withdraw it—he only needed to write a request and they'd return his passport. But nobody could guarantee that he'd be accepted again if he returned with wife and child, because Sweden no longer accepted refugees from Bosnia. He was in a dilemma and didn't know what to do. He thought back to the last conversation with his wife: maybe she'd just been shocked, maybe there was still some way of her getting out. Maybe he

BEKIM SEJRANOVIĆ

could get a false passport from smugglers, travel to Bosnia, and try to make it through to Sarajevo somehow.

"But even if that worked, what then?" he asked, probably himself not knowing if he was asking me, the interviewer, or his own stern conscience.

"What was your child's name?" the composed public servant said, driving bamboo under his fingernails.

"Mirela," he said, extracting the name of his child buried and covered with an impregnable layer of pain.

I wrote "Mirela" on the paper and passed it to the interviewer under her pointy nose, because every personal name, as well as the names of cities, villages, streets, rivers, and institutions had to be written down on paper by the interpreter to avoid spelling mistakes.

"And your second wife?"

He gave the name of his second wife.

He was silent for several moments, and then, though the interviewer hadn't asked him a question, he started talking again with the voice of a man who wanted to make a confession, and he explained that he'd been single for a long time and very much wanted to get married, but the girls in Sweden didn't appeal to him—neither the Swedish girls nor the Yugo girls in Sweden (in fact, he found the latter even worse). He wanted to marry a young woman from Bosnia, but he couldn't go to Bosnia—he simply couldn't. He'd never gone back, nor would he. He got to know his second wife, a Bosnian woman, via the internet. They wrote to each other for a time, and then after a while he arranged a sponsorship letter for her and she came to visit him in Sweden. She was young, beautiful, and there was nothing wrong with her, so they got married and she stayed in Sweden. But as time passed she began to change, she began to behave ever freer, to go out by herself until late, and he couldn't tolerate that, so they quarreled a lot, there were harsh words and fights, you name it. Then, after three years had passed and she attained right of residence, she filed for divorce and moved out. That was a blow to him, he said, and he started to drink. Once, when he was drunk like that, he called on her and they started to quarrel and fight. The next day, the police came to get him and he ended up in jail for rape.

"Where is your former wife now?"

"In Sweden, where else?"

After that, the interviewer asked him about his parents and all their personal information, including their religion. She asked him about his brothers and sisters, and if he had any relatives in his native country, or any relatives, friends, or acquaintances in any western European country. She asked him when and where he'd done military service, asked about his political views, activities in any social organizations, his sexual orientation, consumption of drugs, and his state of health, both physical and mental. She asked him all this with the voice of a well-oiled and finely tuned machine, and each answer he gave was increasingly tired and quiet.

4. *The peach tree*

What scared me was that I was shaken not by the man's fate, but by his readiness to accept it. What was my misfortune compared to his, what was my sniveling cowardice compared to his will? That's what ate away at me every day. When I fled from myself, from my life, I ran to the end of the world and met a man who had reason to hate life more than anybody, and I'm sure he did. At least he didn't freak out.

And then I decided I had to put an end to it somehow. Now we were sitting in his room, in his hut, with a plastic bottle between us. It had three interlocked hearts on it, covered in watery bubbles. But there were no bubbles in the bottle because it had rakija in it. I'd saved it up from my last visit to Bosnia, when the clay covered up the cancer-eaten remains of Uncle Alija.

When Grandfather Kasim said to me as I was leaving, his tongue feeble and disobedient from several strokes, "'Ere, take some of this. It's slivovitz from the ranch."

Grandfather purchased the "ranch" after he retired. It was a small, steep field on the slopes of the Majevica mountain range, not far from his native village, and there he planted an orchard of 120 plum trees. I was four or five at the time and helped him dig holes for the saplings. Then I planted a slender peach tree in a hole that was reminiscent of a child's grave. Grandfather explained to me with refined words and solemnity that it was now my tree. Just as it grew, so would I. But years passed, and the tree was always the same. Sometimes I thought it even got smaller, until Grandfather ended up in the hospital one spring with prostatitis and I saw that the peach tree had died. The mountain wind and sharp frosts of northern Bosnia had cruelly shaken off its pink petals.

Several days later I saw Grandfather's half-brother Alija pulling up the old stem and planting a new one in the same place. Perhaps a bit larger.

I understood everything. Afterward I tore it out and used it to kill four frogs. Three green ones and a small brown one. The little frog croaked much more than the big green ones.

XIX

1. *Doll*

I SUDDENLY STARTED talking. Rakija and the long solitude had an impact. I confessed like an asylum seeker, and Aljoša listened coldly like a public servant of the Norwegian Aliens Department.

I wanted him to give me an idea for how to survive this kind of life. I wanted to ask him what we were doing in that room, on that island, or, if he liked, in this world. Because, beneath the thin membrane of my skin, I felt I was already living my own death. I was withering like the peach tree in Grandfather's orchard.

The more I talked and acted out the misery of my life with drunken tackiness, the more I realized my woe. I wasn't sure what I really wanted from him in the end—for him to pull me up or push me down, to the very bottom of this mire of a life. I wanted anything, only no more of "this," whatever they called "this." Because this "this" here and now didn't even have a name.

Then he suddenly asked if I liked *sevdalinkas*, melancholic Bosnian love songs.

"Oh, how I'd love to hear a sevdalinka!" burst out of him.

His eyes livened up and their color changed from green to yellowish. He ran his fingers through his dense black beard peppered with gray. He was reminiscent of Karl Marx.

BEKIM SEJRANOVIĆ

"I've listened to everything, you know," he continued, as if as an excuse. "All sorts of music. Now I don't listen to anything. Just the radio sometimes, when I go to bed, and then quietly so as to make no noise. I can't stand silence, but I can't stand music or songs either, fuck it. But do you know any sevdalinkas? Just now I feel I could sing. But a good one."

I knew some sevdalinkas. But to sing them for him? Now? After I'd finished talking in my maudlin voice, I felt as if a bugle had sounded taps. Everything that was even remotely alive inside me, everything that was true, had now withdrawn completely into an emptiness that was probably even greater. Only my hollow body was left. It demanded physical pain to prove it was still alive, it sought loud, aggressive, and painful music, like the knife-sharp sound of a guitar to cut my throat, a muscled heavy bass to rip through both lobes of the lungs, a dull and hard drumbeat to knock in my skull. That's exactly what I wanted now. Or that's what the rakija wanted, and this island, and Selma. An unborn child hungry for love. A bit like me.

But Aljoša wanted a sevdalinka. He looked at me, waiting for me to start singing. I knew it'd be best if I did. "It's always better to sing than to talk," Uncle Alija would probably have said if Bosnia's tiny, yellowish maggots hadn't long since eaten his tongue.

I swigged a bit more rakija and continued the torment. Every scamp in the street would later have grinned with innuendo: "You want a song and a blow job too, eh?" But I wasn't a scamp, nor did I have a street.

A song welled up, a well-known one, "*Džidžo moja*," and I started softly, "O girl, o my doll . . . o girl, o my doll . . . your mother dressed you up fine . . . dressed you up fine . . ."

Then he joined in. He threw back his head and repeated the line like a chant or an oath.

That's how Grandfather Kasim used to sing. Unlike him, Al-joša had a good ear. Grandfather knew quite a few sevdalinkas, but when he'd had a bit to drink he'd mostly strike up the girl and the doll. He'd sit and drink outside the crooked, improvised shack at the ranch, sipping rakija, and repeat that short song ad nauseum, until Grandmother snapped at him and stormed back into the house, cursing.

That's how it was when I came to visit from Norway for the first time after the war, in 1996. Grandfather and Grandmother had fled to Croatia during the war, but the moment the armistice was signed they returned to Bosnia. They lived at the ranch, in those first several years after the war because they couldn't go back to their house in the city. Other refugees were living in it.

Grandfather was glad to see me again after quite a few years. He got the barbecue going, opened a bottle of the previous year's rakija, and people came, mainly close friends or relatives. Later on, when it was dark and the guests had all gone, just the three of us were sitting there. Grandfather was drunk and it was only a matter of time before he'd start singing his minimalist mantra about the girl and the doll. As soon as he began, Grandmother gathered up all the dishes she could carry and, hissing angrily through her nose, waddled back to the shack.

"He could've skipped it at least today, to give me a break. That doll's got on 'is brain, all 'e knows about is that damn . . . doll!"

She emphasized that last word with fury. Grandfather was a little startled and only added that it didn't seem to bother his grandson.

"It doesn't, does it? How could it bother anybody? Her nerves have gone."

And then he continued singing again. I can't say I enjoyed his singing, but what could I do? The man had his whims. There were worse whims, of course, and his was to get drunk and sing that old song. Who knows why he repeated that particular song or why it so maddened Grandmother. Maybe any other song that enthralled him like that would've driven her up the wall too. Maybe a female possessiveness meant she couldn't bear the presence of another woman, not even in a song. And if that song stopped annoying her one day, maybe he'd have to find some other to put her out of joint. Maybe that's the way it had to be.

When we heard the rattle of dishes from inside, Grandfather stopped his song. I had to use the opportunity to ask him something, to broach a topic, anything, so that he wouldn't keep singing. But it seemed he was no longer in the mood for singing. He asked if I knew that his half-brother Ahmet had died two years earlier. I answered that I knew—I was tired of the subject—but he went on to describe his half-brother's long and painful death with a masochistic passion. He'd gotten colon cancer, they cut out a large part of his intestines, and after that he needed to relieve himself in a plastic pouch directly connected to his bowels with a tube. I didn't want to hear any more and asked about Alija.

"Oh, 'e would've come today, he would've, yeah, but 'e couldn't."

And there Grandfather fell silent. He puffed and then sighed deeply. I feared he'd start singing again, but he didn't.

"Ah, my Alija, you too 'ad your fill of trouble in this world," he whispered.

Then he raised his voice. "'E worked in the mines, first in Labin, where 'e was best miner. And 'e earned good money. Whoever wanted to work could earn, and Alija was a 'ard worker. But it's true 'e liked to drink, and so much for everythin' else. One time 'e got drunk and smashed up the whole canteen, 'e 'ad 'is fill of trouble there and 'ad to scram. 'E came at dawn one day, in the rain. The was a ringin' an' a bangin' at the door. I went an' opened, and there was Alija. Skinny, with a scraggly beard, an' 'e didn't 'ave that moustache no more. 'E was in miner's gear, rubber boots, covered in mud, wretched, and miserable. Where 'e'd been, what 'e'd been doin', God only knows. Was 'e drunk or 'ungover? You could never tell."

Grandfather stopped. He pushed away the plate in front of him, which was a sign that he didn't feel like any more food. He took his glass and—bottoms up. Not the song now, please, for God's sake, I prayed. But he just mentioned that he had to take his tablets: some for blood pressure, some for his heart, and some sleeping pills. He and Grandmother each had a shoebox for their medicines. Grandfather's was a Borovo shoebox, and Grandmother's a Šimecki.

"'E would've come, but 'e don't like it so sociable. 'E comes at times, drops by with the goats and 'is flute, and a dog trottin' alon' behind 'im, 'e goes about the forest, gathers 'erbs and berries, picks mushrooms. Oh, nobody's got it better than 'im," he concluded with sincere envy.

He stopped again, probably thinking he'd got something mixed up, that the rakija had led him off in a different direction, into a quaintly touched-up and tweaked past, and then suddenly he continued. "But 'e keeps smokin'. I say to 'im, you've gotta stop, bud, and 'e just says: 'It's too late now, quit or not.' Smokin's all 'e's got left, 'e told me. Whaddaya say to 'im? 'E's never listened, and then again, maybe 'e's right. And I pretend to look after myself, take my medicine, I don't drink, I only smoke with coffee, but I've still gotta lie on a bier and be buried six feet under. There's no changin' it, everybody's gotta go sooner or later. And nobody knows who'll go first," Grandfather added finally, a little lost in thought, as if he was hoping.

I'd rather it be later, I caught myself thinking. If possible.

Aljoša and I drank all the rakija, smoked, and repeated the "doll." Now one of us would sing, now the other, and sometimes together. From time to time the shutters on the window would be showered by tiny, prickly snowflakes borne in gusts of the powerful north wind. Then we'd both fall silent and listen worriedly.

XX

1. *Waking up*

I WAS AWAKE. I didn't know exactly why I felt I was awake because I was neither willing nor able to open my eyes, and I couldn't move my body or stop my thoughts. Everything I tried to remember I couldn't summon, and things I didn't want to think about crept under my swollen eyelids, made their way through my corneas, and traveled to my brain.

I rolled over in bed, incapacitated. It was dark in the room and the wind howled furiously outside. I tried to remember how I'd managed to make it home through the snowstorm last night. All I could remember was Aljoša's bearded face and the plastic bottle of rakija.

I lit a cigarette, but my mouth and throat had been corroded by booze and burned by nicotine smoke. I got up to drink some water but, instead, I heaved yellowish foam and acid from my stomach into the washbasin. Then I brushed my teeth for a long time, looking into the smeared mirror dully with half-closed eyes. The smell of toothpaste brought a bit of freshness and soothed my nerves, as if an essence of freshly picked plums was entering my nostrils, as if I was hearing the buzz of the tiny flies that gather above the two purple vats containing at least three tons of plums. I heard the powerful motors of hornets' wings that come up to the vats ominously like Russian army helicopters. I smelled the hot rakija and heard it lazily dripping from the copper cauldron.

2. *Miki with rice*

It was the fall of 1997 when I went to visit Grandmother and Grandfather for the second time from Norway. We were sitting outside our hut at the ranch. It was the last evening before I went back.

I'd prepared for that visit for a long time. And Sara, who I was still with then had wanted to come with me, but I wasn't keen on that idea. I'd been looking to break up with her, but I didn't have a good reason, except that she was too good to me. That really brought me down. I needed somebody who was worse than me for me to feel good.

A week earlier, Grandfather had called the people who harvest the plums and put them in the plastic vats. A few days later, the distillers came with the cauldron and in two days made almost sixty gallons of slivovitz. I also helped, mostly by tasting the fresh product. The distillers said it wasn't good to drink it too hot, it could harm your intestines. A young man had died from that a few years earlier, they said. I waved dismissively and took an even longer swig. When they'd finished the last cauldron of weak rakija, they packed up, loaded their cauldrons into the trailer behind their tractor, and rumbled off down the dusty road.

The hoot of an owl came from somewhere. It seemed very close. Grandfather nodded toward an old apple tree on the other side of the orchard.

"I know the bird," he said. "It stops me sleepin' at night. It 'oots all night long. Once I went out and threw stones at it. In the mornin', at coffee, I says to Grandmother, 'If I 'ad a gun I'd go and shoot it now.' And she: 'Come off it, 'ow did you get to that? Your nerves've gone to pot, you can't sleep, it's not the bird's fault. It's got its business, and you've got yours.' That's what she said. My nerves? 'U! I could live another thirty years. Whaddaya think? 'Ere, 'ow old would you say I am? Not more than sixty, right?"

I looked away and said nothing. Grandfather would never shoot at owls. He couldn't even kill a chicken, something Grandmother loved to complain about to her friends: "'E's useless, 'e can't even chop the 'ead off a chicken. That's not what I call a man."

And so Grandmother had a bloody block in the garden where she used to hatchet the chickens brought to us by Lucija, her friend from the village. Lucija, who we all called Luja, brought us Easter eggs—and not only me, but all the children in the neighborhood. She never married, and Grandmother forever teased her because of that. She never wanted to say how old she was, until Grandmother once sneaked a look at her identity card. Luja was almost Grandmother's age, but she looked much younger. She wore a black leather jacket. Grandmother said she ended up in a madhouse after the war. Because she'd been single all her life.

Once, when I was little, Luja gave me a little rooster as a present. I instantly decided to call him Miki and tied a cord around his right leg. And so we ran like crazy about the courtyard, like the simple-minded roadrunner and the ingenious but despised coyote. I wrapped one end of the cord tightly around my small, thick hand, and the other was tied with a bowline to Miki's leg. And beep, beeep, zooooom. Sometimes I was disappointed because Miki didn't raise dust behind him. So I tried to achieve

BEKIM SEJRANOVIĆ

the same effect by dragging my feet in the gravel. Grandmother got angry and said I'd ruin my sneakers like that.

I came home from school one day for lunch and we had Miki with rice. Grandmother only told me once I'd eaten a drumstick and gone outside to look for my cockerel. She said Miki had been sick, so they had to . . . and then she used pantomime—a short, swift downward movement of her open hand.

I went outside and found Miki's cord. It lay stretched out across the courtyard.

3. Soccer cleats

I washed myself in my room on the island of S. and couldn't help but sigh.

I remembered a scene from that same fall of 1997: I lit a Drina cigarette from Sarajevo and looked at the little glass of rakija in front of me. Grandfather looked at it nostalgically too.

"Hey, Grandmother, bring our medicine boxes," he ordered affably, as if weighing up what to have, medicine or rakija.

There's no more rakija, Grandfather, I thought. What you've drunk, you've drunk.

As if he read my thoughts, he suddenly started talking about his illnesses. Since his stroke the previous winter, from which he recovered surprisingly quickly and with virtually no visible consequences except walking slowly and mumbling a bit, he talked about nothing but his own and others' illnesses.

"Sonny, I was sick even before you were born. They pensioned me off. An ulcer burst, I was pissin' blood, you've no idea. I was lucky to scrape through. The pension was small, and I was young. Oh, those were 'ard times. Luckily I was able to get a job at the factory as a travelin' salesman. I wore out nine cars."

Then Grandmother came with Grandfather's box of medicines and began to gather up the dishes from the table. Neither Grandfather nor I lifted a finger to help. Then, maybe for the first time in my life, I thought she could use some help with washing the dishes. Her legs were swollen like balloons full of water about to burst. She walked holding on to the wall, staggering like Frankenstein's monster because of her stiff joints, knees, and hips. I didn't get up.

"And I 'ad no end of trouble with Alija," Grandfather continued, rummaging through his pills and the warehouse of his memory at the same time.

"When 'e ran away from Labin, 'e kept drinkin' and lookin' for trouble again. I was always findin' work for 'im—pull a string 'ere, pull a string there, ask people to 'elp 'im—but Alija just kept on like before. Nobody could put 'im in his place. That's 'ow 'e was."

Then Grandmother came with her own box of medicines.

The darkness became ever thicker. The moon would have to appear soon, I thought. The only noise was from them rummaging in their boxes. After a while we heard Grandfather snoring.

"'E always falls asleep like that after dinner," Grandmother said. "Then you can't wake 'im—it's not a joke. 'E's grown old, my child. What can you do, everybody ends up under the ground."

I gladly would've listened to anything other than that. If only the owl would start its hooting, but it was probably off hunting. It'd come later to wake Grandfather.

"That's 'ow it was with Alija, nothing was left of 'im—," she continued babbling mercilessly, "lung cancer."

I replied that I knew, I'd heard all that. Everybody just died and decomposed. Life was one long funeral. You saw people you knew to the grave, and also those you didn't know, and in the end you died yourself. You always died yourself.

　　　　　　　　　　　BEKIM SEJRANOVIĆ

Grandmother sighed and said quietly, "You're right, my child, it's best we pass over it."

We said nothing and smoked. But again it wasn't good, it was never good. Grandmother started talking again.

When it came to the story of Alija, Grandfather would often go sentimental, while Grandmother talked like a twisted Bosnian Hemingway. Precise and derisive. She was the exact opposite of Grandfather. Tall and heavy, she radiated fierce determination. She had a difficult character and a heavy hand. When she flew into a rage, it was best to take cover and wait for it to pass. Because anybody who got in her way was in big trouble. Sometimes I got a beating from her, which was sort of predictable, but once she even caned Aunty Zika although she was already married and had two children. And it was just because she said "no" to her. Grandmother fanatically believed that you mustn't say "no" to your elders, and only if you had a really good reason could you say "I can't." Saying "no," "I won't," or "I don't want to" led to a caning. Always just on the bottom, because one didn't hit children in the face, she explained earnestly.

"Not that Alija changed at all when 'e got married," she continued out of nowhere.

She explained that he sold one part of the land he'd inherited from his mother, and so that he wouldn't drink it away they managed to marry him. He also got some dowry and they built a simple house at the end of the village.

"You couldn't really call it an 'ouse'," Grandmother said. "Alija did everythin' 'imself, but God knows where his skills went. 'E built so many 'ouses for other people but 'e made 'imself an 'ut of earth and beams, all crooked like, a real slipshod job. 'E even built the range inside by 'imself. Alija called it a fireplace, but it was nothin' like a proper fireplace, and you couldn't stick your nose into that 'ovel 'cos it stank of smoke so bad. And inside nothin': no bed, no chair—nothin'. 'E didn't even 'ave electricity. The only one in the village. 'E got work again for a time at a mine, but 'e 'ad an accident, a rock 'it 'is leg when they were blastin'. Nothin' serious, but they arranged disability pension for 'im. The pension wasn't much, but enough for 'im. 'E 'ad a few goats and went up on the 'ills with 'em all day, gathered a few 'erbs for teas, drank a bit of rakija, smoked a few cigarettes, and so 'is life passed. But nobody was 'appier than 'im, and whenever you met 'im, 'e'd let you know. 'E'd say to me, 'Sister, nobody's got it better than me. Fuck I've got it good.'"

I looked out into the darkness and listened. Grandfather snored occasionally, and there was still no sign of the owl.

Grandmother took a sip of coffee and continued in an almost reproving tone. "Once we was sittin' nice in the courtyard, drinkin' coffee, and lookin' down the street, when there comes a clatter, a bit like an 'orse and cart. And, lo and be'old, it was Alija, in 'is green blazer, strollin' with 'is umbrella. 'E wore a fur 'at, like the guy in the kefir ad. Dark and bearded. You got a fright when you saw 'im. And the din an' racket like an 'orse-drawn wagon—those were 'is shoes. I don't know what kind of shoes they were. Afterward they told me they were the ones they use for playing ball."

"Soccer cleats," I said and laughed loudly.

I could just see him limping down Brotherhood and Unity Street in the boots with plastic studs that resounded on the worn sidewalk like a herd of well-shod horses, making people turn around, children shouting out to him, walking like an extravagant, whacky artist, his head raised high, staring pensively into the sky above the small Bosnian town.

"I don't know the word, my child," Grandmother said, offended by my laughter, "but 'e mostly clattered around in the courtyard, so full of 'imself. Quite a character, 'e was. 'What brings you 'ere, Alija?' you'd ask, and 'e says, 'I just wanna see what's new in the bazaar.' It was 'is way of dressin' up."

I laughed so impudently that Grandmother got childishly angry about Alija's "art installation," and I thought I should buy some soccer cleats myself.

4. *The raft*

The first opportunity to buy cleats presented itself just two months after that evening. After I returned to Norway, both Sara and I realized that our love was spent. But neither of us could say that to Jon, looking into his brown eyes. He started preschool that year. I'd walk him to school in the morning and guide him across the road, and was waiting with lunch when he came home in the afternoon. He'd throw off his bag, run toward me, jump into my arms, and give me a kiss on the mouth. I'd trim his red locks, make a Mohawk of his shampooed hair, and teach him to sing songs by the band Let 3. He liked "Nafta" most of all and kept repeating the line, "There's no wine, no balls." I taught him to make a bow and arrow, put war paint on him with Sara's rouge, and gave him an Indian name: Fierce Squirrel.

Now I had to explain to him that all of that would stop. That depressed me, and the painful dejection drove me to bouts of fury. I didn't break anything, only the occasional glass and one picture of me and Sara grinning, but I swore repulsively. In my native language. There was no point in Norwegian. And I began to drink. Not excessively at first, but over time more and more. I worked only on the weekends, and during the week I was supposed to be studying, but I no longer knew what I was studying.

Of course, a hangover followed a drinking spree, which was ideal for starting a quarrel with Sara. Afterward I'd have good reason to continue drinking, and things would come full circle. When I turned up at the door at eight one morning, drunk and hungover at the same time, Sara said through her tight, thin lips that she'd had enough and I should go where I'd been all night. And not come back anymore. I laughed and told her I loved her, to which she just squeezed her lips even more and said she didn't want to see me when she came back from work. I kissed her, took the hash out of the drawer by my bed, and started to roll a joint. She grabbed the hash, and it was in the toilet in no time.

"You're not going to do that in my house anymore," she hissed.

Then she vanished through the door. We never saw each other again.

Several months later she moved back to her village of L. in the south of Norway and got married again to her former husband, Jon's father. They then had another child.

The day she threw me out, I went back to my little room in the suburb of Oslo, where I didn't stay often, but I didn't venture to give it up because of exactly this eventuality. I had a bit of hash there, too, which I really needed just then. Because if there was one thing I was afraid of, it was hangovers. Hash is the only thing that helps. I read somewhere that Danilo Kiš said the only cure for a hangover was suicide. What prevented me from using suicide to cure my hangover was the torment that God punishes you with in hell. I thought, What if you kill yourself when you're hungover, and God punishes you with an eternal hangover in hell?

And so after splitting with Sara I continued to drink and get high. One day I was invited to a party thrown by a few people I knew. I decided to go along in style. I bought a pair of soccer cleats at the flea market in Grønland, and I had the blazer— actually gray rather than green—from before. I replaced the fur hat with a cap of llama wool like the Latinos sold at the market in Youngstorget.

The party was pretty average: alcohol, hash, music, attractive young women, lifeless, boring young men. I felt neglected, maybe more than was truly the case. I wanted to be noticed for my uncle's fashion creation, but since I was rather drunk nobody took me seriously. I had the impression that everybody was laughing at me behind my back. And they probably were. There was one girl there who I hassled all evening, and she tried to get out of it as decently as possible. I made it hard for her. In the end, she decided to go home, and I declared I was escorting her, which she politely declined, saying she already had someone to escort her home. She went into the room where all the guests had left their jackets. I went in after her, and suddenly a cocker spaniel appeared and started nuzzling up to her. Then it came up to me too, wagging its tail cheerfully, probably wanting to sniff at me or whatever, and I kicked it in the belly as hard as I could. Remember, I was wearing cleats. The dog yelped loudly, and afterward whined and whined. The girl looked at me contemptuously and told me icily that I was stupid. Stupid and mean. She took the dog in her arms. The people in the corridor saw and heard it all, but nobody said a word to me. Their eyes weren't full of hatred, but of some inscrutable cold. They looked at me like I belonged to some human subspecies. And, at that moment, maybe that wasn't far from the truth.

I then began to make excuses for myself, and was on the verge of tears. I looked everybody in the face and said I didn't really mean to do that, and they answered that it could happen to anyone. Then I tried to atone for my deed and explained that I'd write a poem about the poor dog that very night, that it was the best I could do. They nodded and said I must definitely do that, and that it'd probably help the dog get better. I could even read it out to him, and he'd probably accept the apology.

Finally, the young woman who was the host of the party asked me to leave. Politely and resolutely. Since I didn't do as she asked, some guy said the same thing, only a bit more rudely. I started the bit about the poem for the dog again, but he replied that he'd already heard it and told me to get out of his sight and that everybody was sick of hearing about my fixation on the dog. When I heard the word "fixation," I left without arguing. On the way home I tried for a long time to remember where and when I'd first heard the word "fixation." I had a feeling I'd feel better if I remembered.

I was about ten at the time and had long dreamed of being a pirate, an astronaut, or at least Za-Gor Te-Nay, the forest spirit from *Darkwood*. But after reading *The Adventures of Tom Sawyer* and *The Adventures of Huckleberry Finn*, I knew what I had to do. A raft, that's what I needed. I'd build a raft, run up the skull and crossbones, and set sail—down the Sava all the way to the Danube, then on to the Black Sea, and then who knows where. For a raft you need two barrels that you connect with boards, you knock in a mast with the flag, and that's it. I found one empty plastic barrel in the garage. The other, a wooden one, was in the basement and full of cabbage that Grandmother had put in to pickle for the winter. I soon threw it out of the barrel, though it stank like hell. Grandmother caught me just when I'd roped together the boards and the barrels. She quickly realized what I was doing and started to thrash me, uttering a whole stream of invectives and curses. I yelled through my tears and explained how I was going to raft to the Black Sea. That made her madder still and she beat me even harder.

"I'm sick of your fixations!" she shouted at one point.

I'd heard all of her curses and insults before—"Up the blasted foxhole," "Carc it, you animal," or "You're gonna cop it now," —but I had no idea what a "fixation" was.

I cried for a bit, and when Grandmother calmed down I asked her what it meant. She had only had two months of schooling and was illiterate. She could write her own name, but that was all, and she didn't believe me when I told her the earth was round. Who knows where she'd heard the word and what she associated it with. She told me, after calming down, and now stroking me on the head with her heavy hand, that a fixation was when I got the idea of building a raft and sailing down the Sava. And what's more, of making it from her cask of sauerkraut.

As I walked through Oslo, trying and failing to find the best shortcut home, I pondered what a fixation really was: wanting to sail away on a raft to the Black Sea or to write a poem about a cocker spaniel I whammed in the belly with a soccer cleat?

Then my eyes opened and I saw my hungover face in the mirror. I was still in my room on the island of S. The wind was still violating the landscape. Acid rushed up again from the depths of my stomach and I spewed it out like the rotten remains of my memory.

XXI

1. *The bear*

WE GOT OFF the snowmobile and started to cautiously climb the icy rise in elevation. The day was cold and dazzling. I was with Marko Niemennen, a taciturn Finn whose room was across from mine. Steam came out of our mouths as we crawled on all fours. The cold air nipped our nostrils. When we reached the top, we lay down and glanced all around us. Although we were wearing heavily tinted glasses, we had to put a hand on our foreheads when we wanted to look into the distance. The polar day had begun several weeks earlier. The April sun was low and beat straight in our eyes. Snowy, desert whiteness stretched all around us.

And then we saw *it*, swaying lazily along the edge of the crusty ice. The sea by the ice was bluish green and crystal calm. I caught my breath with excitement. It was the first time I'd seen a polar bear, if we exclude the one I saw at the Zagreb zoo. The creature that Marko and I were now watching was a huge specimen of immaculate whiteness. It was hard to follow against the white background. When it moved along the edge of the sea, it was a bit easier.

We watched for a long time without words. It was about two hundred yards away from us and heading away. That calmed me a little because I'd heard they could be difficult. They said a woman had been attacked and killed by a bear several years earlier. And it often happened that you had to shoot in order to scare them, Marko explained.

When the bear came to a peninsula of ice, it sprang into the sea like a lively child, dived, and emerged after a time on the other side. Then it kept on swimming until we could no longer see it. We remained glued to our spots, as if hoping for something.

On the way back to the snowmobile, I asked Marko if it was the same bear that'd broken into the cabin?

"Yes," he replied, stretching his lips into a malicious smile.

"But how can you be sure?"

"I know the fellow," he answered laconically in his broken Norwegian with a strong Finnish accent.

We got on the scooter, as we called the snowmobile, and rode toward the cabin in question. It wasn't far from there, about twenty miles from our settlement.

I sat behind Marko, holding on to him tightly. I'd stick my head out from behind his shoulders and let the polar air carve my face. The whiteness that was finally lit up by the sun's rays instilled a feeling of timelessness and soulless purity in me. This was how paradise looked, I imagined, and this was how death looked. One big, white silence.

2. *Emptiness*

It's hard to explain the darkness that prevails in a person's mind after four months of night. I began to doubt that I'd ever see the sun's light again. Later, the doubt grew into panic and, in the end, complete submission and numbness. But the light came back after all in late February. First of all timidly, and then the sun began to peek out indistinctly behind the horizon every day, giving us some shred of hope.

After meeting Aljoša, I continued to spend my time on the island of S. in the same way as before. I stared at the wooden shutters on the window, drank vodka, smoked hash when I could get it, and tried to work out the exact date when Selma would be giving birth. The meetings and conversations with Aljoša soon became arduous for both of us. We avoided each other like a dying person avoids medicine that won't help them.

The hardest thing, though, was to be without female company. I bought porn magazines and survived by masturbating regularly. But I soon noticed that porn only excited me if there was a young woman in a picture who reminded me of Selma. I feverishly pawed through those pages, searching for anything that'd give me the feeling she was mine again. Although I didn't know anymore if I wanted her or if I was more excited by the thought of somebody else having her. I searched for the shape of her full lips, her skinny butt, her short black hair, her small, pointy tits, anything. It helped to be stoned because a fantasy then emerged from my brain that blended with an indescribably pleasant sensation of emotional pain that penetrated my marrow and wedged somewhere near the very root of my dick. Still, cumming brought an intolerable feeling of emptiness with it. I'd never feel so empty as when I'd blow a load looking at one of those greasy pages, imagining Selma with somebody else. I knew exactly with whom. But just fifteen minutes later I'd repeat the whole process: a glass of vodka, a joint, a porn magazine, wanking, emptiness.

3. The enzyme

Somewhere around the turn of the year I started to spend more time with Marko. He was a carpenter by trade and could make anything from wood, except a woman, he said.

As the New Year came closer, the millennium celebration needed to be prepared in the settlement, and everybody participated as best they could. So it was that I got to know my neighbor better. He had the job of setting up the Cultural Center ahead of the celebration. He built another bar, raised extra shelves for the drinks, brought benches up from the basement and fastened them, and widened the stage so that the locals would be able to get up on it with the band, which was to come all the way from Oslo, so we could all sing and count down the seconds until the new millennium.

Marko worked with a hand-rolled cigarette in his mouth, with concentration and devotion. He swore loudly and melodically in a strange mixture of Norwegian, Swedish, and Finnish.

I managed to remember his *"Saatan i helvetti! Fy faen, perkele!"* and it sounded powerful. I started to swear in a foreign language for the first time.

Maybe it's not quite correct to say that Marko was taciturn. His Norwegian was poor, and he always answered in short, simple, grammatically inconsistent sentences delivered in a heavy Finnish accent. You could see he'd been through a few tough episodes in his life. He was bitter and caustic, but witty. His looks were almost Asiatic, with slanting eyes, dense black hair, and a stony face. He told me he came from a place in the far north of Finland whose name was hard to pronounce, let alone remember. He added that Finnish was the most beautiful language in the world.

When it came to alcohol, Marko could be extreme. He didn't drink during the day, but at night he'd sometimes get drunk and then he morphed completely. He wasn't violent, but he could be a real pain sometimes. He wanted to buy everybody a drink, sing with them in Finnish, and dance naked, while trying to explain his suffering in broken Norwegian. He probably just wanted a little company, human warmth, and a woman's soft lap. When he got drunk, everybody would avoid him with their polite Norwegian cold and whisper despicably to each other, "The crazy Finn, he's drunk again. All Finns are like that when they're drunk."

On one occasion he got so drunk that he could no longer stand, and nobody wanted to help him home. I had a hell of a time dragging him to our house and getting him into bed. Then I went back to the pub and ordered a double vodka. A pudgy young physician from Oslo sat down at my table and began explaining to me with his watery blue eyes and effeminate movement that it was all because of an enzyme. The absence of that enzyme meant the Finns, along with all Asians, including Inuits and Native Americans, couldn't cope with alcohol like whites do. I'd heard that theory before, but I was certain the doctor was wrong. Human misfortune probably had a big influence on that enzyme, I reflected furiously and stared with undisguised revulsion at that fucker with his smooth white skin and mouth like a parrot's beak. It was pain that drove people to get drunk the way they did, not some damn enzyme. He smiled at me as if we were allies against people without that enzyme. He didn't know that I lack that enzyme too, that vaccine against unhappiness, because it couldn't be said that alcohol only had a mild effect on me. Not at all.

The doctor drank his juice and whispered that we—he and I—were the only real intellectuals on the island and that it was

BEKIM SEJRANOVIĆ

great there was somebody he could have a cultured conversation with. The guy had a German accent for some reason. I didn't want to ask him why.

I knocked back my vodka and said, "*Sieg Heil und auf Wiedersehen, Herr Doktor!*" and left.

He laughed and probably found that witty. As I was going out into the icy, eternal night, I thought, Herr Doktor Mengele has arrived in town.

Afterward I started to hang around with Marko. We were connected by the absence of that enzyme, whose name I can't remember anymore. Mengele thus remained the only intellectual on the island of S.

4. *The new millennium*

When Marko got drunk and everybody in the pub avoided him, as always, he'd withdraw into a corner, take out his phone, and call somebody in Finland. He'd sit alone, drink vodka, and chat in Finnish. He'd laugh, bang his fist on the table, toast, talk loudly, and shout. Sometimes he'd cry too. Once he complained to me that all his money went to his wretched phone, but he didn't give up. It happened that somebody rang him, but seldom.

The New Year's Eve celebration was nothing special, as is usually the case. Everybody was there and everybody was drunk and desperately cheerful. Marko and I sat lonely at a table, drinking and toasting each other. We didn't talk much, we'd just swear—he in my language and I in Finnish—touch glasses, and drain them. At midnight we wished one another a happy New Year without any of the great enthusiasm, which the others in the place were melodramatically squeezing out of themselves. The island's president, barely able to stand, made a short New Year's toast with his tongue blundering around inside his mouth. After that, people continued to drink, sing, and whoop, the women on the stage swung their hips wildly and pulled at the members of the band, who were encouraged, stepping up the rhythm and playing even worse. Marko took out his phone and thumbed the numbers aggressively. It seemed hard to get a connection, and even when he did, it broke off, or the reception was poor, so he yelled, swore, threatened, and banged the device. I was still sitting on the other side of the table and listening to his language, which I liked more and more. Probably because I didn't understand a single word, except the curses.

I had a phone too, but nobody to call. Sometimes I took it out of my pocket to check if anybody had tried to call me, but they hadn't. I couldn't decide if I was glad or not. Maybe I felt better that nobody had rung, but my vanity was probably hurt. It's hard with vanity, but otherwise it's okay when nobody calls to wish you a happy New Year. Fuck the New Year, I thought, turned off my cell phone, toasted Marko and whoever it was from Finland he was yelling to over the phone, emptied my glass, poured myself another, and knocked it back too. So began the new millennium.

A month before the beginning of the new millennium, sometime in November, I'd felt that Selma had given birth. Nobody informed me, I wasn't in touch with anyone from Oslo, and even if I had been I don't think anybody would've told me. It would've sounded like this: "Your wife (former wife, to be exact) has had a child (who knows, maybe it's yours) with her new (and once former) bearded guy. The baby boy is large and healthy, almost nine pounds. Congratulations, and all the best in life."

A month after the beginning of the new millennium, Grandmother died. The news sounded like this: "Grandmother died.

BEKIM SEJRANOVIĆ

All the burial arrangements have been made. Don't worry about Grandfather, everything's okay."

Grandfather died a month later. The wording was almost the same as in the message about Grandmother, apart from the last sentence. And so began the new millennium. I didn't worry anymore because nothing was, or could've been, okay. I waited for weeks for the sun to reappear in the naive belief that it'd bring some relief. When it appeared, everything was still the same except that I raised the shutters on the window of my room.

5. Mai kuntri

I hung around with Marko more and more in the New Year. We didn't actually talk much. We drank together, swore, toasted in different languages, laughed, and exchanged porn, forming discerning opinions on the women who twisted and posed on the glossy paper. Gradually I found out how he got there from the north of Finland.

He'd once been married in a place near Kilpisjärvi, a town right on the border with Norway in the region of Lapland, which was divided between four countries: Norway, Sweden, Finland, and Russia. The region was home to Lapps, the original inhabitants of the Nordic lands, a nomadic people that rode reindeer, sang traditional *yoiks*, and listened to old myths retold by the mystical voices of shamans as they gazed at tiny pieces of polished reindeer bone. Marko said that he himself was partly of Lapp descent. In the not so distant past, the regimes of the four countries mentioned tried to forcefully assimilate the Lapps, while in more recent times this was done by modernization: the lowing of reindeer was replaced by the chug of snowmobiles, and the shaman's absorbing voice by poorly distilled alcohol, which had a ruinous effect, like it did on the Native Americans.

Unlike his father, who'd once raised reindeer, Marko built houses, cabins, and saunas, fastened benches and tables with wooden nails, and even carved cups from soft birch wood. He built himself a house of expensive, quality pine, covered the roof with humus, and planted grass on it—a time-honored form of thermal insulation in Nordic countries. He soon brought a wife to the house, a pure-blooded Finnish woman, and put two sons in her belly. He taught them to track hares and foxes in the snow, milk reindeer, and ski cross-country on the endless plateaus of Lapland. Marko explained to me that men's main pastime was getting drunk in sooty saunas, which they heated with birch logs. The nearest pub was fifty miles away.

"The sauna is the place where real men drink," he told me, raising his gnarled index finger into the air. But work was hard to come by because people had mainly moved away to the cities in the south—houses now were not built, but abandoned. One summer, he heard that carpenters were in demand across the border, in the northernmost Norwegian province of Finnmark, and that the Norwegians paid well. He went there, and it wasn't a mistake—he earned good money. But money is infernal, Marko warned, raising his almost hairless eyebrows. He took a liking to it there, so he stayed on and visited his wife and children when he could, at first often, but then ever more rarely. He had it good there, and after sending money to his wife and children, and even his parents, he'd still have enough to go carousing in Norwegian pubs. There were some cute little sluts there too, he explained like a letch, and he'd dip his wick with them now and then. Still, under the influence of alcohol he'd sometimes be seized by nostalgia that caused euphoric pain, primeval melancholy, and longing for his home, wife, and children, for his village, and, most of all, language. That was the hardest thing for him, he said—not being able to talk. He knew enough Norwegian to do his job, but when the man wanted to go out and cheer himself up, have a chat, and tell a joke or two, his throat, brain, and soul would seize up, and the story would freeze. Nobody laughed at his jokes or could sympathize with his pain.

"*Mai kuntri iz mai kuntri*," Marko emphasized stubbornly.

6. *Maybe he's humping her right now*

Marko started telling an episode that I sensed would have an unhappy end. Once, in a bout of drunkenness and a fit of yearning, he got in a taxi and set off for his village in Finland. Apart from the driver, there were two girls with him in the taxi, "damn sluts" he called them in Norwegian, and added in Finnish: "May the devil himself take them to hell!"

It should be said that taking a taxi to Finland is no small thing, and the fun cost him 8,000 crowns. It all started as a drunken joke. He drank with those girls in a pub all evening, and afterward they decided to share a taxi. When the driver asked where to go, Marko said he should drive him home.

"Could that be Finland?" the driver asked sarcastically.

"Finland, yes," Marko shouted in a burst of drunken delight. "Drive me home to Finland, *perkele, saatana, helvetti*!"

The girls started to giggle, saying, "Yes, yes, drive to Finland, to Finland, ha ha ha!"

They stopped at Marko's on the way to get more vodka and money for the taxi because the driver didn't want to leave until he saw the dough. And so, warmed by the midnight sun of the polar circle, they left for the town of Kilpisjärvi and Marko's nearby village.

The next morning, when Marko and the taxi arrived in front of the house he'd built with his own hands, he paid the driver 4,000 crowns in cash and told him he'd get the rest if he waited, because he had to go back to Norway very soon, for work on Monday. The embracing girls had fallen asleep on Marko's lap in the back seat and now, slowly and drunkenly, they started to open their gummy eyelids covered with smudged makeup.

Marko opened the unlocked door of the house, quietly climbed the stairs, and peered into the children's room. His sons weren't there. Sure, he thought, it's the weekend, they're probably at his parents' place. Then he went to the bedroom, tiptoeing to avoid the creak of the pine floorboards—and there was his wife lying on the shaggy chest of the village shopkeeper Hakke. The summer sun didn't set, and the light penetrated the venetians, fell on her blonde hair, and made it even brighter. He yelled and shouted and cursed all the saints he could remember; the lovers woke up with a start and jumped out of bed. His wife started to scream, but the shopkeeper gathered up his clothes that lay neatly folded on the chair by the bed. Marko whacked him on the head twice, leaped onto the bed and grabbed his wedding photograph, which hung over the bed, broke it over his knee, and threw it at her; she cried, called for help, and implored him not to do anything stupid. Marko ran outside to the taxi, which was still waiting; his wife, barefooted and in a dressing gown ran after him, while the shopkeeper rushed out a moment later and bolted in the opposite direction. Marko's wife caught up with her husband just as he was getting into the car. She stopped him, screamed his name like crazy, and begged him not to go. Then she looked in the car and saw the two girls, who were giggling loudly and heartily at this soap opera, which they weren't separated from by a TV screen but just by the window of the old Mercedes. At that sight, Marko's wife became furious, swore at Marko, and beat him in the face with her small clenched fists. He gave her a hard slap, shoved her away, and she fell butt-first onto the soft, dewy ground. Marko got into the car and ordered the driver to take him back to Norway. He never returned to the village. He hadn't gotten a divorce yet, he said, but if she sent him the papers, he would.

Worst of all, he admitted with sincere disappointment, he didn't have sex with either of the girls who were with him in the taxi. But the shopkeeper was probably still screwing his wife.

"Maybe he's humping her right now," he squeezed through his narrow lips.

7. The cabin

Apart from the two settlements, there were a number of cabins on the island that served as summer cottages. Sometimes polar bears broke into them and wrecked everything in their path in search of food. People said they'd even seen bears in our settlement. When a roguish bear devastated a cabin, the damage could be considerable, so Marko would go there to clean up, do repairs, and reinforce the door or the wooden shutters on the windows. This time he took me along with him.

First we had a look at the cabin and identified the damage, and then Marko gave in to my persistent urging, though maybe a little reluctantly at first, that we try to find the bear's trail. I hoped to see a polar bear, from a safe distance of course, and when I climbed that hill, my wish was fulfilled. Now we returned to the cabin where we'd spend a day or two, depending how much work Marko would need to do. There was no really great damage, more just a huge mess. The door had been smashed down, one chair was broken, and the others scattered about. The pantry had been ransacked and bags of flour ripped open, so that everything inside was as white as outside.

Marko began repairing the door, and I cleaned up. I swept together the flour, the remains of a ceramic dish, and the feathers from a cushion that the bear probably snagged with a claw.

As I was cleaning, I found a small cupboard with three bottles of Russian Troika vodka. One of them was open and half-empty. I whistled to Marko and eyed my discovery. Marko just nodded and continued his work even more devotedly.

We'd arrived in the afternoon, and by evening we'd finished the job. Marko said it was better we spend the night there because we needed two hours to return to the settlement. Although the sun shone the whole night, it was cold. Clouds began to build up, and a snowstorm could've swept up at any moment. With our work done, we sat down at the table and lit cigarettes. Marko went to get the open bottle of vodka, came back, and sat on the chair he'd fixed half an hour earlier. He started to rock on its back legs as if to check if he'd done his work well. Then, with a look of satisfaction, he opened the bottle and took three short, greedy gulps. He handed the bottle to me, I took a little swig and made a sour face.

After a while, I asked Marko fearfully if he thought the bear could come back. He shook his head and clucked.

"The cabin at the entrance to Tempelfjord is next," he scoffed and pointed almost cheerfully in the direction of that cabin and the bay.

After half a bottle of vodka, strange zoological questions started to stalk about my head. How many bears were there really that broke into cabins? Maybe we were dealing with a well-organized gang. After a whole bottle of vodka, Marko maintained that it was one single bear that went around, and instead of devouring seals it ransacked cabins. He'd been on the island for four years already and could write a whole scientific study about the bear that roamed around and whooped it up in the cabins. Both of us laughed drunkenly. Then we pretended we were drunken bears walking in the cabin on all fours and overturning the chairs.

"I'm a drunken bear," Marko roared. "Give me vodka and five, no, ten she-bears. They don't have to be white. Black and brown bears are welcome too."

"I only want white ones," I shouted, "and they have to have nailpolished claws and shave their pussies."

"Yes yes, ha ha, shave their pussies—that's it!"

I tittered with Marko and rolled on the floor laughing.

Afterward we calmed down a bit, and when Marko opened another bottle he continued to belabor his theory about a bear that was clearly trying to get back at people, who knows why. Maybe it lacks some enzyme, I thought.

8. *The hangover*

The next day we woke up late and with frightful hangovers. The wind was raging outside, the sky had gone dark, and it started to snow. Marko was pale in the face. It seemed he wasn't the best. I ate an abundant breakfast, and Marko drank two cups of coffee with vodka. Then he vomited, but he kept drinking a little. I had a bit of hash, so I rolled myself a joint. Marko didn't join me because he was against drugs, he said. We decided to stay one more day in the cabin.

By afternoon, Marko had drunk almost the whole bottle of vodka we'd begun the previous day. He vomited several times, first bile, and later a bit of blood. But he still continued to drink. Afterward he took out his phone and tried to call Finland, but the reception was poor. He went out and wanted to climb up a snowbank in the hope that the reception would be better. I objected because it was blowing a real blizzard outside. He didn't listen, of course, and off he went. I stayed in the cabin, threw a few birch logs into the heavy metal stove, and rolled another joint.

When Marko turned up at the door of the cabin half an hour later, he was red in the face from the cold. That made him look a bit healthier, but you could see from his eyes that he wasn't well. He hadn't managed to climb the snowbank, and now he was furious and swore. He even seemed to be crying.

We sat in the cabin, and Marko drank and vomited in turn. The hash had made me hungry and I cooked fish soup. Marko didn't want to eat. He watched my slurping with undisguised revulsion and spoke chunks of Norwegian backed up by a few acrid Finnish curses. He finished telling me about how he got to this remote island.

After returning from Finland by taxi, he stayed for a few weeks more in the northern Norwegian town of Tromsø, mainly drinking himself into a stupor, and then headed south, to Oslo. There was no shortage of work there, so he worked fourteen hours a day and earned phenomenally good money. At first, he admitted, he drank a lot, had a good turnover of "sluts" (it was impossible to tell whether Marko meant prostitutes or if he referred to all women that way), and things were going well. Except that the phone bills ruined him, he said, because he often called Finland. And he was sacked from several jobs for drinking.

"Fuck, I had to drink so as not to go round the bend," Marko said almost apologetically, and then he concluded that he had to stop, mainly because of his health. Otherwise he'd just have kept drinking. Then he got hooked on gambling. He mostly played poker, and sometimes he was lucky, but more often he wasn't. Once he got ripped off by a group of Vietnamese. He was certain it was a setup and he was furious.

"But there's no messing around with them," he added helplessly.

They threatened to cut off his fingers one by one if he didn't pay. A sizeable amount of money was at stake, and the Vietnamese stopped at nothing. Fortunately he found a well-paid job over the winter as a shock-worker, even sleeping at the construction site. Sometimes he worked there all night under powerful lights—and all that in a frantic attempt to return his debt in those three months. But when the house was finished and the owner of the firm that Marko worked for (off the books, of course) met with the client, they discovered numerous flaws. Some walls were crooked, one room was smaller than it was supposed to be, two windows were missing. In general, the client was dissatisfied with the work. He didn't want to pay the rest of the money to the owner of the construction firm, who in turn blamed Marko. He told him that he hadn't been able to sell the house because of him, a Finnish tippler. And so Marko was up to his neck in problems, or, as he'd say, "up to his nose in shit." He didn't have any money for the Vietnamese, and the boss didn't want to pay him for the three months' strenuous labor. After a short quarrel, Marko whammed him in the mug with his gnarled carpenter's fist, packed together what few belongings he had, and took off back to the north of Norway. He stayed there until the summer and then he heard they were looking for carpenters on the island.

"I would've gone even farther, but there's nowhere farther than this island," he concluded disappointedly.

"Fuck," I said. "Gambling really fucked you around."

"Not gambling, but the Vietnamese. For the first few months on the island I kept looking back, I was afraid they could find me even here. When I gambled, I drank less. If I'd kept drinking like before, I'd probably be dead by now."

"So why do you drink now?" I asked dopily.

"Because I don't gamble."

9. The angel

We sat like that for a while longer, and then Marko, drunk and exhausted from vomiting, went to bed. I rolled myself one more and also turned in. I switched off the light and smoked the joint in the dark.

Yes, I reflected, it seems people can only get rid of one bad habit by falling into another. Charles Bukowski stopped drinking and got hooked on betting on the horses. He wrote that it saved his life.

Alija got off alcohol too, though nobody could've imagined it was possible.

They say Alija didn't change after he married, not even after he had first a son, and then a daughter. He lived in poverty in his hovel at the end of the village, without electricity and water, took his goats around the hills, and gathered medicinal herbs and plants that he'd sell at Biljana, a small local firm that produced herbal teas and natural medicines. Sometimes he'd find paid work—carrying coal, picking plums, or digging wells for people. He kept drinking, and now and again he also played the *saz* when somebody persuaded him to or when he felt like it. He drank more and more, and played less. Everybody had given up trying to change Alija, to "set him on the right path," as they said, so that he'd stay off rakija, achieve something in life, and not live "like a nobody."

Once, probably after several days of boozing, an angel appeared to Alija in a dream. He claimed it wasn't an ordinary dream but something almost real. Delirium tremens, my mother said.

The angel said to him that it was bad that he drank, neglected his family and relatives, and most of all himself; he should renounce drink and turn to the only god, Allah. The angel also told him that, when he woke up, he should go to the chest in the corner, take out the bottle of rakija he'd begun the previous night, pour it out, and swear to God he wouldn't take as much as a sniff of rakija from then on. It should be said that Alija was never a believer, neither in God nor in the Party. He believed solely in the intoxicating power of rakija, which helped him less and less. The angel also told him to wash and go to the mosque for morning prayers.

Alija awoke with a jolt. It was still dark, and it would soon be prayer time. When he got up, he didn't vacillate. First he tipped the rakija out the window and then flung the bottle toward the stream that flowed below the house. He didn't hear if it smashed, but he knew the stream would carry it away from his door sooner or later. After that, he stripped down to the waist and washed at the well, panting from the shocks of the cold water. He stuck on his fur hat and, bearded and swarthy as he was, with conspicuous signs of a hangover, he set off for the mosque. It was open and he went in.

He started to pray as he'd learned in the few months he lasted in a Koran school before the Second World War. He spoke the words of the prayer quietly and indistinctly, partly due to lack of habit, and partly because he'd forgotten some of the words.

Then the hodja appeared in the gloom of the mosque, and when he saw Alija, sullen and unshaven, with eyes spasmodically squeezed shut in a deep trance of enlightenment, he got a fright, jumped, and shouted, "The devil!"

Alija was startled, glanced at him out of the corner of his eye, and continued praying. When he'd finished, he went past the astonished hodja in silence and left. He was never seen in the mosque again, but he never drank another drop of alcohol. He read the Koran, fasted regularly, and sometimes even prayed to Allah, but he didn't go to mosque.

10. *As if we were dead*

I woke up before Marko and started to prepare breakfast and coffee. The bottle of vodka—the last one, which Marko had begun last night, before he couldn't drink anymore—was still standing on the table. I took it and poured it into the snow a little way from the cabin, not without a few qualms. Outside, a sunny day was fighting its way through the fog. The air was cold and fresh.

When I went back in, Marko was awake, sitting on his bed and smoking. I put coffee on the table for him and started to eat. He looked even worse than the day before. His face was puffy and gray. After he'd smoked the cigarette, he went to the toilet and vomited. Bile and blood, I imagined, though I couldn't see.

I ate breakfast and drank coffee, but I wasn't calm. I knew Marko would want vodka in his coffee. He didn't ask me anything but just milled around the cabin looking for the bottle. When he found all three bottles empty in the cupboard, he started to wonder. As far as he could remember, he'd only just begun the third bottle.

After drinking coffee, he went and vomited again. I began rolling a joint.

He came back and screamed at me, "Where's the vodka? You can't have drunk it all yourself, what am I gonna do today, huh? I have to have a drink before we go, understand? Do you understand?"

I understood—even if I hadn't been one of the island's only intellectuals it was easy to realize what he needed. I lit the joint, took several long tokes, and offered it to him. He refused my outstretched hand and hissed like an angry gander. I shrugged and smoked with relish. Marko started to pack his things. He seemed to be in a hurry to head back to the settlement. I wasn't in a hurry to go anywhere. I took my warm sleeping bag, spread it out in front of the cabin, sat on it, and leaned back against the thick logs. I put on my sunglasses and enjoyed the spring sun.

After a while he came out and stood in front of me. He demanded that I go and pack and that we then leave. As he talked, his lips trembled. His hands probably trembled too, but I couldn't see them. I answered calmly that we'd be staying one more day.

"It's gorgeous here," I added.

He flew into a rage and dashed back into the cabin. Soon he came back carrying his things and started loading them onto the snowmobile. I, on the other hand, started rolling another joint.

He shouted, "I'm going now, and you can do as you like!"

Then he started to cough, probably from all the shouting, and went around the back of the cabin to vomit. When he returned, his eyes were dark and bloodshot. Mine were probably red too, but I felt incomparably better than he did.

"Okay, we're going back today," I said. "But we don't have to leave immediately. Here, if you smoke this joint with me, we can go as soon as you say."

He was silent and frowned. I thought he'd go and vomit again.

"Vodka doesn't help anymore anyhow," he said, putting out his hand to take the joint. "And then we're going?"

"Yup."

Ten minutes later, Marko was sitting next to me in his shades, sunning himself. He didn't need to vomit anymore. We didn't talk, simply enjoyed the silence.

"When we get back, we'll say that the bear drank all the vodka," he said, stretching his thin and cracked lips.

"Do you always say that?" I asked with a smile.

"Always."

"You should be grateful to that teddy."

"He is my love—" he now started to snicker.

"But what if he comes back?!"

"We'll shave his pussy," Marko said and thumped his knee.

The sun shone with a harsh, cold light that seemed unreal. We stayed sitting on my sleeping bag for a long time and laughed occasionally. Between the fits of laughter we were silent. Then I'd stare into the whiteness and imagine with relief that we were dead.

XXII

GRANDFATHER AND I finally exited the graveyard. He'd stopped crying, and only turned back toward Alija's grave one more time. I was still irritated by his mawkish tale about death, and I pulled him along by the arm to make him go faster. We walked down the wet asphalt road. His green Zastava that he called Greenie was parked fifty yards away.

Grandfather began going on about wanting to drive from the village to the city. I snapped at him and said there was no chance of him driving. He could hardly move his left leg and arm, and his reflexes were like those of a dead horse. The bit about the dead horse offended him and he got sad again. Then he added that I could take Greenie when he died. It was all he had left and he wanted me to have it.

"Oh, thanks a million," I said peevishly.

1. *Whose tears are they?*

I went from the island of S. to Oslo and I stayed for a few months in a small, borrowed room in the Sogn student hostel. I decided to visit my native country for the last time, and one morning I took a flight to Zagreb.

The plane flew lazily over the snowy peaks of the Alps. Soon, like a bird of prey when it catches sight of a field mouse, it would begin to descend nimbly into the Pannonian Basin. The plane was packed with tourists, along with several stiff business-people and a few Bosnian refugees. A family with two children caught my eye; they'd been traveling from Texas for two days. The woman told the children several times over where they'd changed planes, as if they were learning a little ditty by heart that they'd repeat when they arrived in Bosnia. Her husband, dark and scowling, was forever looking at his watch. The whole family was in new, totally identical cuffed jeans. The children, a boy and a girl aged about twelve and thirteen, sat calmly and looked dully at their mother. None of them seemed happy about the trip. They looked like stamps that'd been franked twice.

It was fair weather and most of the passengers were looking out through the windows. One or two people gasped or called out, full of the dutiful tourist's earnest enthusiasm. Digital cameras were taken out and pictures taken that nobody would ever look at without yawning.

I, on the other hand, stared at the stewardess—at her breasts and hips, to tell the truth—and I decided to go to the toilet and masturbate. I did that often when I traveled by plane. Fairly often on a train, too, but always on a flight. And not just once.

Selma and I had traveled to Zagreb two years earlier in the same sort of plane, but with a few less passengers. We sat at the back by ourselves, clenched each other's hands, our fingers intertwined, our tongues probing every opening on our heads, our lips lapping all the smooth parts. After Frankfurt, my bon-er was bursting my nostrils and I could feel my balls throbbing. Sometimes Selma ran her thin fingers over them. Later we went to the bathroom. First me, then her. Here I'll skip a description of the plane's cramped toilet. I let down my pants and boxers

BEKIM SEJRANOVIĆ

and sat on the toilet. My cock bloomed and tensed. I rubbed it with squelchy gel. Then she came, knocked, and entered. She immediately turned around, raised her skirt, let down her panties, and slowly, like in a slow-motion film, sat on my cock. We almost always did it anally because she liked it that way, and I didn't object. At least not at first.

In the beginning, the landscape of our love shone like a sunny seaside day on ecstasy: our first time out together, the drinking spree, catching the white parrot that we later had to take to the vet, and our first kiss in the corridor of the vet's. Then we went back to my room, carefully returned Lars's bird to its cage, and covered it with a white sheet. I put on some music, took a piece of hash out of the drawer, and laid it on the low, dark table among the moldy bread crumbs and tobacco ash. She took out a little tin box, in which there had once been menthol candies. She opened it adroitly, and inside there were several pink candies printed with hearts.

After an hour the music enveloped us, gently caressing our goosebump skin as we stood in the middle of the small room and followed the monotonous electronic rhythm, dancing, slowly swaying, licking each other with our eyes, and I sent her kisses with my heart and fed hungrily on her love. The music slowly rose and we danced ever more wildly, sometimes coming close to each other, to within a micromillimeter, but we didn't touch, our lips brushed but didn't burgeon into a kiss. From time to time we sat on the sofa, I rolled a joint, lit it, and passed it to her, she puffed out smoke to the rhythm of the music, I spoke, but the voice that came out wasn't mine, the thoughts that turned to pictures in the semidarkness of the room weren't mine. I laughed, we giggled bleatingly, she looked at me and shook her head, threw it back when she inhaled the smoke, and laughed too. Then she hopped and danced dissolutely with her eyes closed, got up on the table, turned her back to me, and danced just with her slender butt. She danced just with it, and I watched that derriere and touched it with my eyelashes, only brushed it with my eyelashes.

Afterward we climbed to the top of St. Hanshaugen Park to watch the sunrise. There's a house at the top with a tower totally reminiscent of a minaret. I fell to my knees and started to pray and yell "*Allahu Akbar*" in a distorted voice. Selma stood aside and laughed loudly. When I bent over in my "prayer" she gave me a kick in the butt, and we started chasing each other around the "mosque," shouting like mad and laughing. We ran into a guy who was taking his dog out for its morning shit, and only then did we realize how smashed we were. The animal, a hulking pedigree with a distended neck, cocked its head toward us distrustfully when we hid in the bushes.

Later we went to a bench, lit a joint, and laughed at the sun. We talked and chattered nonstop, recited each other our hopes, painted our wishes sincerely and without any repulsion. The very next moment I couldn't even grasp what she was saying because I'd turned into one big eye that hung on her lips and one huge keen ear that picked up her nasal sighs, and I was a sensitive index finger that touched her neck. I was everything that could feel her and her pulse and her breathing, I was everything, but I had no idea what she was talking about.

Next, we went back to my room and lay awake all day long, looking at each other with dilated pupils. We rolled on two mattresses joined together on the floor, listened to music, smoked joints, and fucked. First we started to make love slowly and delicately, like silkworms. I'd already told her I was hopelessly in love with her, and now I said theatrically and loftily that I was all hers and she could do with me whatever she wanted. And I kept going on and babbling, stringing together all the words a guy like me, in love and high, can think of. We licked and nuzzled every naked pore, little hole, and bulge of our bodies. We made love tenderly and savagely. I felt like a bull with a huge dong violating a fragile calf in vengeful sadism, and at the same time like the most delicate sprite with a goosefeather or a rabbit's paw instead of a cock, caressing his sweetheart with it more gently than a ray of light. I felt raped when she mounted me and started to grind and scour me like I was the deck of a worn-out ship. We used heaps of gel, but in the end we were both still bruised and raw on the most exposed parts of the body. After I was finally able to have an orgasm, we collapsed alongside each other like two exhausted soldiers who had only just survived a battle. We tried to slow the fluttering of our diaphragms and listened fearfully to the frenzied thudding of our hearts, trembling like rare birds in the spasms of death. I tried to speak, but my tongue wouldn't obey me and my jaws shook uncontrollably. We fell asleep, or maybe unconscious, I don't know, but afterward we started to deliriously squeeze and rub one another again, and soon we were screwing again and continued till we were sore.

As soon as I managed to get my tongue to speak, I asked if she wanted to be my wife. In a frayed voice she said she did, kissed me, and gave me a painful bite on the lip. She took the gel, rubbed down my cock, and turned her slim, tight ass toward me again.

The weeks that followed passed quickly. Selma moved in with me in the bedsit, I kept working on the ship together with Lars, who'd just come back from Sweden with pinpoint pupils. Selma continued waitressing at Sigi's pub, I ferried her to the island every day at 12:15, and he brought her back to the land late in the evening in his red speedboat. We got married three weeks later at the registry in Oslo. The witnesses—the only wedding guests—were half-drunk Sigi and deviously grinning

Lars. Instead of a suit and a wedding dress we had tracksuit tops. Mine was yellow, with "Brazil" on the back, and hers was blue and said "Venezuela." We were happy, truly happy, and stoned. This is the love of your life, Selma Aasen is the love of your life, you love her, oh how you love her, a harmoniously foreign voice rang in my head. I wasn't sure if it was making fun of me or trying to persuade me.

We all piled onto Sigi's boat and went to his pub. There he made food for us and opened champagne. We were joined by two girls and one young man who worked with Selma. Music played, we ate a little, drank more, and danced a bit. I rolled joints and played the husband. Selma gave me a hard kiss and a candy rolled from her mouth into mine. I bit it and then needed ages to rinse away the bitter taste with champagne. Lars hung around the waitresses, while Sigi raved drunkenly in my ear. I drew away from his beard-ringed lips. Later he hugged me with one arm and pressed Selma to him with the other and tried to kiss her. He was struggling to say something about happiness, but I could see very well that his hand was searching for Selma's butt. I smiled and tried to pull away from both of them. Selma managed to tear away from his embrace, took me by the arm, and dragged me into the woods behind the pub. As I walked after her, I heard a rustling. I asked myself if it was somebody's tears dripping on the leaves or if we were being followed by red-eyed rabbits. We stopped under a pine tree and I asked if she could also hear the rabbits coming after us. She said there were no more rabbits because Sigi had called the hunters the week before to kill them all and now he had a freezer full of them. They'd been our wedding meal. But they'd multiply again by the next year and he'd have to eradicate them once more.

"They breed . . . like rabbits," I said, trying to be witty.

BEKIM SEJRANOVIĆ

"In theory," she said. "But they can't anymore, you see. There are no more rabbits."

It still sounded like somebody's tears.

We landed on the Zagreb runway. I'd long since emptied my balls and done up my seat belt again, and now I waited listlessly for the plane to come to a halt, after which I'd head for the border police desk with a fear that by now was innate. An unfriendly officer would look probingly at me, then at the photograph on my passport, and after several moments he'd return it indifferently and give me the signal with his eyes, without words, that I could proceed. And I'd keep asking myself whose tears were following us through the darkness of our first nuptial night.

XXIII

1. The Adriatic

HOWEVER GOOD IT is to travel, it's even worse to arrive at your journey's end. You should travel without a goal, without hope, without anybody waiting to meet you or remaining behind on the platform, and without anybody who'll miss you and badger you to go back to them. If life is a journey, then reaching your destination means death. By that logic, I was already dead. But it seemed I wasn't, because I hoped death didn't look like that two-bed room in Zagreb's Hotel Jadran on old Vlaška Street. Death couldn't look like that, I tried to convince myself, because how would it then be different from life? Death had to be at least a little different.

I'd taken the bus into the city. I stood at the station for several moments wondering what to do: if I got on the first bus to Brčko, I'd be putting off the death of the journey but hastening my own.

So I decided to stay in Zagreb, at least for that evening, maybe get in touch with somebody, and try to buy a bit of hash, if nothing else.

From the hotel room, I rang Čombe, an old buddy from Rijeka who now lived in Zagreb. We agreed to meet that evening. I mentioned hash, and he said he didn't know but would try to get hold of some ganja if he could. Then I called Goran in Rijeka. He was glad to hear from me again after so long. He told me to come to Rijeka straightaway. I asked him about Kole.

"Oh, forget it," he puffed. "You know how it is . . . Y'know, let's go to Rab and have some fun on the island, huh? C'mon on, bud, don't be such an old woman."

Goran said all that in his usual stutter but quite fast, so that you couldn't grasp the individual words in his explosive verbal torrent. He'd always switch the syllables in particular words if he found them easier to pronounce that way. He made me smile for the first time in a long while. The sand of Lopar Beach on Rab got under my eyelids, the smell of sunscreen, gusts of wind filling the sail of my windsurfer, bare-bottomed German girls on air mattresses.

I got him off my back and said I'd ring him the next day.

I hung up and felt the room clinging to me like a cold leech. I went to the window and looked down into the street. It was a sunny afternoon. People were going home from work, leaving offices chilled by air conditioners as if on cue, and heading for their dining rooms. I thought about how to kill time until Čombe arrived: get drunk at the nearest pub or stay in the room and wait to be consumed by the voracious termites of memory?

2. It's not like this every day

Selma and I had been at the very same Hotel Jadran two years earlier, two weeks after we got married—in the very same room, just two stories up. We rolled on the bed and tickled each other. She squealed like a guinea pig and begged me to stop, then she bucked like an animal, switched to counterattack, and started tickling me, pinching me, and twisting my balls in a knot.

After we had a shower, we went for a walk.

"Zagreb is lovely in the evening," Selma warbled.

"All cities are lovely in the evening," I said.

"Yes, but they aren't lovely by day. Zagreb isn't."

I asked her why, and she said she felt it was full of small, thin, pointy pricks during the day.

She compared everything with pricks. She'd say somebody was as dumb as a prick, as good as a prick, as ugly as a prick, her coffee was as cold as a prick, the pizza as hot as a prick, a movie was "a prick of a film"—everything for her was pricks, and she described, measured, and compared everything with them.

After a few days in Zagreb, we went to Brčko to visit Grandfather and Grandmother. I'd called to tell them I was coming with my new wife. They sounded happy and hid their concern.

We sat in our house in Brčko, which Grandfather and Grandmother had recently returned to after several years of staying at the ranch. The house had warped, become crooked, and the living room window was covered with a sheet of plastic printed with "UNHCR." The inside walls were bare and had yellowed like old photos. We drank coffee together, Grandmother talked endlessly, asked tedious questions that she gave the answers to herself, teased Grandfather a bit nastily, and laughed with an all too chipper, forced cheerfulness, while Grandfather sat there and sighed, staring at the fildžan in front of him, and intermittently crying and whining like a beaten dog. Grandmother asked all about Selma: where she was from, where her parents were, and why she had a name like a Bosnian girl. I answered sarcastically that it wasn't just a Bosnian name, it was quite common in Norway, that she was Norwegian, and that she had no parents.

"'O can she 'ave no parents?" Grandmother jumped in. "She 'as to 'ave, nobody just springs out of an 'ole in the ground. She 'as to 'ave parents, 'ow can she not?"

And then she continued some story of her own, going on and babbling without end, as if she feared that one second of silence could break that impotent idyll.

"What's there to cry about?" she chided Grandfather. "Our grandson comes to visit with 'is young wife, and you, Grandfather—what's got you so soppy?"

At that, Grandfather raised his head, and his whimpering changed to a furious roar. "Why are you being such a bore, woman? You'll drive the young people round the bend? Don't make me 'it you with this stick on your foul mouth. You just go on, and on, and on."

Grandmother's lips passed from a smile into an angry grimace, and she grinned maliciously. "You should beat that tart of yours from Tuzla, the one from Slatina, you know full well who I mean! I'm sick of you too, you limp old letch!"

Selma gazed at them; she didn't understand the words, but everything was more than obvious.

I yelled at them to simmer down. They should be ashamed of themselves—here I was, visiting for one day, and they had to quarrel just then. We'd leave immediately if they were going to be like this, I warned.

They calmed down like scolded children. Grandfather stared into his fildžan again, and Grandmother apologized.

"Really, it's not like this every day, I tell you."

3. Selma, jump out the window!

After coffee, Selma went to have a little rest in the other room because she didn't understand anything anyway, and I didn't feel like translating Grandmother's monologue.

Grandfather groaned and shat, Grandmother changed his diaper. I looked the other way and tried to find a point on the wall I could nail my eyes to.

Afterward we sat together and I told them about Selma. I told them that her parents died when she was small and she grew up with her aunt and uncle, that she was kind and smart and studying to be a manager. They nodded, Grandmother looking at me with the distrustful eye of an old provincial wife.

"Well, that's good," Grandfather said, "to be a manager."

I didn't lie to them, though the story about Selma could've been told differently. I could've used other words and constructed my sentences differently, could've added clearer motifs and mentioned more details. Lies and truth are a question of literary style and its function in the given context.

I could've told them that Selma was born the same year as me, that she spent her childhood in the eastern part of Oslo, in the working-class neighborhood of Vílerenga. I could've told them in detail about Selma's vague memories, images of her father masturbating while he held her on his lap, of him touching her coochie, of him making her lick ice cream while he lustfully pulled back his foreskin, of him rubbing ice cream on the head of his swollen cock and persuading her to lick it off, and of her not understanding at the time why she shouldn't do that. He was her dad, the strongest and most handsome man in the world. And the taste of vanilla ice cream wasn't bad. I didn't tell Grandmother and Grandfather that she only realized all that at the beginning of puberty. She told her mother everything and begged that they leave, that they run away somewhere, but her mother silenced her and warned her not to tell anybody—what would people think? In the end, Selma's homeroom teacher suspected something strange was happening to the slim, tall girl with large eyes and wide, full lips. Her spectrum of moods

BEKIM SEJRANOVIĆ

was too broad for a thirteen-year-old. Her wild aggressiveness, exhibitionism, and licentiousness with boys were painfully intertwined with her quiet melancholy, long bouts of depression, and silent, deep-seated spite.

It all came out when her dad, a former hockey player and then sportswear salesman, went all the way for the first time and penetrated her, splitting her open like an unripe walnut, and left her bleeding on the perfumed pink sheet her mom had covered her bed with just that evening.

When she went to school in the morning, she felt everybody knew what'd happened, shame began to rise from her toes and climb up her skinny body, soon it coiled around her, tightening like fine wire. She vomited in the middle of the classroom and then fell unconscious. They drove her to hospital and the doctors there shrewdly suspected that something was wrong. She squeezed her legs together convulsively, held her belly, bawled implacably, then screamed and showered the doctors with curses, only to start bawling again. Afterward they put her on sedatives, examined her, and established with cold, medical certainty what'd happened.

The child protection service then took over care for her, moved her to a home, and sent the police to her parents' door. Her father got a short jail sentence, and her mother was paroled, with the obligation to pay her compensation for the sexual abuse, psychological maltreatment, and parental neglect.

I could've told Grandfather and Grandmother that Selma talked about her adolescence, when goodhearted foster families alternated with cold, bare rooms of homes for abused children—a toing and froing like on a faulty conveyor belt. My own fantasy could've helped conjure up images for them, in which her life was an orgy of alcohol, hash, and parties with rough, mean, significantly older boys. Or maybe I could've told them that she was finally paid her compensation when she turned twenty-one. Her dad changed his name and got married again, somewhere in the north of Norway, and he wished to visit her and beg forgiveness. Her mother didn't even try that but began consuming pills, later alcohol too, and seeing psychiatrists, before she became completely docile and ended up in an institution for the mentally ill. Selma took the compensation money, around 200,000 crowns, and left on a long trip, planning to never come back; she wanted to go anywhere, just far away from that city, from the institutions and the devout, well-intentioned foster families, whose stable lives made them clueless. I could've mentioned all the cities and all her great and failed loves. I could've told them about a successful, rich German lawyer, who she went to China with on the Trans-Siberian Railroad. She traveled all the way to the shores of the Pacific with him, afterward they watched the sun set on Thai beaches, and she felt she was pregnant and felt that he adored her, she felt he loved her too much, wasn't prepared to lose her, was weak, and couldn't resist her—and she felt a growing disgust. He promised her everything: a wedding when they returned to Hamburg, a new house for her alone, any car she wanted. He knew she loved BMWs, and he'd buy one for her, she just needed to choose the color she wanted. Maybe I should've mentioned to Grandfather and Grandmother that the guy was tall and handsome, attractive and rich, but that he smothered her with his cloying love, and despite everything, he had, in her words, a small prick. Maybe Grandfather and Grandmother would then have realized why she ran away from him. She really did tear herself from his arms because he held her like a vice at the bolted door of his house and wouldn't let her out. She was bearing his child, for heaven's sake. He cried, begged, and threatened; he squeezed her tight and tried to kiss her. Then she bit his ear, as hard as a hyena, he howled, and blood spurted. She unlocked the door and ran. Still, she only went to the next-door neighbor's for a Band-Aid. She came back, gave it to him, and left, promising him she'd be back; he stood at the door completely crushed, and rubbing his aching ear like in a sit-com. I could've told them that after the abortion she fled to Paris together with some gay friends, went up to the top of the Eiffel Tower, and contemplated the mesmerizing drop. After that, she went to Berlin and fell in love with a young woman she'd be in a relationship with for the next three years. There she earned her living as a professional dancer at raves, where, all done up in black leather and high-heel boots, she'd hang in a cage above an ecstatic crowd of five thousand. She danced with her whole body, her eyes, lips, and tongue, giving herself to them and feeling the erotic lust of the masses in their trance. And then, at the end, I could've told them how she returned to Oslo empty and deflated, enrolled in economics at university, and found work at Sigi's pub on the island of Gressholmen, where she worked on and off from Easter till late summer. I also could've confessed that she told me I shouldn't be jealous of that young-looking, bearded sixty-year-old because he got her out of trouble, gave her a job, and a room above the pub where she could stay for free whenever she wanted.

"He's like a father to me," she'd told me.

"Just like a father, huh?" I asked with a heavy dose of sarcasm.

She sprang at me, shrieking, slashed my face with nails like razor blades, scratched me bloody, spat in my face when I grabbed her hands. Then she kicked me in the balls, I howled, she attacked me again with her claws, aiming for my eyes. I slapped her with all my might, she fell to the floor in slow motion, only to spring back to her feet the same instant, unnaturally fast, like a wildcat on speed, and again she slashed me across the face. I slapped her several more times, and each time she fell but always rose again. Then she leaped toward the window, opened it with a crash, and started to climb onto the sill, screaming that she was going to jump and wanted to die. I grabbed her by the neck from behind and threw her to the floor.

"You're gonna jump, huh? Fucking hell. You're gonna jump, are you? From the first floor? Go on then and jump, jump you stupid cunt!"

In the end, she knelt on the floor, tore at her hair and cried in pain, banged her head against the wall, and savagely scratched her face. The red furrows she tore with her nails stood out. Her howling gradually changed to bawling, and later to crying, and finally just to a quiet sobbing. I could've told Grandmother and Grandfather that I took her in my arms like a small child, hugged and comforted her, and never again said anything about Sigi or her father.

I could've told them all that and nothing would've been different. My own voracious memories would go on devouring my life, and I'd still be in the same hotel room waiting for Čombe to come with the ganja. I'd jerk off and then shower. I'd still sit on the bed and light a cigarette, still stare at the hotel telephone, and not call Kole.

BEKIM SEJRANOVIĆ

XXIV

1. *Greenie*

MY STAY IN the hotel room in Zagreb became unbearable, but finally in a new way. I opened the window, stuck out my head, and immersed myself in the sunny afternoon. I inhaled the bustle of the city and shook off the dust of memory, ruthlessly, like out of an old carpet.

I went out, walked with the crowd, looked into people's faces, and sized up women's asses. I went along the street, grazed by fragments of people's conversations, and assembled them into entire life histories. Slowly, with a lazy reluctance, a feeling of freedom and summer started to flow through me—the sweet turmoil of a new beginning. Maybe this was the end of one journey, but perhaps also the beginning of a new one, my burgeoning optimism told me.

I crossed the city's main square, passing the bronze statue of Ban Jelačić, welded onto a huge horse and with a saber in his hand for him to brandish forever. I walked up the narrow streets into the Upper City and found the restaurant where Selma and I had eaten dinner two years earlier. I was in a good mood and decided I wasn't going to let any putrid memories spoil this sudden new lease on life.

I chewed the raw meat, greedily digging my teeth into it, and devoured it with the help of red wine. Every bite was a piece of memory that I tore from myself and consigned to the abyss of my intestines. And here was one very tough little piece that insolently resisted my eye-teeth—it was for the night two years earlier when we'd gone to visit Grandfather and Grandmother.

When we'd turned off the light and lay down to sleep, cockroaches the size of Matchbox cars teemed from the rotten floorboards under the bed and out of every recess and started to traipse over our bodies. I switched on the light and they disappeared again with frightening, unbelievable speed. We stayed up all night with the light on killing cockroaches.

"Bravo, my love!" Selma shouted when I crushed one of the sinister, cat-sized varmints and kissed me as a reward.

The next day I asked my grandparents about the cockroaches, but they said they had no idea. They took sleeping pills before going to bed, so they wouldn't notice "even if a bullock cart ran over them," Grandmother quipped, getting her tongue into gear for the day.

That morning, after much effort, I managed to persuade Grandfather to give us the keys of his old jalopy, the Zastava, aka Greenie. He couldn't drive because his left arm and leg were like foreign bodies, but he'd bribed a police clerk to extend his driver's license for another three years. Sometimes he'd get into the car, start the motor, put his hands on the steering wheel, and weep.

We drove almost every day, and Greenie broke down every second day. Several times I was on the verge of abandoning it on the roadside, shooting it like a dying old nag, but I didn't have the heart to. Where would Grandfather go to cry in peace? We went to raves on Adriatic beaches and danced to exhaustion, rolled about in hot rooms of monstrous, kitschy new apartments along the Dalmatian coast, fucked on the altar of a church in a ghost town in Istria, got high and walked the peaks of the Gorski Kotar region, and fed bear cubs in the wilds of Lika, near Otočac.

2. Murderer!

I went back toward Hotel Jadran, bought several bottles of red wine on the way, and went up to my room to wait for Čombe. After half a bottle of wine he finally arrived. He knocked, I asked who it was, he answered, "Water, neighbor," and barged noisily into the room. That was an old gag of ours, from the Surrealists. He told me to pack up my things and said I could stay at his place for as long as I liked. He'd grown visibly thin since our last meeting, spoke through his nose, and now sounded like a Zagreber. We stayed sitting in the room, rolled joints, sipped wine, and went back to time-worn shared memories. Sometimes our stories didn't match up, but neither of us wanted to spoil the wistful idyll of the past and kill it with the harsh acuity of the truth. Čombe, like Dalton, had been a press photographer. All three of us once worked for the same newspaper. But Čombe and I had known each other even longer, our history went back to the Paranoya period when Kole and I were inseparable, when we were kids and kept telling and retelling the awesome story about Čombe stealing an Autotrolej bus from the parking lot at Školjić at three in the morning and driving half of Route 2, Zamet–Pećine. He made all the scheduled stops and took on passengers.

Čombe asked if I'd heard from Kole. I just shrugged and said I'd be getting in touch with him.

After all the old stories, it was time for sparse reports on the period from when we last saw each other. He said everything was the same: he worked, had a girlfriend, sometimes he went to Rijeka for the weekend, and there he often chanced on some old acquaintance. Recently he'd seen Kole.

I told him in a vague way that I'd spent the last year on an island in the north of Norway, working as a librarian.

He puffed on his joint in silence, greedily inhaled the smoke, leaned against the wall, and placed a pillow under his head, as if waiting for a movie to start. He saw I was hesitating and generously passed me the joint. I inhaled and wondered what to say. Should I tell him that, when Selma and I returned to Norway, we found that our best man Lars had vanished without a trace, leaving behind a ruined photo with "hoka hey" on the back and a dirty white parrot that shrieked "hasta la vista, hasta la vista, baby" like a specter? Or describe to him in detail how my marriage slowly turned into a quagmire that fiendishly smothered all our movements, sucking us into its quicksand?

After we went back to Norway, Selma continued studying and I found work as a university tutor. Life was a calm and peaceful river. But a morbid possessiveness gradually began to emerge in her, a panicky fear of being abandoned, and an unspeakably strong need for attention. At the very beginning, I believed blindly in the correctness of such a concept of love. I let Selma carry me away like an empty larva to her realm of limited thoughts and sentimental dramatics. After a while, the ring of her demands and aggressive tantrums, which would always end in nervous breakdowns, began to tighten around my heart. I tried to save myself as best I could. I expended all my long-cherished thoughts, new invented theories, and proofs of love, I tried to assure myself and implored her like you beg the executioner to spare your life.

She was maddened by the idea that I was teaching young female students with firm, bulging Norwegian boobs under their

T-shirts, who I sometimes went for a beer with after lectures. When we went to bed in the evenings and smoked a joint before sleeping, she'd demand that I tell her how I'd fucked one of those students.

She'd say, "Come on, tell me how you kneaded that little freckled one in your office."

I felt uncomfortable the first time, but the second time it turned me on. Saucy little stories took shape all by themselves. From night to night, we wove a web of maddeningly exciting details. I was ever more absent at the lectures, and I was ashamed to speak to a student I'd ravished on the desk in my fantasy the night before. Sometimes, on the other hand, I watched them furtively and imagined which girl I could have that night together with Selma. But Selma was only interested in the female students if she was horny. If I ever mentioned that to her outside of that context or if she simply wasn't in the mood, she'd fly into a rage, call me a pervert, scratch my face, and threaten to cut off my cock. Half an hour later she'd implore me, gnashing her teeth like a mare in heat, to tell her about one of them and describe how I'd touch them, raise their shaven legs onto my shoulders, and fuck them, and to do her just like that at the same time. She particularly loved it when a big blonde with sassy melons was on the program.

At the end of the winter semester, I started to cheat on Selma with students. First of all with a big blonde with sassy melons. I met her occasionally during the winter vacation. I tried to put into practice what Selma and I fantasized about together, but it wasn't as good, except that I finally stuffed it into the right hole.

One day at the beginning of January, Selma was waiting for me at the door and shouted that she was pregnant. I asked her in disbelief how that was possible, given the way we had sex. She cried, swore, and tore out whole tufts of hair, screamed how should she know how it was possible, but she knew she was pregnant. I didn't say anything, but there wasn't a trace of paternal happiness on my face. She bawled for two hours, yelling, "Murderer, murderer, murderer . . ."

After she did several tests, it turned out she wasn't pregnant after all. I roared at her for the unnecessary panic, and she fell into deep depression. In the end, I felt guilty for the nonexistent pregnancy, the nonexistent child, and the nonexistent murder of that nonexistent child.

3. Two heads

Selma checked my phone in well-conceived attacks of jealousy and found ambiguous messages, suspicious but insufficient to prove any wrongdoing. Later, like an experienced angler who throws back irresistible bait, she started sending erotic messages from my phone to that number. She finally had me in her hand, and there was a glint of satisfaction in her eyes because her jealousy and possessiveness had finally turned out to be justified. Her reaction was meeker than before, when she'd had no reason to be jealous. She punched me in the head several times, screamed, and only cried for half an hour. I didn't try to console her. She said I'd lost her forever. Those were her favorite words when we quarreled. Mine were that I didn't need anybody in the world, and least of all a crazy bitch with tiny tits. The bit about the tiny tits maddened her most of all. I actually liked hers.

Several days later, Selma vanished and didn't come home for a couple of weeks. I called her, but she didn't answer. I knew she was at Sigi's, and that made demons rampage in my head. Not even the blonde could comfort me. When Selma came back, she was still mad at me, and I was weary of her jealousy. We didn't quarrel, but we slept separately, she in the bed, me on a mattress on the floor. We'd only see each other in the mornings or late in the evenings, and we went past one another like you hurry past an unpleasant sight. But one morning, still half asleep, I crawled into her bed, and we started to hug and press up against each other. We made love like blind bats, our eyes still gummy from sleep, and I finally poked into the right hole and came and came and came. When the last twitches of love's spasms ebbed away from our bodies, we pulled apart in surprise and revulsion.

A week before the Easter vacation she coldly informed me that, like every year, she'd be working at Sigi's over Easter and that it'd be best that she live there for a while, at least during the vacation. She didn't feel like the rigmarole of shipping out to the island every day. I told her to go to hell and bought a plane ticket to Zagreb the same day.

I stayed in Zagreb for one day and then left for Rijeka. I was there for several days and spent them mainly with Goran, driving around Istria in his "bug." We sat on the terrace of the tavern in Hum, the smallest city in the world, in the rays of the April sun, eating boiled ham with spring onions and washing it down with local wine. I told Goran about the female students in Norway.

He chuckled and stuttered in disbelief, "Really? Jou're yoking ... Really?"

Back in Rijeka that evening, we went to meet Kole. We had beer at the Palach Club. Kole was nervous and his eyes flitted under his peaked cap. He talked skittishly and smiled like a wooden puppet. He said his mother's pension hadn't come and that she herself had asked if I could lend her two hundred kunas until tomorrow. I gave him the money, he sat with us impatiently for several more minutes, and then said goodbye and left. I watched him vanish from my life like a phantom. I never saw him again.

Two days later, I went to Brčko to see Grandfather and Grandmother. There I heard the news that Uncle Alija had died. When I returned to Norway after his funeral, the emptiness of my own life grinned at me from the door of my bedsit.

I waited several days for Selma to turn up, called her and let it ring and ring. Every time, I heard her recorded voice asking me to leave a message after the beep.

On Saturday I went down to the harbor and took the boat out to Gressholmen. The captain was that old guy who Lars and I had worked with the previous summer. I went up to the wheelhouse to say hello, but he didn't show any great joy at seeing me. I wanted to tell him that Lars had disappeared, but I gave up the idea and got off with the handful of other passengers when the boat reached the island.

I joined the small line of people going up the winding path that led to Sigi's. The day was dazzlingly bright and chilly. People's lungs let out almost invisible puffs of steam.

I entered the pub, the floorboards creaked ominously, and the rays of light that made their way through the fogged-up glass illuminated the blue of the smoke-filled space. Selma was standing at the bar, where a heavyset man with a long moustache was paying for his beer. Two heads turned toward me for a moment, first one, then another.

XXV

1. Get those pictures out of your head, man!

I DIDN'T TELL Čombe about any of that, but the pictures sprang into my mind irrepressibly like a plague of locusts during a sultry summer twilight. Several times I opened my mouth as if to say something, but I still couldn't. The struggle was over within just a few moments after several of Čombe's sighs, which were creaky from excessive smoking. No, I didn't want to tell him all the things that'd happened before I entered that pub with the pervasive odor of rabbit stew, and I felt even less like talking about what happened afterward. Selma told somebody in the kitchen behind her that I'd arrived, as if seeking support and assurance in what she was about to do, and I knew, of course, that the person was Sigi. His head appeared in the pass-through where he put the plates of food to be served. How could I possibly describe her avoidance of eye contact and the strange resolve with which she came up, took me by the hand, and led me out of the pub?

I don't know how to describe what I felt as I followed her along the little path behind the building to the very place where we made love on our first nuptial night. She stood me up against the trunk of a knotty pine, as if she was afraid I'd collapse and wanted to prop me up. I knew she wanted to say something to me, something that'd change our relationship and our lives forever, and that I hadn't even dared to think about until then. I sensed that, and it made my heart pound like a tiny rodent's when a swift and merciless snake slithers into its burrow.

I don't ever want to tell anybody what a feeling of decay spread through my body when she hugged me, pressed up to me, but flaccidly, and held me in her arms without words and without a kiss, like when you hug a child you're abandoning. I also don't want to ever admit to anyone what trenchant pain sliced through me when she detached herself from me for the last time, stepped back and made it clear to me that there wasn't the slightest trace of salty moisture in her eyes. There was a rustling in the bushes, but I didn't turn to look in that direction. I knew the loose, fecund, red-eyed rabbits had populated the whole island again. Sigi had bought them so they'd multiply and he could kill them all in the fall and fill his freezer with meat again.

I don't want to think of it anymore: the sounds were suddenly gone, all movement ceased, the wind stopped, the tips of the pines no longer swayed, and the nose of the rabbit watching us from the bushes stopped twitching. I don't want anybody to ever remind me of the pain I felt when she informed me in a skillfully worded sentence that she was pregnant, this time for real and confirmed several times, and that she wasn't sure if the father was me or Sigi.

I went back to my bedsit, poisoned to the core by jealousy, consumed by morbid thoughts and hatred toward life. I paced about the room from wall to wall and loudly repeated the final words I exchanged with her:

"How could you, how could you, how could you, how could you?"

Then I answered myself in her voice, cold and spiteful:

"How could *you*, how could *you*, how could *you*?"

I continued and asked how it could be that she didn't know who the father was, and then, imitating her voice, I repeated that it wasn't important; she was the mother. I fell to my knees on the hard, cold parquet of the room and whimpered:

"And what of us, what of us, what of us?"

Her voice poured from my throat and said it was over, that she loved Sigi, and had only ever loved him. She felt sorry for everything, she told me, and blathered on about how she hoped everything would be okay with me, and wished me happiness. She said I was a good boy and would undoubtedly find somebody who I'd be happy with, like she had. At the end, she finished me off with a blunt knife by consoling me that I needn't worry about the child because it probably wasn't mine anyway. And now, banging my forehead against the floor, I asked the question to which I already knew the answer: why she thought the child wasn't mine, and how she could know if she wasn't sure. She didn't answer, she was silent there beneath the knotty pine on the island of Gressholmen, and that silence reigned in me. I closed my eyes, wrapped my head in my hands, and curled up on the floor.

I wanted to dispel those pictures, and I spoke out loud, "Get those pictures out of your head, man, get those pictures out of your head!"

Afterward I lay in bed for three days and masturbated to those same pictures until I was raw.

2. Fuuuck

Maybe it would've been good if I'd been able to share all that with somebody, to get it off my chest and free myself of the demons that beset me without end. Instead, I told Čombe that work at the university had bored me, I wanted to experience something new, so I went to the island of S., but Selma didn't want to go with me, so we split up, mostly because of that. He drank a little wine and looked at me kindheartedly. He started to roll a new joint, smiled, and shook his head.

The truth was that rumors had begun to smolder in the corridors of the History and Philosophy Faculty in Oslo just before the end of the spring semester about the youngish tutor who downed tequilas with female students in dubious bars, crumbled hash and rolled joints at private parties. One student brought him a narghile as a birthday present, which he tried out there and then and offered his students to try it too. Malicious tongues also mentioned certain students in open, wantonly tight tops, who often went up to the tutor's desk, leaned forward, rested the load of their bosoms on the varnished wooden surface, and asked ambiguous questions, which he was unable to answer. In the end, the tutor in question was called to a meeting with the director of the Institute of Literature. The topic was responsibility in the workplace, the theme, immorality, and the moral of the story—dismissal at the end of semester.

Afterward I replied to several advertisements, without success, but finally I managed to get a job as a librarian on the island of S. I was to leave at the end of August and didn't know how to get through that month and a half of summer in Oslo. The sun shone without letup from four in the morning until midnight and mercilessly made its way through the cane blinds. Sleep was impossible, be it because of the sun or the cries of the gulls, magpies, and crows, which would begin as soon as the sky ruddied in the east around three in the morning. Later a hostile voice in my head would start to ask questions, and another voice would answer. There were pictures that corroborated the answers. They showed her lying spread-legged beneath Sigi, the muscles of his hairy ass working like an animal's, and his member, uncircumcised, crooked, and fleshy, thrusting into her little cunt that'd only opened up for me once. His hung, mature balls slapped against her skinny bum and she moaned, quietly and devotedly, like a boy crying alone in a dark corner after a beating from his father.

Čombe lit a new joint, took two long tokes, filling his cheeks like a bagpipe, and then handed it to me. I did the same, and as I let out the smoke I told him that Selma had found a new guy and last winter they'd had a baby, a daughter as far as I could remember. Or maybe a son. I wasn't sure, I lied.

Čombe took the joint back, raised his eyebrows high into the air, glanced away to the side, and let a long expletive exhalation through his nose: "Fuuuck."

3. The father

I also tried to say "fuuuck" to myself when I saw them walking in St. Hanshaugen Park a week and a half before I left for the island of S. His beard was longer, the fruit in her belly had begun to swell, and the dark circles around my eyes from insomnia were ever darker. They saw me too and came up without hesitation and said hello with saccharin-sweet smiles. She spoke like the hostess of the lottery draw on TV, smiling only with the lower part of her face and emphasizing particular words with unnatural clarity. He stood aside, nodded seriously, and mumbled in approval after every second sentence. I watched her lips spreading into a smile, coming together and moving apart again. For a moment I also saw her tongue moisten them in the pause between two utterances, and I begged somebody inside me, that somebody who operates my insides, to stop the pictures and voices that now intruded from the back of my mind. I begged that stranger to let me say something in reply, to stop me from showing weakness, and to give me a chance to make their life hell.

She explained in the voice of a legal adviser that we'd have to apply for a divorce, but in accordance with Norwegian law you first need to apply for a separation certificate, and then, only after a full year has passed, do you get a divorce.

"That's why," she continued, "when the baby's born, you and I will still officially be married and you'll automatically be registered as the father."

He joined in and said he knew it was perhaps a bit awkward, but it could be rectified later on.

She said they didn't intend to do DNA tests to determine who the father was—that wasn't important at all—so why should they worry about it? I could also have contact with the child after it was born, they'd even be glad.

"Yes, we'd really be glad," he added.

I nodded, unable to say anything. After all, what could I have said?

She also asked me to bring her some things that she'd left at my place: several books that she needed for uni and a few documents. She added that I should apply for a separation certificate so we could get a divorce as soon as possible. It was simply a matter of filling in a form and sending it off together with a copy of the marriage certificate, she said, as if encouraging me.

That day I drank myself into a stupor. I sat in the room and stared at the glass-topped table. I listened to music and talked loudly with myself. I lay on the floor and counted the minutes, hours, and days since our last meeting, struggled to suppress the pictures, and wanted the whole world to die together with me. I did the same for the next three days.

On the fourth day I gathered my strength, raised myself off the floor, and thought I'd gotten over the raging river of bile. I repeated to myself Nietzsche's trite phrase about what doesn't kill us making us stronger, as I cleaned up the room and purged the last remnants of that excruciating love. Then I let a jet of water in the shower wash away the mold of memory, and I imagined leaving for the far north in several days, for the island of S., and putting all of it behind me.

Afterward I started to look for the books and things that Selma had asked me to return. I took a folder of documents out of the bottom drawer of the desk. It had compartments and I browsed through the contents. I found several birth certificates, high school reports, and the findings of various medical commissions. I also found our marriage certificate, looked over it, and saw the date—soon it'd be our anniversary.

I also found a twice-folded, old piece of paper. I opened it and saw that it was a baptismal certificate, thirty or so years old. It gave the date and place of the ceremony and the full name of the child: Selma Kristine Aasen Johansen. It also mentioned the names of her parents: Marie Johansen—née Aasen—and Sigmund Johansen. At the bottom was the illegible signature of a protestant priest.

4. Sweet lies

The phone in the hotel room rang once. Čombe raised his eyebrows questioningly and looked at me with a slight dose of paranoia. I heard its ringing, but I still saw Selma's baptismal certificate in front of me and sensed the same shiver of disbelief and enlightenment that'd seized me when I first looked at the names.

The phone rang a second time, and I tried to tear myself off that murderous hook of the past that had snagged me a year earlier. It was one of those moments when you feel that all the building blocks in your brain have finally fallen into place, but the image they form is tainted with horror. It's a feeling like when you're reading the last page of a novel and expect some resolution, but the last sentence annuls and devalues everything. It leaves you without any kind of compass, any realization about good and evil, lies and truth.

The phone rang a third time, and I thought this was the last chance ever to at least try and tell somebody what I felt when I read her father's name on the baptismal certificate: Sigmund. Sigmund Johansen. And how my eyes whirled when I looked at our marriage certificate again and read the names of the witnesses: Lars Karlsson and Harald Johansen. Harald Johansen, whom Selma alone called Sigi.

I spoke with sincere admiration: "Bearded, fifty-year-old Sigmund Johansen, who sleeps with his daughter—my wife—and went to her wedding as best man."

I sat on the floor looking over the two documents and enthusiastically repeated those words, propelled by the realization of the unpredictability of life. Several minutes later, that philosophical awe dissipated and gave way first to jealousy, then to repulsion, and finally to sexual excitement that serves as a final line of defense against unbearable pain.

After I'd masturbated, emptiness and an awareness of the complete uselessness of that realization came as inexorably as a sledgehammer. What should I do with the fact that I still couldn't believe? Get back at them by reporting them to the police? What for exactly? Because she was his daughter and lived with him, and he'd been a marriage witness for her without me knowing he was her father? Demand a DNA test to ascertain if the child was his or mine? All that would achieve, if it turned out the child was really his, was all-encompassing misfortune.

Sweet lies are better than true misfortune. Sweet lies are all we have.

Then again, I had no proof of the claim that Sigi was her father. Apart from the surname Johansen, which is common in Norway.

And what about Sigi—Sigmund? The devil's advocate in me started again.

And what about . . . ?

The phone rang a fourth time. I picked it up. It was Goran. He stuttered more than usual.

"Hi, y-y-yeah, d'you know what happened?"

I said nothing, as if wondering, and then stammered back to him that I really couldn't know. Would he like to tell me, or should I guess?

"How about you start with the first letter," I teased.

"Y-y-yeah . . . K-K-Kole killed himself. This afternoon."

Then, stuttering a little less, he informed me of all the details. I asked him to tell me when the funeral would be so I could go.

I hung up and conveyed everything to Čombe, who'd understood it all anyway.

"Fuuuck," he said.

XXVI

After the funeral

THE CLOUDS STILL hung heavy on the hills when Grandfather and I finally made it to Greenie and left for the city.

The next day I traveled to Zagreb, from there to Oslo, and then on to the island of S.

As I drove toward the city, Grandfather tried to rehash an anecdote about Alija. It was the last time I'd seen him.

We were going to the ranch, and when we'd passed through the village and were driving along the macadamized road, we came across Alija and his goats at the first bridge. He was sitting in the shade and reading a book. We stopped and got out to say hello, but Alija didn't take his eyes off his book. When he finished the sentence, he told us with astonishment that he'd found the book with quotes from Marx on a trash heap in front of the community center.

He read a few more sentences, looked into the sky, and said in admiration, "Wow, this Marx is a brainy character."

He waved after us with the book as we disappeared again, leaving a cloud of dust behind us.

"D'you remember those things?" Grandfather asked with his heavy tongue as he tried to smile.

"I do," I said, trying to avoid the potholes.

The next morning I packed, and Grandfather and Grandmother drank coffee and enumerated all the things I mustn't forget. After a second fildžan, Grandfather got up and went to the other room, dragging his left leg behind him. Grandmother leaned toward me and whispered in confidence that Grandfather watched saucy movies on TV and then wanted to canoodle.

"'E's gone quite crazy, 'e can't even go to the toilet by 'imself, but 'e wants to 'ave a bit of, you know," she said with a chuckle and tugged at my arm.

I tried helplessly to pull away.

Grandfather came back slowly with a plastic bottle that read "Radenska Three Hearts Mineral Water" but was full of rakija that I'd later drink with Aljoša on the island of S. He handed it to me like it was a holy grail.

Grandmother didn't stop her blathering, she just changed her tone of voice and the topic as smoothly as a talk show host. And every little while she'd flog her favorite hobbyhorse.

"And 'ow's Selma? When's she gonna 'ave a baby? Tell 'er that we can't wait forever," she blabbed, biting off half a cube of sugar and slurping coffee at the same time.

"Oh, you're a nuisance—why are you meddling again?" Grandfather said.

"Could it be she's already pregnant and 'e don't wanna tell us?"

"Impossible," I lied unintentionally.

When I returned to Oslo, Selma informed me that she was really pregnant.

Before we parted forever, Grandfather said he had something else for me. He gave me a yellowed photograph from 1945 showing him and Grandmother. They met for the first time at the celebration of the city's liberation. Grandfather soon had to move on, so they'd had their photo taken as a keepsake. He was in a Partisan uniform and had a cocked cap. Grandmother was wearing traditional pantaloons, sandals, and a necklace of imitation pearls. She held Grandfather's Schmeisser in her hands awkwardly like some detached phallus.

Grandfather moved the photo back a bit and squinted to see better because he didn't have glasses.

"There you are, sonny. To think of all we've gone through since then . . . And now you tell me, is that love? What is it? What the dickens is it?"

"Is that love?" I asked myself, gazing at the yellowed photo as the plane lifted off.

Below me, Zagreb was becoming smaller and smaller. I closed my eyes. When I opened them again, there was nothing more below me.

WILL FIRTH was born in 1965 in Newcastle, Australia. He studied German and Slavic languages in Canberra, Zagreb, and Moscow. Since 1991 he has lived in Berlin, where he works as a translator of literature and the humanities—from Russian, Macedonian, and all variants of the "language with many names," aka Serbo-Croatian. From 2005–07 he translated for the International Criminal Tribunal for the former Yugoslavia. Firth is a member of professional associations in Germany (VdÜ) and Britain (Translators Association). His best-received translations of recent years have been Aleksandar Gatalica's *The Great War*, Faruk Šehić's *Quiet Flows the Una*, Miloš Crnjanski's *A Novel of London*, and Robert Perišić's *Our Man in Iraq*.

willfirth.de

About Sandorf Passage

SANDORF PASSAGE publishes work borne from displacement and movement that creates a prismatic perspective on what it means to live in a globalized world. It is a home to writing inspired by both conflict zones and the dangers of complacency. All Sandorf Passage titles share in common how the biggest and most important ideas so often are best explored in the most personal and intimate of spaces.